I0678568

HEADLESS IN LONDON

LUKE RYDER
BOOK 5

JOHN G. BLUCK

ROUGH
EDGES
PRESS

Headless In London
Paperback Edition
Copyright © 2025 John G. Bluck

Rough Edges Press
An Imprint of Wolfpack Publishing
1707 E. Diana Street
Tampa, FL 33610

roughedgespress.com

Paperback ISBN 978-1-68549-531-2
eBook ISBN 978-1-68549-530-5
LCCN 2025930693

HEADLESS IN LONDON

ONE

WEARING leather driving gloves and a hooded, black jacket, a man studied the alley entrance of the ancient apartment building. It stood in East London in the Crows End neighborhood next to a noisy pub.

Seeing no one nearby, the bloke pulled the apartment building's heavy door open. Carrying a sturdy paper shopping bag, he rushed inside along the empty hallway. His heart thumping, the man began to pick the lock of the baroness's low-rent flat, number nine.

The mechanism clicked open within four seconds. He sighed. As he eased the flimsy door inward, it creaked. He stopped.

Listening, he heard nothing but a raucous crowd in the street in front of the large pub next door. He eased into the out-of-date lodging. Glancing at its furnishings, he saw a worn couch, a coffee table, two easy chairs, and a double bed. Here, Baroness Anne Thorpe entertained guests, men for the most part, in her flat, a secret hideaway.

He eased the door shut and twisted its lock knob to set the deadbolt. Reaching into his shopping bag, the intruder removed a cheap plastic raincoat, a dark ski mask, and rubber gloves. In seconds, he put these items on. Then he pulled the living room drapes aside, set the bag on the floor next to the window, and took a lug wrench out of the paper tote.

Now hidden behind the curtains, he leaned on the wall next to the window, exhaled, and coughed. After two deep breaths, he tried to relax, but his heart still galloped.

Odds are Anne would enter her flat at eight thirty. He knew her routine. Early Friday evenings she attended her London Readers Book Club meeting. The gathering often ended at eight. He'd arrived in plenty of time to lie in wait in case she'd arrive sooner. He planned to approach her in silence from behind and knock her out. He felt no need to kill her at once.

His pulse pounded at his temples as he thought what it would be like to murder a woman. He didn't relish the thought of becoming an infamous killer. He wished to remain anonymous, ignored.

As the minutes ticked by, he thought about Anne. He took a deep breath. *It's a shame to erase her from the world of the living. But it has to be done.*

He judged her to be easygoing, agreeable, and complacent. Anne also had a stubborn streak, though she avoided conflict and regarded herself as a peacemaker. But she ignored problems instead of trying to solve them. Because she couldn't face reality, she found it difficult to dump lovers. She led everyone on. That would be her downfall.

* * *

8:35 P.M., FRIDAY, NEAR ANNE'S APARTMENT

A mist drifted downward, and the wet pavement glistened under a Crows End streetlight. The weather was chilly when Luke and Layla Ryder neared the front door of the sizable, but not huge, Red Feather Pub. This Friday was the second to the last day of their London honeymoon. A wooden sign dangling from chains above the establishment's front door displayed red, vivid artwork—a cardinal's crimson feather. The quiet sounds of the happy, but modest-sized crowd inside seeped through the entryway.

In contrast, the street outside the pub was extra noisy this Friday night. Pedestrians talked and laughed. Once in a while, a scream echoed across the roadway. Hustle and bustle made the neighborhood seem festive, even warm, though the wind bit at Luke's skin.

Handsome and muscular, thirty-eight-year-old Luke had married weeks ago. Six foot two inches tall, he appeared confident. His black hair hinted at his half-Italian heritage.

Luke took a deep breath, sucked chilled air into his lungs, and admired his new wife, Layla.

In her twenties and inches shorter than Luke, Layla had a slim, athletic build with an ample bosom and dark, ebony skin.

Below their second-floor Airbnb apartment, the Red Feather Pub served as a convenient place for them to eat and socialize.

Across the street from the Red Feather a larger, noisier pub, the Golden Sword, stood. This bigger pub was next to an old, sprawling apartment building.

Unlike the Red Feather, the Golden Sword was often jam-packed with huge, boisterous crowds. This evening, despite the damp, misty air, a throng of drinkers had overflowed onto the sidewalk and the slick, brick-paved street. At least fifty men and women milled about, holding beer glasses. Unsteady, as were his mates, one man splattered the sidewalk with a splash of his brew. Their loud, drunken talk sounded happy to Luke, who had grown up in a quiet Kentucky holler (a small, wooded valley).

All of a sudden, a dozen more revelers emerged from the Golden Sword. They wore bright-colored plastic top hats and blew toy whistles. Seconds later, they broke out into a drunken rendition of "Happy Birthday." The rest of the sizable gathering joined in with raucous singing. A middle-aged man in a neat suit smiled, and his white teeth gleamed. His companions slapped his back.

As the off-tune singing grew louder, echoing from across the street, Luke and Layla paused in front of the smaller Red Feather Pub. They were about to enter it to compete in its weekly pub quiz contest.

Luke stared across the road at the happy revelers. "Let's watch 'em for a second. You ain't gonna see anything like this in Kentucky." He spoke with a Southern drawl.

Layla grinned and nodded. "Sure." Her voice was warm and feminine. People often assumed she was well educated, though she'd merely attended two years of high school before going on her own.

* * *

8:40 P.M., FRIDAY, CROWS END

Anne wove her way through the noisy, jam-packed street filled with loitering people. She passed the crowded Golden Sword Pub and headed toward her old apartment building next to the large drinking establishment. But Anne's mind was elsewhere. *Estrella Bach is overbearing. The woman dictates what books the club reads. She's officious. We need a new club president.*

Once inside her apartment building, Anne took her keys from her purse, made her way down the carpeted hall, and unlocked the door of her secret flat.

* * *

8:45 P.M., FRIDAY, ANNE'S APARTMENT

The cheap lock of the apartment door clicked. Hinges squeaked.

The intruder's ears perked up. He peeked through a crack in the drapes.

The thin, wooden door swung open. Anne Thorpe, a thirty-eight-year-old baroness, entered from the hallway. People regarded her as attractive in a classical way.

She wore a blond hairpiece. This surprised the intruder. He knew the wig hid her brown, curly hair which normally hung down to her shoulders.

Exceptional, her face grabbed his attention like it always did. He reckoned her prominent cheekbones gave her a unique appearance. She was not beautiful by today's standards, but easy to remember.

She removed her wig, tossed it on the couch, and took off her white jacket.

* * *

ANNE'S back faced her heavy living room drapes. Outside in the street, the raucous throng sang another rendition of "Happy Birthday." The revelers blew cheap, plastic horns. Despite the rowdy noise from the street, Anne heard the floorboards behind her squeak. A tingling stream of unease rushed through her body. She turned. The sight of a disguised intruder shocked her.

Dressed in work clothes and a cheap plastic raincoat, the man also wore a dark blue ski mask and green plastic gloves. His eyes stared at her, cold and steady.

Fear cascaded up, down, and throughout Anne's entire body.

He rushed her.

She felt a surge of adrenaline. Grabbing the man's mask, she ripped it away. His familiar, angry face stunned her. Her automatic scream startled her. She wondered how her primeval instinct had launched such an ear-piercing alarm. *Why him?* To her, everything seemed to happen in slow motion. She froze.

He raised a steel wrench. As fast as an alley cat swatting a mouse, he swung his weapon down onto her head. A sharp pain shocked her. All of a sudden a cool blackness and a sense of peace and quiet enveloped her. Then there was nothing.

* * *

8:49 P.M., FRIDAY, NEAR ANNE'S APARTMENT

From his vantage point across the street from the Golden Sword Pub, Luke heard a muffled, but sharp scream come from the vicinity of the swarm of drinkers. *Sounded kinda like someone in distress.* He stared at the throng of revelers. *Or could it be a drunken woman?* He gazed at Layla. "Did you hear a cry?"

"What?"

"A loud scream."

"They're having a crazy, wild time." Layla grinned and then paused. "I'm cold and wet. Let's go in."

* * *

8:50 P.M., FRIDAY, ANNE'S APARTMENT

The intruder's stomach quivered.

Anne had collapsed like a marionette puppet whose strings had been snipped. Unmoving and silent, she lay on her back, blood streaming from the ugly gash on her forehead. Her eyes stared upward at the ceiling. They didn't blink or move, as if they were the eyes of a stone statue.

Her assailant touched Anne's soft throat as he checked for a pulse, his fingers lingering on her skin. At first, he hoped he'd feel the throbbing of blood traveling through her body. But he did not detect even a slight movement from her blood vessels. A fleeting feeling of regret ran through him, followed by sudden fright.

After shoving the bloodied, heavy wrench into his bag, he picked up the tote. He wished to leave at once. But after two long seconds, he dropped the bag to the carpet. The evil, yet logical, side of his brain had told him, *There's still work to do.*

He steadied himself. As cold as a skater on a frozen lake, he walked into the kitchen, grabbed a heavy butcher knife, and shivered. After removing his honing stone from his pocket, he began to sharpen the knife blade.

This death needs to appear to be the work of a madman.

Satisfied the blade was as sharp as he could make it, he set to work on Anne's neck. His hands shook. Still, within five minutes, he'd cut her head off.

* * *

8:58 P.M., FRIDAY, THE RED FEATHER PUB

The warmth of the cozy Red Feather Pub rushed across Luke's face when he opened its front door. When Luke opened the tavern doors, sounds of the customers grew louder all at once as if someone had turned up the volume on a radio. Luke counted ten tables bathed in the dim light of the place. The wooden bar glistened like it had been coated with five clear coats of lacquer and polished with pumice. Spotlights lit shelves behind the bar where at least a hundred bottles of liquor sat. Having a fine time, the patrons drank, ate, and talked.

Luke smelled fish and chips, bangers and mash, shepherd's pie, corned beef sandwiches, and ale. The odor of alcoholic beverages tempted him. A recovering alcoholic, he'd order a lime cordial made with soda water to keep on the straight and narrow. He hadn't been able to find American ginger ale in the UK.

Luke caught sight of the bartender, Alexander.

The heavy man grinned, and his pale face flushed red. "Hello, Luke. Want the regular for you two?" Layla had taken up Luke's habit of drinking lime cordials. Pregnant, she wasn't drinking alcoholic beverages.

Luke nodded at Alexander. "Yep. Thanks, Alex." Luke

realized he and Layla were well-known in the pub, though they had been in London merely a week. They'd always had breakfast in the Red Feather, and they often ate dinner at the pub, too.

Luke and Layla neared the table at the back wall, close to a dartboard, where they'd made a habit of sitting. Elsa, a secretary, and Marjorie, a store clerk, often sat with them there. The day before, the two women had invited the newlyweds to join them and compete in the pub quiz. The women had named their new team "Hands Across the Pond."

The trivia contest took place every Friday night at nine fifteen. Earlier, Marjorie had told Luke he and Layla would know the answers to questions about the US, while Elsa kept track of both well-known and obscure English entertainers. Marjorie was well versed in many subjects. Luke figured she was an expert at crossword puzzles, too.

As Alexander set two lime cordials on the table, Elsa and Marjorie approached. Alexander caught their attention. "Ladies, I'll bring your usual."

Elsa set her purse on the table. "Thanks, Alex."

Marjorie nodded and slid a chair away from the table before Luke could do so. She eased onto the seat. "Ready for your first quiz?"

Luke shrugged. "We'll see."

Layla grinned. "If they ask about American subjects, we'll have an excellent chance."

Elsa opened her purse, took out a five-pound note, and waved it. "If you give me your money, I can pay."

Luke took a tenner from his pocket and handed it to Elsa, and Marjorie gave her a fiver.

While Elsa turned in their quiz entry fees, Luke peered at Marjorie. She shared a flat across the street with Elsa. "Did you ladies hear a sharp scream in your building a few minutes ago?"

"No, why?"

"Sounded like someone in trouble." Luke creased his brow.

"My neighbors always scream, yell, and argue about politics and everything else. What you heard is normal. In the States I presume a scream would mean trouble. Here it could be a frisky woman who's overindulged."

Luke sighed. A Kentucky deputy sheriff, he often relied on his instincts. His gut told him something had been different about the scream he'd heard minutes ago outside the pub.

Elsa came back with the table's answer sheet, and she showed it to Luke and Layla.

A blond woman stood next to the bar. She raised a hand-held, wireless microphone. "Let's begin the quiz." Her shrill voice boomed across the room. The loudspeaker volume was turned up too high. The woman's amplified voice hammered Luke's eardrums. "The first question is what is bronze made of?"

Marjorie leaned toward Layla to whisper. "Bronze is a combination of copper and tin."

Luke nodded. "Correct." In his mind's eye, he pictured his high school chemistry teacher, Mrs. Nicholas, talking about the periodic table of elements and alloys made from them.

Elsa wrote their answer on their score sheet.

* * *

10:05 P.M., FRIDAY, CROWS END

On his way to rendezvous with Anne, a second man walked toward Anne's apartment building. Anne was his Friday night date. As he turned a corner, he caught sight of her sprawling, timeworn building. It stood next to the Golden Sword Pub.

He pulled his trench coat collar high against his chin to

ward off the chilly, drifting mist falling on the brick street. Stopping for a moment, he observed rowdy drinkers inside and outside of the pub. He moved forward. Like he always did, he stayed in dark shadows when he walked at night. Within thirty seconds, he neared a side door to Anne's apartment building. He kept his head down as he came in view of a surveillance camera over the doorway. Memories of Anne's soft body warmed him, and the damp cold no longer bit into him.

When he reached in his pocket and fingered the key to the flat, he recalled the day she'd gifted it to him.

They had been in her double bed in her secret hideaway early one afternoon. Nude, Anne had thrown the sheets aside and stepped toward an easy chair where she'd placed her handbag. To him, she appeared younger and ultra-attractive without clothes. Many women her age had gained weight and were flabby. Because of that, they often kept their bed chambers dark. But Anne adored making love in a bright room, in daylight if possible.

It was a happy afternoon the day she'd dug into her expensive purse.

She'd returned to the bed with a key, holding it with two fingers. Bouncing on the mattress, she'd laughed and extended her hand to his. "Here."

He remembered how the well-polished key glistened and felt in his hand.

Her cheeks glowing, she had moved closer to him. "As usual, call ahead, and I'll let you know when you can come over. If I'm late, let yourself in."

A sudden, cold wind brought him out of his reverie. After pulling his collar up yet higher and tilting his head further down, he entered her building's lobby. He started down the hall toward her flat, number nine. Its door was ajar.

Peering into Anne's apartment, he saw a pool of blood and her decapitated head. Like a cobra bite, shock jabbed him, though he'd seen plenty of wicked, horrid scenes before. He tasted bile in his mouth.

Anne's head lay on the carpet next to her body. Her unmoving eyes stared upward at a ceiling light fixture.

He braced himself. He pushed the door farther inward with his elbow. Once inside, he took his clean handkerchief from his rear pocket, grasped the doorknob with it, and closed the door behind him.

The expensive cell phone charger he'd given her sat on one of the bookshelves in the living room. *I must get it and leave at once. Anything else I've left here? No.*

He grabbed the phone charger and stuffed it into his trench coat pocket. Careful not to step in blood, he walked around the corpse and stopped by the flat's door. He stared at the body, and a tear rolled down his cheek.

Again, using his handkerchief, he twisted the doorknob and opened the door a crack. He peered to his right, down the hallway. Then he pulled the door open enough to enable him to see leftward. *No one's in sight.*

He slipped from the apartment but left the door ajar, the way it had been when he'd arrived. He departed the building by its rear entrance and melted into the darkness of the alley.

* * *

10:10 P.M., FRIDAY, THE RED FEATHER PUB

An hour had passed faster than Luke had expected. Throughout the pub quiz, Alexander, the bartender, continued to deliver pints of ale and beer to the tables crowded with patrons. Now the quiz questions focused on American subjects, such as which state has Cheeseheads? Luke knew the answer. "Wisconsin, home of the Green Bay Packers."

Between them, Luke and Layla knew the correct responses to all of the US questions.

The contest's emphasis next shifted to English history. Elsa took the lead when the blond announcer's shrill, amplified voice echoed across the pub. "Name the last king in the Plantagenet dynasty."

Luke shrugged and peered at the two English women on his team. "A dynasty?"

Marjorie straightened. "It's a royal house with roots in France."

Elsa smiled. "The correct answer is Richard III." She leaned closer to her team members. "I'm sure I'm right."

The dynasty question and answer ended the quiz.

Her lips near the microphone, the blond hostess spoke again. "Teams, pass your score sheets in a clockwise direction to the next table, and we'll grade them." She gestured to show which way the contestants should send their answer sheets.

Luke watched as Layla, Marjorie, and Elsa scored the sheet from the table next to them. Elsa glanced at Luke. "Would you like to check it?"

"I trust you."

Elsa stood. "I'll turn it in."

The fair-haired woman who'd been running the quiz examined the sheets and tallied the scores. A second woman with bright red hair double-checked the blond's work.

When the blond woman picked up her microphone from the bar, a loud bumping sound and the squeal of audio feedback sprang from the well-built speakers. "The team, Hands Across the Pond, is the winner by the slimmest of margins—two points. Team leader, come forward to collect your winnings."

Elsa stepped to the bar to claim the prize. Smiling, she returned. "We won fifty pounds." She handed twenty-five pounds to Luke.

Marjorie stood and turned to Layla. "I've had a grand time with you and Luke, but I must go home." She paused. "Too bad you'll soon be flying back to the States." She moved forward and hugged Layla and then Luke.

Elsa embraced Luke and Layla, too. Elsa smiled. "I'll

miss you two. We must exchange addresses. Then we can keep in touch."

Layla took a petite notebook from her purse and on a blank page wrote the address of Ford's Farm, the farmstead Luke rented in their Kentucky holler. She ripped out the sheet. "Here."

Elsa smiled. "Thank you. Here's the address for Marjorie and me."

Luke felt happy. "I'm sure we'll write. You're invited to our farm if you decide to take a holiday in the US." He wrapped his arm around Layla. "Best we get to bed soon. We're gonna go shopping early tomorrow."

Luke watched through the pub's front window as the two Englishwomen left the tavern's front entrance. They began to cross the street toward their outdated apartment building next to the Golden Sword Pub.

* * *

11:05 P.M., FRIDAY, ANNE'S APARTMENT BUILDING

Elsa and Marjorie approached their apartment building. The boisterous noise of people talking, shouting, and laughing inside the neighboring Golden Sword Pub seeped into the evening air.

Elsa turned toward Marjorie. "The US is a big country with lots of places to tour. I wish I could afford to visit it to see Luke and Layla."

"By then Layla's baby will be in school." Marjorie laughed. "At least it would take me until then to save money enough to travel to America."

Elsa smelled food and stale ale when a patron opened the Golden Sword's front door and left the tavern. "One drawback of our flat is it's noisy at weekends."

Marjorie shrugged. "But it's a happy sound." Marjorie increased her pace as they neared their apartment building. After the door of the main entrance shut behind them, the noises of the throng in the filled-to-capacity tavern lessened but were still noticeable.

The two women followed the carpeted hallway toward their flat, number ten. Elsa squinted, peering at the door to flat nine. "Anne left her door unlocked."

Marjorie tilted her head. "I guess she didn't pull it shut enough to lock it."

Elsa began to walk faster toward Anne's door. She peeked through the crack. Sudden nausea hit her like a case of motion sickness on a dizzying carnival ride. Staggering, she gagged, fell against the hallway wall, and then steadied herself. "It's Anne. Her head's been cut off."

Marjorie rushed forward. She glanced through the doorway and saw blood, a headless body, and then Anne's head. Its unblinking eyes stared at the ceiling.

Shaking, Marjorie stumbled. After leaning against the hall wall, she fished in her purse and grabbed her mobile phone. She tapped in 999. "Hello. I need the police. A murder has been committed in Crows End..."

TWO

LUKE AND LAYLA were well rested after sleeping late in their Airbnb second-floor apartment above the Red Feather Pub. After climbing downstairs to the ground floor exit, Luke stepped through a black, iron gateway onto the brick-paved lane. Layla followed him. Bright sunshine bathed them. His foot caught on something standing against the vines growing on the pub's wall. A garden rake fell in front of him. He picked it up and began to replace it against the brick building.

His hand still on the rake handle, Luke surveyed the empty, quiet street. He glanced up and down the roadway as he set the rake aside. The Crows End neighborhood should have been buzzing with life on this Saturday morning.

As his eyes adjusted to the sun's rays, he held Layla's ebony hand. He smiled at her. From the corner of his eye, he detected a slight movement to his left. He shifted his gaze and saw yellow police tape stretched across the street's nearest intersection. The thin, yellow barrier vibrated in the soft breeze. A stocky London policeman with gray hair stood near the tape and stared at him and Layla.

Luke glanced right. In the distance, he saw a second strip of yellow tape blocking the far end of the street.

A warm flush spread across Luke's face. He focused on Layla's brown eyes. "We're walking into a crime scene."

Layla nodded as she peered at the officer. "In our first weeks of marriage you'd think we'd get a break from this sort of thing."

The Metropolitan policeman walked toward Luke and Layla as they stepped into the street in front of the Red Feather Pub. Luke estimated the man was in his late forties and close to five foot ten inches tall. "Hello. May I ask what you're doing here?"

Luke gestured toward the Airbnb. "We have a room above the Red Feather. We're on our honeymoon." Luke took a breath. "What happened?"

The detective sergeant (DS) cocked his head. "I'm not at liberty to say." He assessed Luke and Layla. "You sound like Americans."

Luke put an arm around Layla. "Yes, Officer. We're from Kentucky in the US." Luke wondered if the policeman was prejudiced against interracial marriages.

The sergeant motioned at the apartment house across the lane. "Have you met anyone who lives across the street?"

Luke shrugged. "We made friends with two ladies who live there, Marjorie and Elsa."

"I've met the women," the officer said. "They mentioned you, but for the record, may I see your identification?"

Luke pulled his passport from his hip pocket and handed it to the DS while Layla rummaged in her purse for hers.

The detective sergeant examined their IDs and wrote their names in a pocket-sized notebook.

Luke smiled. "Can we leave? We'd like to catch a Tube train to Sloane Square to go shopping."

The officer's face relaxed, and he seemed cordial. "Of course. Thank you for cooperating." The peace officer peered to Luke's left. "Please go where I'm pointing."

"Okay, but to get to the Underground, we've always followed the street." Luke gestured to his right.

"If you go the way I indicated, walk two intersections and then turn right. Walk past two streets, and you'll see the steps down to the Tube station straight ahead."

Luke smiled. "Thanks, Officer." He glanced at Layla and then back at the DS. "When we come back, can we cross the yellow tape?"

"Yes. I'll give your names to our officers. Then you can re-enter the area."

"Thank you." Luke stepped in the direction the policeman had suggested. After he and Layla were out of the officer's earshot, Luke leaned close to Layla. "I bet there was a serious crime."

Layla glanced up at Luke's clean-shaven face. "I hope it's not more dangerous in this neighborhood than we've been led to believe."

"Don't worry. Not many people carry firearms in the UK."

Luke noticed Layla shivered, though a warm breeze blew along the street. She gazed at him. "But they could carry knives."

As Luke led Layla along the sidewalk toward the Tube station, he glanced backward and noticed the sergeant speaking into his mobile phone. *Must be relaying info about us.*

* * *

9:38 A.M., SATURDAY, TWO INTERSECTIONS FROM THE RED FEATHER PUB

Drake, a plainclothes detective constable (DC) stood on a corner two intersections from Anne's flat and the Red Feather Pub. He wore an earpiece connected to his two-way radio and listened to Detective Sergeant Boutwell's instructions. Three intersections away, two policemen dressed in civilian clothes monitored the radio transmission.

Drake nodded. "Yes, Sergeant Boutwell. We'll follow them. Have a description?" He cupped his earpiece with his left hand. "Yes, sir." The constable paused. "Men, did you hear the DS?"

Drake listened as one of his undercover team members spoke. "Yes. But we're three streets away."

Squinting along the roadway toward the Red Feather Pub, Drake recognized Luke and Layla. "The targets are close." He felt uneasy. The tall man and the black woman moved at a quick pace. "Men, I'll delay the targets whilst you get in position."

* * *

9:46 A.M., SATURDAY, TWO INTERSECTIONS FROM THE TUBE STATION

After Drake, the undercover detective, spotted Luke and Layla coming his way, he stuffed his two-way radio and earpiece in his windbreaker's right pocket. He guessed the targets would cross his position in less than thirty seconds. He turned around, glanced left, and saw his two men two intersections away. Within seconds, his officers blended into the throng of window-shopping pedestrians.

How do I delay the targets? Drake spotted a digital camera dangling from Luke's neck.

Drake turned around to face the targets, and then he hurried forward. He halted in front of Luke at the same time the man turned the corner to head toward the Old Street Tube Station. "Sir, I'd be careful with your camera." Drake eased out a breath. "Bad people steal from tourists."

Luke glared at the undercover policeman.

Drake felt a touch of fear as he peered at Luke's flashing eyes. The man appeared powerful and carried himself like a soldier.

Luke tilted his head. "I can take care of myself. I'll kick

their asses if they try anything." Luke shot a steady stare at the constable.

Drake figured Luke had guessed his true identity. *I must keep playing the role.* "Isn't it a matter for the police?"

"Yep. But when they're not around, you gotta take care of yourself." Luke grabbed Layla's hand. "Let's go."

As Luke and Layla started for the Tube station four hundred yards distant, Drake caught sight of his two men walking fast. One of them raised his hand and nodded. They were hot on the trail of Luke and Layla.

* * *

9:51 A.M., SATURDAY, NEAR ANNE'S APARTMENT BUILDING

Detective Sergeant Boutwell's mobile phone rang. "Hello, Drake." He paused to listen to his undercover man.

"Sergeant, why are we following two tourists?"

Boutwell thought for a moment. "This is more than a murder case. It involves national security. We must follow all leads, even those appearing to be trivial. Report all movements of the targets."

"Yes, Sergeant."

* * *

9:55 A.M., SATURDAY, OLD STREET TUBE STATION

Layla felt her heart beating fast. She glanced sideways at Luke as they neared the Old Street Tube Station. "The man who bumped you acted creepy."

Luke peered at Layla's eyes as they trotted down a flight of stairs into the station. "Don't stare backward. Two guys are followin' us."

"How do you know?"

"The weird guy had a two-way radio in his jacket pocket

with an earpiece hanging out. He stopped me to give two plainclothes cops time to catch up with us."

"Why are they after us?"

"We were behind police tape near a crime scene."

Layla surveyed the interior of the Old Street Tube Station. "They gonna get on our train?"

"Yep."

After Layla and Luke stepped onto their train, she peeked at the two tails. They'd stepped onto the train car seconds before its door closed. They gripped blue poles as the train rumbled forward along the tracks. Dressed in casual clothes, they appeared to be tourists or local workers. The men mixed with the wide assortment of riders who wore expensive suits, work clothes, simple outfits, and even company uniforms. Layla squeezed Luke's hand and gestured at the two men. Sloane Square was four miles away.

Luke led her to the far end of the car. They sat. To Layla, Luke seemed calm. She leaned next to his ear. "Why us?"

"I'm not sure. But I think the detective who stopped me asked them to check us out."

Layla sighed. "I don't think we look suspicious to the average cop."

"It must be a high profile case. They're following poten-tial leads, even minor ones. It has to be a page-one crime."

"Will they quit tailing us soon?"

"We'll have to wait and see."

The train rushed along the tracks. Layla examined her Tube system map. "We need to switch trains."

When she and Luke exited the train at the Cannon Street Station, the two men tailing them got off. After waiting three minutes, a train going to Sloane Square arrived.

Layla felt Luke grasp her hand. He said, "Let's get on a middle car." Layla observed the two men getting on the Sloane Square train, one car away. In less than a minute, the train's wheels screeched ahead on the rails.

* * *

10:05 A.M., SATURDAY, AN OFFICE IN SCOTLAND YARD, LONDON

Detective Chief Inspector (DCI) Rory Calvin, aged forty-eight, a man with a thick, black mustache, sat at his desk in Scotland Yard. When his secure desk phone rang, he picked up the handset. "DCI Calvin, here."

"This is Detective Sergeant Boutwell. As you required, we're following Mr. Luke Ryder and his wife."

"Good." Rory rolled up his sleeves to expose his arms covered with black hair. After he'd spent so much time outdoors, his skin had turned tan and leathery. A wiry man, he stood five feet nine inches tall. "What have you observed?"

He reached for a chocolate candy bar in a fat glass jar on his desktop and unwrapped the treat.

"They've boarded a train at Old Street Tube Station. Luke Ryder told me he and his wife were going to Sloane Square to shop."

"Continue to watch them for the time being." Rory paused and took a bite of his candy. He swallowed. "Be advised I've done a computer check using the new artificial intelligence system. Mr. Ryder has worked for the FBI."

"That's revealing, sir."

Rory studied his chewed fingernails. "Tell your men to treat Mr. and Mrs. Ryder well. We may be soon working with Luke Ryder."

Boutwell sighed, and Rory heard it. "We'll treat them with kid gloves."

"Thank you, DS Boutwell."

Rory hung up. *Had Boutwell and his men irritated Ryder?* Rory didn't only work for London's Metropolitan Police Service. He also worked secretly for MI5. He led a clandestine, specialty unit, code-named the Harmonizers. This unit coordinated police investigations with the UK government's security and intelligence services, which included MI5 and the Secret Intelligence Service (SIS), once called MI6.

Sergeant Boutwell and his men were also part of the Harmonizers. As such, they were required to keep their MI5 activities top secret.

Like a champion chess player, Rory thought through possibilities and a variety of future moves. *It's possible Luke Ryder is working undercover for the FBI or the CIA.*

Rory had learned Baron Thomas Thorpe was privy to top secret information about a robotic battle tank, a US Army prototype. Rory also had unconfirmed intelligence the baron's wife had been in a romantic relationship with a suspected spy.

It's time to update Thames House. It was the MI5 headquarters building in Central London. Rory had been there many times due to his work for MI5. Like his men, he was not permitted to reveal his association with MI5 to anyone unless authorized to do so by his MI5 superiors.

Rory picked up his desk phone's handset, about to tap in a phone number. *Let's see how fast MI5's new artificial intelligence system can dig up information about Mr. Ryder.*

* * *

10:25 A.M., SATURDAY, THE US EMBASSY, LONDON

From the air, the massive US Embassy in London appeared to be a translucent, sparkling cube covered by windows. Twelve stories high, it stood along the Thames River in a revitalized industrial area. The average person could walk from the Vauxhall Tube Station to the embassy in ten minutes.

FBI Agent Henry Dunbar sat in his office on the ground floor. He munched on a corned beef sandwich and then sipped coffee. Five feet eleven inches tall, the barrel-chested, thirty-two-year-old black man tipped the scales at 190 pounds.

A month ago, the bureau had assigned Henry to be the FBI Legal Attaché, or legat, in London. He served as the personal representative of the FBI director in the UK.

Henry's phone rang, and he answered it at once. Few people knew his direct number. "Hello, this is Agent Dunbar." His voice sounded gruff.

"Henry, this is Rory Calvin. We met the first week you arrived."

Henry rubbed his short hair and stared with pale brown eyes at his telephone. "I remember you."

Rory laughed. "How could you forget my black mustache and hairy arms?"

Henry smiled. "I couldn't if I had to."

"I have a favor to ask. A US citizen, Mr. Luke Ryder, is on holiday in the UK. According to MI5, we understand he's worked with the FBI…"

Henry sat up straight. "I know him. He worked undercover at NASA—solved a cold case murder and caught a North Korean spy. I worked the case with him. Luke's got a sixth sense. Remember the pirates who hijacked a cruise ship off the California coast?"

"Yes."

"Luke fought 'em and won."

"Impressive."

"You bet your bippy."

"Bippy?"

"It's a saying from an old TV show, Laugh-In. It means 'of course,' or 'you bet your ass.'"

Rory kept silent for a moment. Then he spoke. "At first we at MI5 thought Luke could be involved in an FBI undercover operation to investigate a man from Belarus, Mr. Yegor Bulot. We believe he's a potential terrorist or a KGB operative. He could be a gigolo, too."

"A gigolo?"

"A gigolo who could seduce a woman to gain information from her." Rory paused. "Is Mr. Ryder working for the FBI in London?"

Henry wrinkled his brow. "What? Luke's on his honeymoon."

"He told a Metropolitan Police officer the same thing this morning near the scene of the decapitation of Baroness Anne Thorpe."

"He was there?"

"Across the street. Two witnesses said he'd told them he'd heard a piercing scream at the presumed time of the murder, but they'd convinced him it had come from a loud party at a pub. We have a video of Yegor Bulot near the baroness's flat last night."

"Luke's an amazing undercover cop. Too bad he can't help you with your investigation and liaison with us at the FBI. But for God's sake, the man's on his honeymoon."

"I'm thinking out loud...brainstorming. From what you say, Luke would be a great asset to help with this investigation."

Henry felt his pulse rise. "No way." Henry felt embarrassed after he'd raised his voice to a near yell.

"Hear me out. We've contacted British Airways. He's slated to fly back to the US on Sunday. Again, I'm thinking out of the box. He could stay longer and help."

"The guy's not an FBI employee. He's a deputy sheriff in Kentucky."

"We can offer him incentives. We could pay for his hotel and expenses. Perhaps fly him home for free. A bonus would be available to him, too."

Henry's pulse slowed. "Let me check with my superiors. But don't get your hopes up."

"Thanks for trying, Henry."

"I'll get right on it, Rory." Henry hung up.

* * *

5:37 A.M. (FIVE HOURS EARLIER THAN LONDON TIME), SATURDAY, LOUISVILLE, KENTUCKY

FBI Agent Rita Reynolds, a rising star in the bureau, sat at her kitchen table, sipping a fresh cup of coffee. Quiet this weekend, her apartment served as a sanctuary from her stressful job. *It's enjoyable to relax.*

A series of rings from her FBI mobile phone jarred her and vibrated the table. Rita inhaled, and then reached for the irritating gadget. *What's up?* She peered at the cell's screen. The call came from FBI Agent Henry Dunbar, stationed in the US Embassy in London. She pictured him, a stocky, strong, black man. Always asking questions, searching for answers, he had the reputation of being an excellent investigator. His skill, persistence, and focus had helped bring him to the top echelon of the bureau.

Rita moved the phone to her ear and pressed the device against her black hair. "Hello, Henry. How's London?"

"Great. But there's news about Luke." Henry's voice sounded gruff, as usual.

A smidgen of fear hit Rita. She stood. "Is Luke okay?" She still had a crush on him, though he'd made Layla pregnant and then married the woman, an ex-prostitute. Rita knew they were on their honeymoon in London.

"He's fine, but he's caught the attention of MI5—in a good way, though."

Rita relaxed and stared out her window with her brown eyes. The trees were swaying in the breeze. "What do the Brits want?"

"After they learned how Luke defeated the cruise ship pirates, MI5 folk got hot to bring him into a homicide investigation. Someone murdered a baroness last night. The case may involve terrorists and espionage."

"What?" Images of Luke posing as a NASA public affairs specialist and catching a North Korean spy flashed through Rita's brain. She had led the task force to investigate a cold case murder at a NASA center in California. She'd chosen Luke to work undercover at the space agency.

Henry coughed. "Sorry. Sandwich meat went down the wrong tube." He cleared his throat. "MI5 had been investigating the baroness earlier because a man from Belarus was sleeping with her. Her husband, the baron, has top secret access to UK military capabilities."

"Sounds like a tangled mess."

"Yep. Witnesses told the police Luke said he thought he'd heard the baroness scream when she died."

"Luke's got ESP. I wish he would've accepted the FBI's job offer after his undercover work at NASA."

Rita heard Henry shift his telephone handset. "The Brits are offering to pay for everything to get him on the case. He and Layla are scheduled to fly back to Kentucky tomorrow. I promised to try to convince Luke to help MI5 and smooth the way with the FBI."

"What do you need me to do?"

"Get Sheriff Pike to agree to lend Luke to the FBI and MI5 in case Luke wants to join the investigation." Henry paused as if he were thinking. "Doesn't Layla have a young daughter?"

"Angela. Luke's sister's watching her." Rita paused. "I'll call his sister to see if she can watch the kid a week longer. Would Layla come home without Luke?"

"I don't know, but I've convinced an embassy secretary to escort Layla to tourist sites while Luke's sleuthing, if we decide to help the Brits." Henry coughed again. "Damn meat's still stuck in my throat. I'd better hang up and call HQ."

"Okay, I'll help. Let's keep in touch."

Henry hung up.

* * *

10:38 A.M., SATURDAY, THE SLOANE SQUARE STATION, LONDON

Standing on the platform, Luke peered backward at the crowd behind him as the Tube train started to leave the Sloane Square Station. Railroad cars vibrated the tracks causing a loud, pulsing sound. He hadn't noticed whether or not the two men who had been following him and Layla had gotten off the train.

When Luke stepped away from the station onto the sidewalk, a chilly wind blew, and clouds raced across the sky. He pulled his windbreaker collar tighter around his throat.

Layla's eyes focused on him. "Let's take our time, wander, and explore."

Luke nodded. As he scanned the parklike square paved with stone slabs, the wind rustled its trees. A man with a bicycle propped against his knees sat at a varnished, wooden park bench. Old-fashioned luxury estates and brick apartment buildings faced Luke as he reached into his jacket pocket and took out his booklet of maps.

He saw Layla point. "See the fountain?"

"Yep."

A structure spouting water stood in the center of the square. The sculpture of a woman knelt on a round, stone pedestal. Holding a jar-like container, she appeared to be pouring water from it.

Layla brushed against Luke's arm. "It's the Venus Fountain," Layla read from a London guidebook.

After exploring the square, they strolled past a neighborhood where foreign flags flapped above stately buildings. Luke gazed at the structures and banners. He spotted the German, Spanish, and Romanian Embassies.

Luke glanced backward as he and Layla walked north along Sloane Street. *Those two guys are still following us.* Luke decided not to tell Layla. *Who the hell do these cops think we are?* He shook his head.

Strolling at a slow pace, Luke and Layla noticed a giant department store on Brompton Road. Luke guessed the old building towered six stories. He glanced at his map. "It's Harrods, a famous store. Let's head over there."

As they came close to the impressive store, Luke saw a man standing upside down on his head. A basket sat next to him, and onlookers tossed coins into it. Had Harrods hired him to do an act near its front door? The gymnast attracted a growing crowd.

Dressed in a green cap and uniform with a yellow-edged collar, a male store employee opened the door for Layla. As Luke followed her, he realized the store's interior was darker than most American department stores. Lantern-like electric fixtures and spotlights highlighted the merchandise. Ornamental plaster scenes of ancient Egypt and other faraway places covered the dim walls.

While Layla began to browse through racks of expensive dresses, Luke peered backward at the same time the two men tailing them entered the building. Luke crossed his arms.

All of a sudden, Luke's satellite phone rang. He glanced at the device's display. The call came from FBI Agent Henry Dunbar. Luke knew his conversation would be secure because the FBI had installed the same scrambler software in his phone as it had put on all its agents' phones.

Luke pushed the "answer" button. "Hello, Henry. What's happenin'?"

"I'm stationed in London. You stirred up a tornado at the Red Feather Pub."

Luke furrowed his brow. "How'd you know?"

"The London police called me. Where are you?"

"Me and Layla are in a big department store, Harrods."

"Go outside. I have a story to tell you."

"Okay. I'm lookin' out a window. I see a park bench." Luke speculated Henry would tell him about a crime committed near the Red Feather Pub.

* * *

11:36 A.M., SATURDAY, HARRODS

Luke put his satellite phone in his left hand and tapped Layla's shoulder. She was staring at a display of English china tea sets and then turned toward him when he began to speak. "Let's go outside for a few minutes. I got a call from Henry Dunbar."

"The FBI agent you worked with at NASA?"

"Yep."

Layla nodded. "I'd have to win the lottery to afford any of these tea sets. Let's go."

Luke spoke into his phone. "Did you hear Layla, Henry?"

"Yes." Henry sounded crotchety like he always did, but Luke realized people who judged Henry's mood from the tone of the man's voice likely would be misled.

After Luke and Layla exited Harrods, Luke saw the two tails leave the store. One of the two men smiled and waved goodbye. Luke waved back. "Did you see them, Layla?"

"Yes. Weird."

Luke guided his phone to his ear. "Hang on, Henry. We're outside Harrods. Gonna sit."

"Okay."

Luke pointed to a park bench. He and Layla sat. "Henry, shoot."

Henry took a breath. "You see the newspapers about a killing across from your Airbnb?"

"No. The police blocked the street this morning and stopped us. Didn't tell us crap."

"Your pub quiz partners discovered a dead baroness in a flat across from the Red Feather Pub last night. They found her body next to her decapitated head."

Luke wrinkled his brow.

Luke heard Henry sigh before he continued. "MI5 learned you've worked for the FBI. The killing is linked to espionage." Henry paused. "The Brits may want to buy a US robotic battle tank, and it has top secret software." Henry paused. "What I'm about to tell you is for your ears only."

"Okay."

"They think you've been undercover monitoring the baroness and her husband, Baron Thomas Thorpe, who's in charge of buying the tank for the British Army."

"Nuts." Luke crossed his legs. "That's why two plain-clothes policemen have been tailing us ever since we left our Airbnb."

"It doesn't surprise me. I told an MI5 guy you're on your honeymoon. I'm not sure if he believed me. Where are the tails?"

"They left." Luke laughed. "They even waved goodbye."

Henry chortled. "Those birdbrains should take a refresher class at tradecraft school. You won't see them again." He paused. "You won't believe what the Brits are proposing."

"Nothing would surprise me after this mornin'." Luke's irritation subsided. He reckoned his curiosity had begun to make him feel calmer.

"They want you to help with their investigation of the murder and a potential spy from Belarus. They're willing to pay your expenses and a bonus—at least a thousand pounds, probably more. Plus, the FBI would pay you, too."

"You're kiddin'. Why?"

"I think MI5 wants to monitor you and Layla in case you're both working for the FBI or CIA tracking the spy."

"CIA? Layla?"

"Intelligence folks have vivid imaginations. You've stirred up a hornet's nest of interest from the UK security and intelligence services."

Luke figured he could use extra money for a down payment on a new pickup truck. About a month ago an assassin hired by a Mexican drug cartel had shot up his rusty, timeworn pickup. It had burst into flames. "What'll I have to do to make the money?"

"Extend your stay in London. Help a policeman with his

investigation. MI5 says they're impressed by how you nailed the North Korean spy, beat a horde of pirates, and helped bust a drug ring."

"What about Layla?"

"She could fly home tomorrow, or spend a few extra days touring London, all expenses paid by the UK." Henry cleared his throat. "If she wants to stay here, I've asked an embassy secretary to guide her around London."

"You guys work fast."

"Rita's helping stateside." Henry knew Rita had known Luke since high school.

"What'd she do?"

"Cleared the way with your boss, Sheriff Pike. Asked your sister to watch Layla's daughter longer, too."

Luke formed a mental picture of Angela, Layla's little daughter. But hunger interrupted his thoughts. "My belly's growling like a starvin' timber wolf. I gotta eat." He glanced at Layla. "And I'll discuss the UK offer with Layla. Call you back soon."

"When?"

"In an hour." Luke smiled at Layla. "We'll eat and then stroll in Kensington Gardens. And my name will be mud if we don't have tea in the Orangery next to Kensington Palace."

Henry exhaled. "I'll be waiting."

THREE

THIRTY-FIVE-YEAR-OLD YEGOR BULOT exited his country's diplomatic home, the Embassy of Belarus, at 6 Kensington Court, southwest of Kensington Gardens. The brick edifice stood four stories high and had white-trimmed windows. Though the Belarus Tractor Company employed him as an agricultural machinery salesman, Yegor was a spy. He worked for the State Security Committee of the Republic of Belarus, better known as the KGB RB, an offspring of the disbanded Soviet KGB.

A stocky but handsome man, Yegor leaned against the black, wrought iron fence in front of the embassy. The red and green flag of Belarus flapped in the cool wind above him. Reaching past the lapel of his tan trench coat, he found a pack of cigarettes in his suit's breast pocket. He put a smoke in his mouth, struck a match, and sucked on the cigarette. After drawing smoke into his lungs, he blew it into the breeze. His dark brown eyes blinked and followed the tobacco smoke as it dissolved into the air.

A workaholic, Yegor spent much of his time thinking

about his principal job, that of a spy. *The robotic tank demonstration will be Tuesday. It's essential to learn about the tank's secret operating system. But how?*

Raven Robotics, a US company and maker of the robotic tank, publicized its steel monster as a sixty-five-ton warrior that soldiers could run from afar using a keyboard, a joystick, and a computer mouse. But Yegor had learned the tank was more advanced than advertised. An intelligent machine, it could survey and analyze its surroundings. Its top secret, neural net brain could "think" and make battlefield decisions. Without human supervision, it could identify targets. The tracked steel warrior could classify a target as friend or foe. When in autonomous mode, it could decide whether or not to fire its weapons. An independent, emotionless, almost invincible fighting robot, the artificial beast would not stop until it had slaughtered all its enemies.

Yegor exhaled. *A scary machine.*

He'd been in touch with Baron Thomas Thorpe, the man in charge of high-level UK armed forces weapons purchases. Yegor had tried to convince the baron cheap armored personnel carriers made by the Belarus Tractor Company would be decent vehicles for the cash-strapped UK armed services to buy. The UK-US-Belarus Agricultural Pact of 2029 enabled the three countries to trade farm products and machinery as well as a limited amount of inexpensive military equipment. *It's strange what politicians will do in the name of peaceful coexistence when their real goal is to make money. Then again, the pact gives us an opening to learn about the enemy.*

Yegor remembered the expensive lunches he'd bought for the baron. The noble hadn't said a thing about the robotic tank, though Yegor had brought it up in conversations. *The baron must have suspected I'm hunting for robotic tank technical details.*

Yegor took another drag on his smoke. He sighed, recalling the day he'd met Anne, the baron's wife. Yegor had judged her to be attractive, though not beautiful. Later, she'd often joined him and the baron for restaurant lunches. Of course, Yegor always footed the bill, though the KGB RB later reimbursed him.

Sophisticated, Anne seemed mature for her age. Yegor reckoned Anne was two or three years older than he. One early afternoon during lunch, the baron had left for the men's room. While the baron was gone, Yegor had found it easy to persuade Anne to meet with him later. Had it been a mistake to bed her? No.

Yegor realized being a man who uses sex to compromise the enemy had its advantages. He figured pillow talk could reveal something useful about the baron. Even one significant fact could give him an edge in his quest for secrets about the frightening US robotic tank.

The loud siren of an ambulance brought Yegor back to the present. He stood tall, tossed his spent cigarette on the sidewalk, and stepped on the butt, crushing it. He saw a newspaper vending machine. Its headline screamed, "Baroness Beheaded." His hands shaking, he reached into his pocket and withdrew a coin. In seconds, he held the paper and began to read about the murder. Were the coppers already after him?

* * *

12:18 P.M., SATURDAY, EN ROUTE TO KENSINGTON PALACE

After Luke and Layla ate omelets at a French restaurant across the street from Harrods, the newlyweds walked toward Brompton Road. From there they could find their way north to Kensington Road.

Luke stopped at a street corner, drew Layla closer, and studied her eyes. "Should I stay and make a bunch of money, or go home?"

Layla glanced up at him. "Stay. You can buy the new truck you've been dreaming about."

"What about you?"

Layla smiled. "I'll see London tourist traps with the embassy secretary. If your gig lasts longer than three or four days, I'll fly home."

"Makes sense." Luke wondered what the Brits wanted him to do during the investigation. *They probably just want to watch me, if they think I'm undercover working for the FBI.* Luke kissed Layla's cheek. "Okay, I'll help the Brits. The embassy secretary guiding you will make your sightseein' stress free."

Layla swayed her hips as she sashayed along the sidewalk. "It'll be fun."

Luke led Layla west along Kensington Road toward the Palace Gate of Kensington Gardens.

"When will you call Henry back?"

"He can wait. You gotta have tea at the Orangery."

* * *

1:05 P.M., SATURDAY, THE US EMBASSY, LONDON

FBI Agent Henry Dunbar studied a newspaper. Its headline seemed to yell like a town crier, "Baroness Beheaded."

Instead of reading the front page news item about the killing, he turned to page three to read a gossip columnist's piece, "Baroness Dallied."

Henry was not surprised by the tell-all tale. *The media often focuses on lewd stories.* He read about rumors claiming Anne had played around, and her marriage had been on the rocks.

A student of history, Henry recalled the story of a young woman from the Isle of Wight, Seymour Fleming. She had married a baronet in the 1700s. In the following years, she had affairs with twenty-seven men. Later, she ran away with her husband's friend. A few years afterward, Seymour paid someone to write a story about her affair with this man. With relish, the public read the missive about her dalliances with her lover.

Henry set the newspaper down. *The British public has devoured scandals of the rich and famous for centuries. History repeats itself.*

The harsh ring of Henry's satellite phone startled him. He peered at the device and saw Luke's name on its screen. "Hello, Luke."

"I'll take the deal. Layla says she'd like to stay an extra three or four days."

"Excellent. You two need to keep quiet about this."

"Okay. I'll tell Layla." Luke paused. "What's next?"

Henry peered out his window at tree branches waving in the breeze. "I'll call DCI Rory Calvin at Scotland Yard to tell him you've agreed to help. He's heading the baroness murder investigation."

"Okay."

"After you have tea at the Orangery, grab a taxi and go to Scotland Yard. I've set up an FBI account to pay for your expenses. Ask for Rory at the front desk."

"What about Layla?"

"I asked an embassy secretary, Sonja Perko, to stand by to be ready to show Layla around London. Sonja will take a cab and meet you at the Orangery." Henry displayed a rare smile when he pictured Sonja. "She's a petite blond, twenty-five years old, and athletic."

"Athletic?"

"Was a star gymnast in college." Henry thumbed through his Rolodex and found Sonja's contact information on a card. He liked paper cards because if a power failure ever hit his building, he could still find phone numbers on them. "A taxi from the embassy to Kensington Gardens could take as long as eighteen minutes." Henry imagined heavy traffic would delay the cab, even though Kensington Gardens was a mere three miles from the embassy.

"How will I know her?"

"She'll find you. She's got your pictures and phone number."

"We'll watch for her."

Luke disconnected his phone.

* * *

1:30 P.M., SATURDAY, NEAR THE US EMBASSY

Sonja Perko stood in front of the US Embassy waiting for a taxi. The wind tussled her short, blond hair. She sighed. *So much for my hairdo.* She blinked and recalled her painful phone call with her boyfriend. She'd called off their Saturday night date at the last moment. *Random problems come with the job.* She fought back anger.

To gain experience on her first CIA deployment, Sonja was playing the part of an embassy secretary. She wished to change the world to make it better like her heroes— Mahatma Gandhi, Al Gore, Ralph Nader, and Nelson Mandela—had done. She had studied to become a high school history teacher, but a CIA recruiter had contacted her during her last year of college. Her high grades, fluent French, and extracurricular activities—gymnastics and the Japanese martial art, aikido, had impressed the agency. Sonja hoped she would be a good fit for her current and future CIA missions.

She exhaled. *Too bad I have to babysit a tourist.*

A black, chunky London taxi approached. Its sides displayed an ad for a bank. Sonja waved her arm, and the driver pulled to the curb. She opened the rear door and got in. "Please take me to Kensington Palace." Because heavy traffic clogged the streets, she knew the ride would take longer than usual.

As the cabbie eased into the flow of traffic, Sonja opened her purse. She grabbed her photos of Luke and Layla and studied them.

* * *

1:50 P.M., *SATURDAY, PALACE GATE, KENSINGTON GARDENS*

Luke decided to wait near the Palace Gate where Sonja's taxi would likely arrive. He felt relaxed holding Layla's soft hand as they walked. Peering ahead through the gateway, he saw a shiny, black cab stop at the curb. A small woman with short blond hair left the vehicle. Twenty-something, she appeared fit and about five foot two inches tall.

Luke glanced down at Layla. "Could be the secretary, Sonja."

At once, the blond woman focused on them, smiled, and waved. She wore a navy blue gabardine pants suit and a light, unzipped windbreaker. A little blue purse hung over her shoulder. As she neared Luke and Layla, Luke noticed she moved in an athletic, graceful gait.

She held out her hand toward Luke. "I'm Sonja Perko." Luke noticed her grip was firm for a young woman. Turning to Layla, Sonja shook her hand, smiling. "We'll have fun touring places in London you've not seen yet."

"Thank you in advance, Sonja."

Sonja scanned the gardens. "It's not crowded today." She paused. "Ever since I've been in London, I've spent my spare time exploring the city. I've kept a journal. It helps me recall details about each place. If you'd like, I can spew trivia about the gardens as we walk."

Layla smiled. "I'd like to learn about them."

Luke gestured to a building with public toilets. "Sorry, ladies, but nature's callin.'" He pointed toward the bathroom. "I'll catch up with you."

Sonja grasped at her purse. "It costs fifty pence to go in. Do you need change?"

"No, thanks," Luke replied.

"We'll be heading that way." Sonja pointed.

* * *

SONJA WATCHED as Luke entered the bathroom building. She glanced at Layla. "We won't go far."

Layla nodded and stepped along the pathway. Sonja strolled next to her. "This will give me a chance to ask you what you'd like to see."

The two women walked at a casual pace. Layla peered backward at Kensington Palace. "After we see the flowers and ponds, I'd like to visit the royal dress display."

"Excellent choice." Sonja stopped, hesitated, and scanned the area. A man in dirty clothes with an unkempt appearance neared them. "Since the gardens cover 265 acres, we can't see them all in an hour. We could…"

At the corner of Sonja's left eye, a sudden motion grabbed her attention. The filthy man rushed toward Layla's purse. Sonja grabbed his nearest arm in two places. His heavy body flew toward Layla. Pulling the man's arms in the same direction he had charged, Sonja added her movement to his attacking force. She threw him down onto the walkway.

Crashing with a thud on the pavement, he landed on his backpack. As he rolled aside, his eyes flashed. He held Layla's handbag by its strap.

Sonja felt relieved, as if she'd taken part in a martial arts bout, not a real attack. Even so, she told herself, *Remain calm.*

As fast as she could, she reached into her dangling purse and pulled out a mini can of mace. She sprang forward and sprayed the attacker's face as if he were an oversized wasp. Pawing at his eyes, the purse snatcher stumbled to his feet, and ran toward the Palace Gate. He still clutched Layla's handbag.

"You okay, Layla?"

"I'm fine."

Sonja pulled her mobile phone from her purse and tapped an icon on its display. "A man grabbed Layla's purse and got away." Sonja nodded and listened. "Let me know when you get him." She disconnected from the call and felt as if Layla's eyes were poking her.

* * *

OUT OF BREATH, Diego walked fast. He was a member of a London gang, the Latin Mob. He smiled, but his hands trembled as he read from an Airbnb printed receipt he'd found in a side pocket of the black woman's purse. Snatching his burner phone, he tapped an icon to call a Mexican man, Julio.

"You got the info, Diego?"

"Yeah. He's staying in an Airbnb above the Red Feather Pub in Crows End."

"Super. We'll send the rest of the cash to your top guy."

Diego said, "We call him 'The Older.'" Diego felt the purse stowed in his backpack.

"Okay. 'The Older.'" Julio disconnected his phone.

The sound of shoes pounding the pavement behind him made Diego jump. He turned to see two men running at top speed toward him. Dropping his phone on the pavement, he stomped on the device, crushing it against the concrete sidewalk.

It's got to be coppers. He raised both hands. "I'm complying."

* * *

LAYLA'S BROW FURROWED, and she rubbed the back of her neck. "Who'd you call?"

Sonja stroked her blond hair and sighed. "A London policeman."

Layla cocked her head. "You're not a secretary, right?"

Sonja glanced away. "I work security. I'm tasked to protect you."

"Why?"

"Luke's assignment involves dangerous people."

"Will I get my handbag back?"

"Yes. Undercover police are watching us. The man I

called told me they saw the incident and were about to nab the perp."

Layla shook her head, closed her eyes, and exhaled. She felt better. "Thank God." She raised her eyebrows. "You know karate?"

Sonja brushed her hands together as if knocking sidewalk dirt from them. "I took classes in aikido. You learn self-defense moves designed not to severely harm an attacker."

The door of the restroom opened, and Luke emerged. He stared at Layla, and she felt the concern he telegraphed to her with his eyes.

Layla figured her facial expression had shown him her distress.

Luke narrowed his eyes. "What's goin' on?"

"A guy snatched my purse." She heard her voice waver.

Luke's eyes flashed and he leaned forward. "I'll catch him."

Sonja grabbed Luke's arm. "I called the police. They saw it happen and will get him."

Luke stiffened his posture. "I should of known they'd still be tailin' us."

Sonja smiled. "It's for your protection."

Layla lowered her head and peered at Luke. "You should've seen her. Sonja tossed him like a stuffed animal onto the ground."

Sonja shrugged. "I used aikido. You use the forward motion of the attacker to throw him in the direction he's moving. A grandmother can deflect a bad guy if she's well trained."

Luke exhaled. "What about the purse?"

All of a sudden, Sonja's phone rang. "Yes?" She stared into the distance. "You got the purse?" She paused. "Bring it to the Orangery." She disconnected. "The snatcher didn't have time to dump the handbag."

Luke rubbed his whiskers. "I wonder if the guy's a simple purse snatcher or something else."

Sonja made steady eye contact with Luke. "I'm sure the police will interrogate him."

Layla felt herself breathing easier. "Do we still have time to go into the palace?"

Sonja smiled. "I suggest we skip the palace tour and garden stroll and go have tea." She glanced at Luke. "Henry told me DCI Rory Calvin's anxious to speak with you."

* * *

2:30 P.M., SATURDAY, KENSINGTON PALACE

Luke, Layla, and Sonja walked toward the Orangery for afternoon tea.

Luke saw a bench. He halted and smiled at Layla and then Sonja. "I should call Henry. I bet he's getting nervous. You ladies can sit for a minute."

Sonja shrugged and sat down. Smiling, Layla joined her.

"Thanks. It won't take long." Luke stepped away and turned his back. After taking his phone from his hip pocket, Luke touched Henry's phone number on the device's contact list.

The phone rang three times.

"What's up, Luke?"

"We had an incident. A guy grabbed Layla's purse while I was in the bathroom." Luke glanced back at Sonja. "As little as Sonja is, she tossed the purse snatcher onto the sidewalk. But he got Layla's handbag." Luke paused. "The police called Sonja back. They caught the perp and have the purse."

Luke heard Henry shift his handset against his ear. "Our MI5 partners phoned me about it." He sighed. "Good thing I asked her to help. Her hobby's martial arts."

"She's a secretary?"

"Okay, she's on the team. Keep it to yourself."

Luke lowered his voice. "FBI?"

"CIA. She's new and in training. Escorting Layla will be

good experience, and Sonja can help with the baroness and robot tank investigations."

Luke sighed. "She's a tiny little thing."

"Yeah, but she's lethal, albeit she doesn't carry a pistol. It's a big no-no to carry a firearm in the UK, even for CIA and FBI agents. The Brits don't even like Secret Service agents to carry handguns when they guard the president during visits."

Luke turned his head and glanced at Layla and Sonja on the bench. "Sure as shooting, Layla will be safe with Sonja."

Henry paused. "As long as I have you on the phone, I need you to keep me up to date on what the Brits are doing. They're reporting to us, but in case they leave something out, you can fill in the blanks."

"Okay. I gotta get Layla and Sonja to the Orangery for tea. I'll duck out early and catch a cab to Scotland Yard to meet DCI Calvin."

"I'm glad to hear it. Talk to you later."

* * *

2:45 P.M., SATURDAY, NEAR THE ORANGERY

As they neared the Orangery, the sunshine warmed Luke's skin. Random, white, wispy clouds moved across the robin's-egg blue sky. He jammed his left hand in his pocket. *Should I leave the women here and take a taxi to Scotland Yard now?* He took a deep breath. *I better take a sip of tea or two and then go.*

Soon after Luke and the two women sat at a table in the Orangery, a London policeman entered the building carrying a shopping bag by its string straps. He stopped near them and caught Sonja's attention. "Hello, Sonja."

"Hi, Ron. Thanks for coming over here right away."

Ron perked up. "You're most welcome. The Metropolitan Police are here to serve."

He turned to Luke and Layla. "I take it you're Mr. and Mrs. Ryder."

Luke displayed a smile. "Yep."

The officer glanced at Layla and removed her purse from the shopping bag. "Here's your handbag." He handed it to her. "We believe nothing's missing. We watched the purse snatcher the whole time."

Luke turned to the policeman. "Learn anything about the perp?"

"He's a well-known petty criminal. Nothing to worry about."

Layla smiled. "Thanks, Officer."

Minutes later, a waitress brought three pots of tea, and the trio ordered sandwiches and scones. Luke watched as the women buttered their quick breads and spread jam on them. Luke picked at his food. *I gotta catch a cab to Scotland Yard soon.*

* * *

3:01 P.M., SATURDAY, AN OFFICE IN SCOTLAND YARD, LONDON

Rory dialed Henry's US Embassy number. The phone rang six times.

"Hi, Rory." As usual, Henry's voice sounded gruff. "You learn anything worthy of note about the purse snatcher?"

"He's a well-known petty thief, a member of the Latin Mob gang." Rory paused. "We recovered Layla's purse and everything in it. We saw the perp talking on a burner phone. He smashed it on the walkway."

"Why?"

"Likely to protect fellow gang members."

Rory heard Henry making sounds like he was sipping coffee. Then the FBI agent said, "I thought you pulled your surveillance off Luke and Layla."

Rory hesitated. "The first two men, yes. But we added a new detail in case of trouble." Rory paused. "Your Sonja's on the ball. Our men saw her toss the assailant aside like he was a puppet."

Henry laughed. "Seems as innocent as a schoolgirl, but she's as dangerous as a leopard."

"Excellent. When should I expect Luke?"

"In a half hour."

FOUR

LUKE STOOD at the curb on Kensington Road and waved to Layla as she and Sonja got into a taxi to check out the Natural History Museum on Cromwell Road. *Too bad I can't have a fancy dinner with 'em later on.*

A boxy, black taxi approached. Luke stuck four fingers in his mouth and blew. A sharp, loud whistle sounded above the din of traffic. Luke saw the cab driver smile as he guided his vehicle to a stop near Luke.

As Luke got in, the cabbie of East Indian background grinned. "I haven't heard such a loud whistle in years." The driver continued to grin as he stared at Luke.

Luke shrugged. "A four-finger whistle comes in handy once in a while." He took a breath. "Please take me to Scotland Yard."

The cab driver accelerated from the curb. "You a Yank?"

"Yep. I'm from Kentucky."

"Do you live near the track where the Kentucky Derby runs?"

"Close."

"You here on business?"

"I'm tourin'."

The driver glanced backward when he stopped at a light. "The New Scotland Yard used to be called the Curtis Green Building. Years before, people knew it as the Whitehall Police Station."

Luke nodded. "Thanks for the history."

"My pleasure. I like to tell tourists about the city."

Luke knew Scotland Yard stood in Westminster near the Thames River. It took the taxi nine minutes to arrive at 35 Victoria Embankment. When Luke exited the black cab, he gazed at the Scotland Yard building. From the outside it appeared to be a standard stone-clad government office structure between seven and eight stories high. He noticed the wide front entry and its outside wall that consisted of a bank of high windows.

After stopping at the desk inside the entry, he caught the attention of the receptionist, a young woman with long, red hair. "I'm here to see DCI Rory Calvin. I'm Luke Ryder."

The young lady picked up her phone and punched a button. She listened. "This is the front desk attendant. A Mr. Ryder is here to see you. Yes, sir." She hung up and smiled at Luke. "You can go right up. He's in Room 837. The lift's to your right." She pointed.

* * *

3:50 P.M., SATURDAY, SCOTLAND YARD, LONDON

Luke found Room 837 close to the elevator lobby on the eighth floor. He stared into the office and saw a wiry man with a thick, black mustache and hairy arms. His sleeves rolled up, the man sat in front of a computer monitor and typed with two index fingers, hunt-and-peck style.

With his knuckles, Luke tapped on the door frame.

The fellow turned and studied Luke for an instant, smiled, and stood. Taking a step forward, he held out his hand. The man spoke with a deep voice. "Luke Ryder, I presume?"

"Yep, and you must be DCI Rory Calvin." Luke felt the man's firm grip.

"Call me Rory. Welcome to the team. Have a seat, Luke."

As he sat, Luke surveyed the cramped office. Smaller than he had expected it would be, the room still contained a lot of equipment. There were three telephones, a fax machine, a two-way Handie Talkie sitting in its charger, and a two-way radio base station console with a handheld, push-to-talk microphone. Six file cabinets lined one wall. Rory's desktop included a slim printer, a Rolodex jammed with address cards, and a chubby, clear jar of wrapped mini candies.

Rory reached into the jar and pulled out a chocolate bar. "Would you like one, Luke?"

"No, thanks. I ain't got a sweet tooth."

Rory began to munch his chocolate. He swallowed. "We are impressed with your background, the murder cases you've solved, and your bravery. I liked reading how you fought a band of pirates on the Alaskan cruise ship." Rory paused. "The British government wired two thousand pounds to your bank account this afternoon."

Luke sat up straight and smiled. "Thanks, but I haven't done anything yet."

"Not to worry. I'll keep you busy all day and into the night."

"What are my duties?"

"Accompany me whilst I interview suspects. Ask questions. Share your thoughts about suspects, clues, and whatever." Rory paused. "I would like to hear your hunches, even if you think they are far-fetched. I'm told you have extrasensory perception."

Luke sighed. "Stories about me are overblown. I'm a normal man, but I've been lucky in three or four cases."

"Don't sell yourself short, Luke. The FBI and even the CIA have well-thought-out reasons to try to recruit you."

"The CIA?"

"I'm positive you'll hear from them." Rory crumpled the candy bar wrapper and tossed it into a gray, steel waste can next to his desk. "Let me explain what we do here. I head a Metropolitan Police unit, code-named the Harmonizers. Its purpose is to coordinate London police activities with the UK government's security and intelligence services—MI5 and SIS, once called MI6."

Luke nodded and crossed his arms.

"I also interface with the FBI through your colleague, Henry Dunbar. On occasion, I contact the US ambassador, Mr. Ralph Caro. He is in charge of CIA agents in the UK, including Miss Sonja Perko." Rory paused and took a breath.

Luke cleared his throat. "As long as yur telling me all this, tell me about the US-built robotic tank. It's somehow tied into the murder of the baroness."

Rory smiled. "Let's talk whilst we drive to the scene of the murder."

* * *

4:10 P.M., SATURDAY, NEAR ANNE'S APARTMENT

Eight minutes after Rory started his unmarked police car, he stopped in front of Anne's apartment building in Crows End. From the car's front seat, Luke gazed at the familiar street in front of the Red Feather Pub and his Airbnb apartment one story above it. Although the lane was open to traffic, yellow police tape still cordoned off Anne's apartment building. A pair of policemen stood in front of the place, holding clipboards.

Luke focused on Rory. "I bet y'all operate much as we do in the States."

Rory scanned the building's exterior. "Yes, and we deal with similar crimes."

After signing their names and entry time on a clipboard, Rory and Luke walked along the hallway to apartment number nine. Sitting on a folding chair, a third policeman guarded the flat's door. He handed Rory and Luke nitrile gloves and crime scene shoe covers. After donning them, the two men stepped into Anne's flat with caution.

* * *

4:15 P.M., SATURDAY, INSIDE ANNE'S APARTMENT

Luke saw a three-foot-wide blood stain on the carpet as he and Rory walked into the worn, medium-sized efficiency flat. A chalk outline marked where the body had been. Luke guessed a smaller chalk circle showed where the police had found Anne's decapitated head.

Luke turned to Rory. "It's an undersized apartment for a baroness."

"Indeed. We believe she conducted secret affairs with men here." Luke noticed Rory scanning the room's furnishings. They included a couch, coffee table, two easy chairs, end tables, a full-size bed, and on the far wall, a kitchenette.

Luke eyed five sets of bookshelves lining two walls. He glanced at Rory. "She liked to read. Must be a hundred books here."

Rory scratched his head as if he were thinking. "She belonged to a book club."

Luke saw a note on top of a thick, heavy book sitting on the coffee table's bottom shelf. He knelt and read the letter. "This says the crime scene techs found papers in a book."

Rory picked up the message. "The techs are gone for a meal break."

Luke fixed his gaze on the heavy, coffee table book, *Volume 2, Best Images of South America.* "May I open it?"

"Of course. Take care though."

Luke flipped the big book open. Someone had hollowed out enough pages to contain a two-inch thick stack of handwritten documents on ultrathin, onion skin paper. Luke glanced at Rory. "Mind if I examine the papers?"

"Go ahead."

Luke lifted the top, lightweight page which read, "My Sordid Life, By Anne Thorpe." To Luke, the neat penmanship seemed to be feminine. Easy to read, the document had been written with a ballpoint pen.

Leaning over Luke's shoulder, Rory glanced at the title page. "We need to go over this in detail." He walked to a box of crime scene tools and supplies and picked up two large evidence bags. "Here." He handed one of the envelopes to Luke. "It appears Anne has numbered the pages." He took the top half of the pile. "I'll read these. You read the bottom ones."

Luke picked up the first page of the bottom half of the stack. "Funny the crime scene guy didn't call you right away."

"He knew I was on the way. Didn't want to take a chance of his radio message being intercepted."

Luke began to read page thirty-nine.

FIVE

HOLDING the bottom pages of Anne's writings, Luke sat on the comfortable couch.

Rory glanced up from the second page of Anne's account. "Anne writes she's been having an affair with a banker, Robert Rothstein—a man of whom I'm aware." Rory wrinkled his brow. "He's under investigation, suspected of embezzling money from his bank. We believe he's an addict, too." Rory took a notebook from the vest pocket of his sports coat and wrote down the banker's name.

Luke held an inch thick pile of the ultrathin papers. "There's a lot here. What if we scan for names first, and then read what Anne says about them?"

"That makes sense." Rory grinned. "The banker is a decent suspect. We need to question him as soon as possible."

"Does he know he's in trouble?"

"He could suspect it. We've begun to audit the Crows End Bank's ledgers. Someone stole more than a million pounds from retiree accounts."

Luke scanned his pages for names. He glimpsed at Rory.

"Why would a high-class woman write this as if it's a book manuscript? Why not put it in a diary?"

Rory shrugged. "It's hard to say what a noble will do. They live in a different world than we ordinary blokes."

Luke saw a name. "I found somethin'."

"What?"

* * *

LUKE BEGAN to read out loud from page forty-three of Anne's handwritten account: "My acquaintance, Estrella Bach, needs to be called what she is, an officious busybody. As I write this, she is president of our London Readers Book Club. She is dictatorial and pushy. I'll see to it she is removed from the presidential office. She may be a gentry member with land and money, but her position doesn't mean she should guide our club."

Luke lifted his eyes from the wad of pages in his hand. "Estrella may be worth talkin' to."

After writing Estrella's name in his notebook, Rory glanced at Luke. "I've heard of the woman. She owns horses and keeps them on her country estate. She's wealthy and throws her weight around." He paused. "I agree we need to interview her."

Luke shifted on the couch. "Could Anne's story be somethin' she wanted to sell to a publisher? You'd think she'd be embarrassed to write about her sexual affairs."

Rory eyeballed Luke. "Indeed."

Papers in his hand, Luke stared out the window. *She must of had a bad marriage. Did she fight with her husband? If she divorced, would she need money? A tell-all book could sell a lot of copies in the UK.* In his mind's eye Luke recalled TV shows about royal scandals. They were of great interest to both the British and American audiences.

Rory rubbed his mustache, and Luke noticed the man's eye movements as he scanned farther down a page. "I found another name, Arnold Beeker, a pro golfer." Rory curled his lip. "She slept with this man, too." Rory shook his head.

Luke lifted his chin. "We're makin' progress."

Rory lowered his head. "At this early stage, I don't see how any of these people could tie into the robotic tank."

Luke flipped through the pages in his hand. "I spotted a foreign name."

Rory jerked his head up from the pages he'd perused.

Luke frowned. "I ain't sure I can say this fella's name right—Yegor Bulot."

Rory sat straighter. "Yegor's been on our radar because he's obsessed with the robotic tank."

Luke crossed his arms. "What kinda name is Bulot?"

"I'm not sure. Yegor's from Belarus, a close ally of Russia. He's an import/export rep for a Belarus tractor manufacturer. A new UK-US-Belarus agreement permits Belarus to sell farm equipment and some military machines here and in the US. We're watching him."

Luke squinted. "Why would a tractor company rep worry about a battle tank?"

"He may want to steal trade secrets to improve farm machines. Or he could be after secret military technology." Rory raised his eyebrows. "What's Anne say about him?"

"She had sex with him."

Luke noticed Rory's eyes gleamed. "Yegor's our number one suspect." Rory sat up. "We could be close to solving this case. I wager Yegor had an ulterior purpose in getting into Anne's knickers."

Luke leaned forward. "What do you mean by ulterior purpose?"

"Yegor wanted to get something more from Anne than sex. He could've blackmailed her, threatened to tell the baron she'd cheated on him if she didn't deliver secret information about the robotic tank." Rory held his chin high. "I'll let you read the dossier we have on Yegor. My team have been tailing him and shooting pictures of his activities. We've also recorded some of his conversations."

"It should be real interestin' to read Yegor's file and see pictures of him." Luke rubbed the back of his neck. "But we can't forget her husband, the baron. Half the women murdered in the US were killed by their intimate partners."

Rory opened and closed his mouth and then spoke. "Anne's written she's had relations with all these suspects except for the woman, Estrella." Rory stared at the ceiling for a moment. "We won't question Yegor right away. He'd figure we're onto him. He could flee the country. But you're right. An obvious suspect is the baron."

Luke leaned forward. "Anne hasn't mentioned the baron in the pages I've scanned. You see anything in yur pages?"

Rory glanced up at Luke. "Anne says her husband, the baron, is infertile, and she can't have children with him." Rory studied the paper in his hand. "She writes about quarrels with him. Says she's thought of getting a divorce."

Luke set his half of Anne's manuscript back in the bottom of the hollowed-out book. "I didn't see any more names."

Rory uncrossed his legs and set the top half of Anne's papers into the bulky book. "I've finished scanning for names, too." He stood. "It's time we pay a visit to the baron, catch him off guard at dinner time."

* * *

WHEN LUKE ROSE from Anne's couch, he heard the flat's door open. Wearing shoe coverings and nitrile crime scene gloves, three crime scene technicians in white jumpsuits entered the apartment.

Rory focused on the tallest man. "Jerry, please see to it a courier picks up this hollowed-out tome and the papers in it ASAP. Tell the lab people these items are to be analyzed at once. Tear this place apart even if it takes days. Examine each square inch."

"Yes, sir."

Rory turned to Luke. "Let's go. We need to surprise Baron Thomas Thorpe before his grief lessens."

Luke studied Rory. *He's stressed, gettin' aggressive.*

Rory took his phone from his sports jacket pocket. "Excuse me, I must make a call."

SIX

ART GRANGER, a slight young man of medium height, sat behind his gray metal desk in Thames House in Central London.

Often compared to the FBI, the UK's domestic security agency, MI5, was much more secretive than the bureau.

Art chewed on a sandwich, his evening meal. After glancing at a crossword puzzle on his desktop, he set his hours-old Reuben on a flattened paper bag. In ink he wrote "architect" in a horizontal row of puzzle squares.

After he again bit into his dry sandwich, he wished he could afford a better dinner. *Playing James Bond is fun.* He felt into his pocket. *But I need a lot more quid.*

His desk phone rang. The incoming number indicated his MI5 boss, Rory Calvin, was calling. "Hello, DCI Calvin." Art brushed his thin blond hair from his forehead.

"Are you tracking Yegor?"

"We were. But we lost him after he left the Belarus Embassy."

"Again?"

"Yes, when he switched trains."

"Get back to me when you locate him again."

"Yes, sir."

Rory hung up.

Art stared at his handset and slipped it back onto its cradle.

* * *

5:27 P.M., SATURDAY, THE KING'S CROSS STATION

Yegor had ridden the Underground for hours, brooding. After his train stopped at the King's Cross Station, he exited his car with a newspaper in his left hand. Walking along the street, he found a coffee shop and ordered a cup of brew and a bagel.

Minutes later, seated in a booth, Yegor smoothed his newspaper on the tabletop and eased out a breath. *If necessary, I'll leave the country before the coppers get to me.* He rubbed the back of his neck. *But I must get the system software for the robo tank before I go. Or should I abort the mission?* Yegor sighed and then took a big breath. *No, I shouldn't leave England. I'll be assigned a broom to sweep the streets in Minsk if I don't get a trade secret about the tank.* He pictured the dreary, Stalinist-style KGB RB headquarters in Minsk on the corner of Independence Avenue and Komsomolskaya Street.

He glanced at the headline once again, "Baroness Beheaded." He pictured Anne. She had lived in a fantasy world. Her tactics of delay had made him irate, though he believed she'd loved him. Too bad she had to die. Why had she refused to deliver what he needed, details of the baron's role in the purchase of the autonomous US battle tank?

Yegor glanced across the coffee shop. Nobody sat close to his booth. He slid his satellite phone from his suit jacket pocket and selected Baron Thomas Thorpe's cell number. *I'll speak in a quiet voice.*

* * *

5:47 P.M., SATURDAY, EN ROUTE TO THE THORPE MANSION

Rory's undercover police car bumped over a rough section of road as he and Luke headed for Baron Thomas Thorpe's country estate. Luke's satellite phone sounded. He dug the device from his hip pocket and stared at Layla's name on its display.

"Hi, sweetie."

"Hi, hon." She sounded out of breath to Luke.

"What's happenin'?" Luke sealed the phone against his ear so he could hear Layla better.

"We're in a nice Italian restaurant, and Sonja's in the restroom. Let's talk fast."

"Why?"

Layla paused. "Sonja's been asking probing questions."

Luke peered out the car's window at the passing countryside. Rory glanced at him as if trying to figure out the other side of the phone conversation. Luke's mind galloped ahead like a racehorse heading for a finish line. He figured he'd have to tell Layla sooner or later Sonja worked for the CIA. But he couldn't do it with Rory tuned into his phone conversation with Layla. Also, Rory and Henry would have to agree Layla had a need to know Sonja was a CIA agent. Luke guessed Layla would have to sign a nondisclosure agreement of some kind. He paused while he considered what to say next to Layla. "What's Sonja interested in seein' in London?"

"I get your drift." Layla laughed. "Is the Scotland Yard cop with you?"

"Yep."

"She asked what I did as an escort. How'd she find out?"

"Tell you later. What places did you tell her you'd like to see?" Luke smiled. *Layla's on the ball.*

"I said I escorted men who wanted to show off young women to business clients, but I didn't go into detail."

Luke felt a flush spread across his face when he shot a glance to his right at Rory. The man appeared to be listening, though he kept his eyes on the road ahead. "How's the food?"

"I saw a Mexican man. I'm not sure if he followed us to the restaurant." Her voice trembled.

"Tell Sonja."

"Okay. We're going to order soon." Layla's phone made a sound as if she'd shifted it from one hand to the other and placed the device against her other ear. "Sonja's coming back. Tell you specifics later."

"Bye, love. Have a nice dinner." Luke scanned ahead through the windshield.

Rory glanced sideways. "Was that Layla?"

"Yep."

"I'm sure Sonja's giving her a fine tour."

Luke lifted his chin. *Rory knows Sonja's CIA. Henry and Rory are in cahoots. Everyone should lay their cards on the table. After Layla signs government paperwork, she needs to learn Sonja's a CIA agent.*

Rory made a right turn onto a country road lined by trees on both sides. "I'll give you some background about the baron." Rory scratched his left ear. "The baron acts polite, but he hides his real personality."

Luke rubbed his whiskery face. *Why is the baron concealing his real personality? Does he keep his feelings secret to appear like he's a normal aristocrat? What's he like under his cloak of secrecy?*

Luke heard himself start to speak. "I picture the baron as a man with a pale face who stays inside, sheltered from the wind, rain, and sun."

"Perfect description." Rory eyed Luke for a fraction of a second and trained his eyes back on the road ahead. "The baron's as white as a ghost. Always dresses in a fine suit. Speaks in a clear voice, with precise words. Soon, you'll see how accurate your intuition about him is."

SEVEN

YEGOR WAITED on a bench in Queensway Tube Station ten minutes from Kensington Gardens. Deep in thought, he felt a tap on his shoulder. Turning, he saw his handler from the Belarus Embassy, Viktor, a short, thin man with a creased face and pure white hair. Yegor leaned away from Viktor.

Sixty-eight-year-old Viktor smiled. "Sorry to sneak up on you, but doing it keeps my tradecraft in tune."

Yegor patted the spot next to him on the bench. "Take a seat, and rest."

The timeworn gentleman sat. "What are you going to do to get meaningful information about the robotic tank?"

Yegor swallowed. "I have leverage, Viktor. Let me explain…"

EIGHT

RORY INCREASED his automobile's speed on a straight stretch of road. "We're close to the Thorpe mansion."

Luke stared along the highway as if his mind were elsewhere.

Rory tapped the brake pedal a moment before he felt his vehicle bump over a rough patch of road. He wondered what Luke thought as the American peered at the passing, green landscape along the country lane.

"How does Thorpe treat people?" Luke asked all of a sudden with an inquisitive voice.

A relaxed smile crossed Rory's face. *Luke's trying to figure out what the baron's psychological type is—what makes him tick. How can I describe a baron to an American?* "Lord Thorpe is a noble who has a different set of attitudes than commoners do."

Luke ran his fingers through his hair. "Different?"

"From an early age, his parents taught him he was better than most people." From the corner of his left eye, Rory saw Luke shake his head. *Most Americans don't understand the UK's social class system.*

Luke crossed his arms. "Sounds like the castes in India."

Rory felt his muscles go rigid. "Not as extreme as in India, but I get why you think what you do." Rory reminded himself the United States, though less than three centuries old, had been forged in a revolution during which people began to consider themselves free and equal. *Luke needs to learn why social class is important in the UK.* He drew breath into his lungs. "Our countries differ because of their separate histories."

"How?"

"Here, for thousands of years, people were born into roles in society like those of the lords, the trades, and specific vocations. Often jobs like bricklayer, shoemaker, or farmer were handed down from father to son. Then the Industrial Revolution came, and attitudes began to change little by little but not as fast as they changed in America after your violent revolution."

Rory felt his car seat move as Luke shifted his weight. "I git it. In America we're different cuz money's king." He paused. "Do barons lord over their womenfolk when they're inside their homes?"

"I don't know." Rory paused and licked his lips. "I'm sure we'll learn more detail about how nobles interact behind closed doors when we read Anne's account with care instead of merely scanning it."

Rory saw the baron's mansion pop into view in the distance as his police car crested a hill on the winding road. "The Thorpe estate is on the right."

Luke squinted. "I see a mansion."

* * *

6:10 P.M., SATURDAY, TUBE STATION NEAR KENSINGTON PALACE

A thick mist drifted across the park on a cool wind. A lone man reached under his trench coat and grabbed his cell phone equipped with a scrambler. He tapped Baron

Thomas Thorpe's home number on the smart phone's display.

The sounds of the baron's slow breathing came through the earpiece. "Hello?" The baron slurred this one word, and he coughed.

The caller felt his mind go into high gear. *Is the baron drunk?*

"This is Range Man. Condolences for the loss of your wife, but we have business to attend to in person."

"When and where?" The baron's voice sounded muddy.

"Do you need to write it down?"

"Not now. A car turned into my driveway twenty seconds ago." The baron's delivery sounded clearer as if he'd begun to sober up.

"We must meet soon."

"Call back later."

Range Man heard a click, and his phone disconnected.

* * *

6:13 P.M., SATURDAY, THE THORPE MANSION

Groggy, the baron stepped away from his window over-looking the front drive. A half bottle of scotch sat on the oak end table next to him. He eased down in his leather easy chair, in a half daze. His vivid blue eyes focused on the last drops of whiskey left in the bottom of his heavy tumbler. Like a mechanical man with a shaky hand, he reached for the bottle of scotch and poured three ounces of the amber liquid into his glass.

His pipe sat next to the whiskey bottle on the table. He always had enjoyed the smell of pipe tobacco. *I should've smoked instead of poured two shots.* But whiskey would ease his sore throat pain. As he gazed at his surroundings, the room began to spin. Steadying himself, he sipped from his refilled glass. *Getting drunk has been easier since Anne died.*

He set his glass on the table next to his pipe. His hands

trembling, he tightened and straightened his tie. *I must get a hold of myself. The damn robotic tank field demonstration will be Tuesday. I should skip it.*

A secret SIS military analysis officer, the baron knew his superiors would not appreciate his being crocked more often than before. He was the chief of the British Army's procurement office in charge of acquiring novel, advanced weapons. But his covert job as an SIS officer was more important.

Should I go to the office Monday? It could take my mind off Anne's death. He stroked his chin. *If I decide to go to the proving ground live-fire demo, I will have to be sober by Tuesday morning.*

He caught sight of Anne's photograph in a frame on top of the bookshelf next to the baby grand piano. As he stood, he lost his balance but grabbed the back of his leather chair. He ran his hand through his black hair, and then shuffled to the picture. He picked it up and stared at Anne's smiling image.

A fine woman. Too bad we couldn't have children. It's a shame she cheated on me.

Lord Thorpe's devoted sixty-eight-year-old butler and chauffeur, Baxter, stepped into the room. He seemed like a malnourished Frankenstein. "I spotted two men standing at the front entrance, sir." He spoke in a low, bass voice. His gray eyes blinked, and his tall, six-foot-one, skinny frame wavered. He brushed aside his gray, stringy hair.

The Thorpe mansion's doorbell rang.

Who would visit at dinnertime? The baron didn't feel like speaking with anyone at the moment, but chances were the visitors had come to offer their condolences. "I'll see them, Baxter."

* * *

THE TALL, heavy front door creaked, pulled open by a uniformed butler with unkempt, long, gray hair.

Then a six-foot-tall man dressed in an expensive, dark blue suit stepped around the butler. He studied Luke and

Rory for a moment and asked, "DCI Calvin, have you caught my wife's killer?" Baron Thomas Thorpe slurred his words. He moved closer to the open doorway.

Luke smelled alcohol on the nobleman's breath from five feet away.

Rory drew his eyebrows together. "Not yet, Lord Thorpe." He paused. "May my colleague, Mr. Luke Ryder, and I come in and chat?"

"Of course." The baron nodded, and the butler pulled the massive door wide open.

Luke felt frigid air as he entered the foyer. The hallway was just as cold. He glanced at Rory as they followed the middle-aged baron to a front room. Coal burned in a fireplace and warmed the space. The room air smelled of burning paraffin. Luke recognized the odor. *It's candle coal.*

The baron motioned toward a hefty leather couch next to an easy chair. "Please sit, gentlemen."

To Luke, the baron appeared thin, but muscular. The noble's mussy, black hair looked as if he'd brushed it with his fingers. He had a straight nose and a pitch-black mustache.

Lord Thorpe staggered and then collapsed into his chair.

NINE

AFTER GRABBING his tumbler of whiskey from the end table next to his leather chair, the baron first aimed his eyes at Rory and then at Luke. "Would you gentlemen like a drink? Glasses and beverages are along the back wall." He waved at a well-stocked, shiny, oaken bar.

Luke felt his body demand a drink, but he'd been alcohol-free for close to a year. His smile wavered. "No thanks." He recalled being drunk. A hangover wasn't pleasant, but alcohol never stopped trying to lure him back into its clutches. *Once an alcoholic, always an alcoholic.*

Rory eased out a heavy sigh. "I'd love to have a cocktail, but I'm on duty."

The baron took a giant sip of whiskey and coughed. "Excuse me, but I need to get my drinking done today." He studied the carpet and then caught Rory's eyes. "I must be sober by Monday. I'm thinking of going back to work to keep my mind off Anne's passing."

Rory drew in his shoulders and scanned the room.

The baron waved his arm, gesturing at his surroundings.

"Search the entire place if you wish. No need to get a warrant."

Rory smiled. "Thank you." He took a wallet-sized cardboard box from his sports coat pocket. "Then you won't mind if I take a routine DNA sample?"

"Go ahead." The baron grinned. "But won't alcohol ruin the results?"

"It could. Let's go to a sink, and you can rinse your mouth." Rory put on nitrile evidence gloves, and withdrew a swab, a vial, and a folded evidence bag from the box.

With difficulty the baron stood and walked in a clumsy gait. "A toilet is over here." The baron gestured and walked into a side room. He grabbed a paper cup and swished water in his mouth.

As Luke watched, Rory said, "Please open your mouth." The baron parted his lips, and Rory rubbed the swab inside the man's inner cheek. Rory bagged the swab and vial and dropped his evidence gloves into a wastebasket.

Afterward, the baron walked at a slow pace back to his chair. He lifted his glass and swallowed a gulp of scotch.

Rory leaned forward. "I have key evidence I must ask you about before we examine your house."

The baron straightened. "What?"

* * *

RORY SAT on the edge of his chair, leaned forward, and focused on the baron. "In Anne's flat we found a manuscript in her handwriting. It describes her friendships with three men and a woman." Rory launched a gaze like a laser beam toward the baron's pale face. "Were you aware she wrote this document?"

Blinking, he bit his lip. "No." He peered sideways. "But she admitted she'd cheated on me many times." He took a quick breath.

Luke thought the baron calmed after he exhaled. Then the man emitted a rough cough, and his face turned red.

Luke kept his eyes on the nobleman. *He's lyin' about something.*

Rory took his palm-sized notebook from his sports coat pocket. He flipped the memo book open. "I'll read names of persons Anne listed in her manuscript. I'd like to know if you recognize any of them."

The baron glanced away from Rory and gazed out his window.

Rory studied his notebook. "First, Arnold Beeker, a pro golfer."

The baron's blue eyes flashed. "Never heard of him."

Rory wrote in his notebook, and then eyeballed the baron. "Robert Rothstein, a banker?"

The noble shook his head, indicating no.

Rory flipped a memo page. "Ever heard of Estrella Bach?"

"Yes. Anne mentioned her many times. The woman's president of a book club. We've met once. She's pushy, haughty, and rich."

"Do you think Estrella would wish to harm Anne?"

"I know Anne didn't like the woman, and Estrella didn't like Anne either."

Rory nodded as he studied the baron's face. Luke thought the nobleman appeared relieved. Did he think Rory considered Estrella a person of interest?

Rory glanced at his notes once again. "Have you heard of a Mr. Yegor Bulot?"

The baron sat up straight and his pale skin turned red. "Yes."

Luke saw the noble's mouth drop open for a moment. He seemed dazed. Then he touched his lips, rubbed them, and spoke. "He's a salesman with a Belarus tractor manufacturing company. He's been trying to sell cheap armored personnel carriers to the British Army." The baron stood. "Has the bastard been sleeping with my wife?" The baron pounded his end table. His bottle of whiskey began to fall, but he grabbed it before it tumbled onto the shiny, oak floor. His quick reflexes surprised Luke.

Rory leaned forward. "According to Anne's writings, she had relations with Yegor." Luke saw the London DCI raise his eyebrows. "Do you think Yegor may have harmed Anne?"

"Yes. I surmise before long Yegor would've threatened to make his dalliance with Anne public if I wouldn't buy those shitty armored personnel carriers." The baron sat down on his leather chair and lifted his chin. Breathing fast, he flared his nostrils.

Rory tilted his head to the side. "Did you know for certain Anne slept with Yegor?"

"No, but it makes sense. Yegor's sleazy and would do just such a thing to enrich himself."

Rory flipped to the front of his notebook. "You have worked as chief of the British Army procurement division for a decade. How long has Yegor been trying to convince you to buy Belarusian military equipment?"

"A year." The baron jutted out his chin and crossed his arms.

"How would Yegor have met Anne?"

"Yegor and I had business lunches after he made sales calls. One time Anne joined us."

Rory nodded and then sat straight up.

Luke believed Rory felt confident. Would he stick an imaginary pin in the baron's snobbish ego? "Before her death, were you aware Anne had rented the flat in Crows End?"

The baron cracked his knuckles. "Hell no."

Luke had to go to the bathroom. "Excuse me. May I use your toilet?"

The baron displayed a slow smile. "A larger one is down the hall, past the library on the left."

Rory shook his head. "Nature calls at the worst times."

Luke stood and left the room, stared into the library, and saw a camera on a copy stand. He started moving again, quickening his pace along the wide hallway as he neared the bathroom.

* * *

LUKE LEFT THE BATHROOM. *I should step into the library to check out the camera stand.*

The carpet felt thick under Luke's shoes as he entered the sizable, book-filled room. He thought the library with its tall ceilings, bookshelves towering against each wall, and fireplace would make a fine location for a Sherlock Holmes movie. But the twenty-first century digital camera and copy stand combination on the reading table seemed out of place. The camera peered downward from an adjustable steel arm toward a two-by-three-foot wooden base. A document sat on the pine platform, ready to be photographed.

Luke saw a cable that ran from the camera to a computer sitting on the carpet. The side panel of the computer had been removed and sat on the rug. Squatting down, Luke glanced inside the computer. He opened his eyes wide. The machine's heavy, four-by-six-inch hard drive was gone. *Must've broken, or had the baron removed it to get rid of evidence?*

Luke started back to the room where the baron and Rory were talking. *I gotta ask the baron what he'd been copyin'.*

* * *

WHEN LUKE RETURNED to the sitting room where the baron relaxed near Rory, the two men were smiling. Close to empty, the aristocrat's whiskey bottle sat at the nobleman's side. Lord Thorpe caught sight of Luke. "Find the loo?" His words were barely distinguishable from each other.

Luke figured he'd ask about the photo setup in the library right away. "On the way back from the bathroom, I stepped into yur library. I saw a document copy stand sittin' on the long table."

The baron rubbed his face. "I've been copying historical

documents I found gathering dust in the attic." To Luke, Lord Thorpe appeared to force himself to grin.

Rory leaned forward.

Luke felt as if a burst of energy traveled across his body. "How come the big hard drive is gone from the computer hooked up to the copy station?"

The baron shifted in his chair and loosened his tie. "The damn thing died on me. I've ordered a new one. Should arrive Monday." He covered his mouth and coughed. "I must rescan everything."

Rory cocked his head. "I know someone who may be able to recover what's on your hard drive."

Lord Thorpe bit his lip. "I started to copy the items a week ago. It won't be difficult to rescan them." He paused. "I tossed the drive into the wheelie bin for recycling this morning."

Rory leaned forward in his chair. "Is it still in the wheelie?"

The baron shrugged. "No. I heard the bin lorry come by before noon. It's noisy as hell."

Rory stood. "Excuse me, Lord Thorpe, but I must step out to make a quick phone call."

The aristocrat appeared apprehensive.

TEN

RORY STUDIED his mobile phone's contact list and tapped Art Granger's MI5 number at Thames House in Central London.

"Hello, DCI Calvin." Art spoke in a tenor voice.

"Art, I need you to send a crew to search for a computer hard drive. This one's about four-by-six inches, an inch thick, is heavy-duty, and weighs about a pound and a half. It may have been dumped wherever the local bin lorry tips out the metal recycle load it collected from Baron Thomas Thorpe's country estate."

"Yes, sir. How soon?"

"At once." Rory paused. "Also, please send Tom and Roger and other crime techs they can snag to examine the baron's manor house. He's agreed to a search. But do begin warrant paperwork. We may need one later."

"I'll get on it straightaway."

* * *

THE BARON SNORED, and his chair back tilted rearward until it rested almost at its horizontal setting. Luke thought the baron had to be enjoying his rest. *Meanwhile, I should take a second gander in the library.* Luke reckoned he might find a key document near the copy camera.

After entering the library, Luke saw a rolling ladder on a track along shelves on the back wall. *This is interestin'.* As he rolled the ladder along the track, it vibrated. He stared upward and saw an empty space where a book had been on the top shelf. *What kinda books would these folks store up high?*

After climbing the ladder, Luke noticed *Volume 1, Best Images of South America* sat to the left of the vacant space. He imagined Anne climbing the ladder. *She took the second book in the series and hid her writings in it. I gotta tell Rory.*

Luke took a moment to think. *Did Anne pick Volume 2 to hide her manuscript because the book sat high on the top shelf? Why would she set it on the bottom of her coffee table in her flat in plain sight, if she wanted to conceal the volume?*

* * *

LUKE FOUND Rory standing in the hallway. He glanced at Luke and gestured for him to come closer. "The baron's sleeping it off. A team will be here soon to search the mansion. We should leave to speak to Estrella Bach. Her estate is fifteen minutes away."

Luke made strong eye contact with Rory. "I went back into the library. I found an empty space on the shelf where Anne's hollowed-out book, *Volume 2, Best Images of South America,* had been."

Rory's eyes widened. "Is it obvious from a distance the book is missing?"

"Yes."

Rory scribbled in his notebook. "Why wouldn't she stick a replacement book in the space?"

"Good question."

The butler approached. "Would you gentlemen like refreshments?"

Rory anchored his thumb in his belt. "No, thank you. We'll leave in a minute." He paused. "Please let our investigators in when they arrive. The baron has agreed to let us examine the house."

The butler made a discreet bow with his head. "Yes, sir. I'll see you out then."

Rory turned to Luke. "Estrella owns a sprawling country estate, a manor house, and several fine horses."

Luke felt hungry. "Do you think she'll offer us tea and some cake?"

"There's a slim chance she will."

ELEVEN

RORY'S mobile phone sounded as he and Luke approached the undercover police car in the baron's driveway. "Hello, Art." Rory pictured the thin young man, eager to please.

"Sir, our people photographed Yegor Bulot entering and leaving the Belarus Embassy three times this week. Later today, we observed Yegor in Kensington Gardens near the King Arm's Gate sitting on a park bench. An elderly man joined him. We're working to identify him. They talked, but we were unable to get close enough to record their conversation."

Rory widened his stance. "You're getting excellent intel."

"There's further info. The research team learned Yegor has been contacting many UK farmers to sell tractors to them. He's made half a dozen sales in the last two months."

"Keep up the good work." Rory disconnected from the call.

TWELVE

THE BARON SNORED during his deep sleep, but the ring of his cell phone jarred him awake. Groggy, he pulled his phone from the breast pocket of his suit coat. "Hello. Who's calling?" The baron's voice was raspy.

"You know."

"What do you want?" The baron wheezed.

"Anne was pregnant. We were in a relationship."

The baron flipped the lever on the side of his leather easy chair and sat up straight. Pain pounded his head. "You're a son of a bitch."

THIRTEEN

LUKE GLANCED at Estrella Bach's manor house as Rory
stopped his unmarked police car in her wide, paved
driveway in front of a closed gate. Luke guessed a remote
control could open the expensive barrier.

After a quick visual assessment of Estrella's mansion and
land, Luke judged her estate to be much bigger and more
impressive than the baron's house and grounds. A lush,
well-kept lawn and stately trees surrounded Estrella's large
house.

As Luke and Rory exited their car, a handsome, brown
horse standing behind the gate near a stone wall lifted its
head. The animal studied Luke and Rory with probing eyes.

Luke peered back at the steed. *Sure is handsome.* Luke
nodded toward the gate. "I can press the push-to-talk button
to get 'em to open the gate." He paused. "But first I wanna
take a close-up gander at the stallion."

Rory nodded. "Go ahead."

Luke walked to the horse. Its eyelids opened and closed
as it took a step in Luke's direction. Feeling in his trousers
pocket, Luke took out his satellite phone and focused its

camera on the fine animal. At the same time as Luke pushed the shutter button, static hissed from a speaker next to the gate. "Stop taking pictures, at once." The high-pitched female voice seemed to burn holes in Luke's eardrums.

* * *

7:13 P.M., SATURDAY, THE US EMBASSY, LONDON

Henry sat at his FBI office desk in the US Embassy, chewing the last of his microwaved TV dinner. *I better contact Ashton Boxman ASAP.*

After arriving in the UK, Henry had met Ashton twice. As director general (DG) of MI5, Ashton was the sole person of its five thousand employees to be identified to the public.

Henry recalled his first meeting with Ashton. At first glance, Henry had thought Ashton was too young to be the head of MI5. Ashton had the appearance of a young college graduate, even though he was in his late thirties.

The day Henry had met him, Ashton had worn black-rimmed glasses and had combed his brown hair straight back. His outfit had consisted of a cheap, mass-produced suit he must have bought in a department store; a blue dress shirt; and a gray tie.

Henry had heard rumors Ashton often worked seventy hours, seven days a week. Henry studied the phone on his desk. *There's a decent chance he'll be in his office.* Henry pressed the speed dial button labeled "Ashton."

The phone rang twice. Henry heard a click. "Hello, Henry. Have you worked Saturday and late into the night, like I do?"

Henry scanned the remnants of his food on the TV dinner tray sitting on his desk's ink blotter. "Since the murder of the baroness and its connection to Yegor, the Belarus citizen, and our robotic battle tank, I've been working my ass off."

"Would you like an update?"

"Yes." Henry's smile broadened. As the FBI director's personal representative in London, Henry was the liaison with the main UK law enforcement and security agencies.

"DCI Rory Calvin's people told me your man, Luke Ryder, has worked well with our team."

Henry rubbed his rough, ebony face. "Don't you think all of us should get on the same page?"

"Aren't we working together?"

"No. Luke should know Rory's on your MI5 payroll. Why tail our man and his wife? It's a waste of resources."

"I agree. I'll tell my people to identify themselves to Mr. Ryder."

Henry raised an eyebrow. "We have an alphabet soup of groups working this situation: MI5, FBI, CIA, and your SIS. Let's coordinate better."

"I'll make it happen." Ashton remained silent for a moment. "I have much to report. I'll email you an encrypted message." Ashton rushed his words. To Henry, the DG sounded embarrassed and eager to cooperate. "Here are highlights. Odds are the Belarus national, Yegor Bulot, is a spy. He's slippery as an eel and has often evaded our surveillance. Baron Thomas Thorpe is in charge of evaluating the robotic tank for possible use by the UK armed forces. He is vulnerable, and Anne's murder is related to Yegor's efforts to uncover information about the tank."

Henry thought he hadn't heard anything useful. "I don't want to cut you short, Ashton, but I'd better call Luke ASAP. I'll read your report as soon as I get it."

"You need to know something else. We'll send extra agents to the upcoming robotic tank live-fire demo at Poppins Proving Ground on Tuesday to protect the tank. Spies from countries besides Belarus may be attending, and we'll keep an eye on them."

Henry grinned. "I'll make sure Luke, Layla, and Sonja will go, too."

* * *

7:15 P.M., SATURDAY, ESTRELLA'S COUNTRY ESTATE

A tall, blond woman rushed from the front door of Estrella's manor house, jogging toward the horse. Luke saw the woman's blue eyes flash. He guessed she must've been in her early thirties. She waved her cell phone in the air. "Leave at once. I don't allow pictures to be taken of my horses."

Luke's brow furrowed. *Why the hell is this woman irate?* He stood taller. "This is outside of your fence line. Where I'm at is a public right-of-way. I have every right to take a picture as long as I don't sell it to someone." Luke figured the lady had the potential to explode like a vial of nitroglycerine.

Estrella appeared strong and athletic to Luke. She narrowed her eyes. "People take pictures of horses and then steal them for buyers."

"I'm no rustler."

Rory got out of his car and snapped its door shut.

Next to her horse, Estrella tapped her foot. "Why the bloody hell does a Yank think he can tell me what's permitted in my own country?" She lifted her cell phone. "I'm going to call 999 and have you arrested."

Rory held up his badge. "Madam, we *are* the police."

Grasping her mobile phone, the tall woman dropped her hand to her side. "Why's a Yank working for the Metropolitan Police?"

Rory moved next to Luke. "He's helping with the investigation into the death of Baroness Anne Thorpe."

Estrella sighed. "I heard she'd been murdered."

Rory stared at Estrella. "We're here to ask you questions because you and Anne were acquainted."

Estrella huffed. "It'll have to be fast. I'm late for a dinner engagement." She brushed her hair with her hand. "Sorry I yelled. People do rustle horses around here. I'll open the gate." She walked along her driveway and pushed a button on a post. The gate rose.

As Luke passed through the gateway, his satellite phone

vibrated in his hip pocket. He glimpsed at the device's display. "Hello, Henry."

"This is important, Luke." Henry's voice sounded deep.

"One sec." Luke tapped Rory's shoulder. "I've got to take this. I'll be right in."

"Okay." Rory and Estrella entered her manor house.

FOURTEEN

LUKE PRESSED his satellite phone against his ear. "Go ahead, Henry."

"Rory isn't only a Metropolitan policeman. He's with MI5, too."

Luke recalled MI5 was one of the UK's secret security agencies, but he didn't remember what it did. "Is MI5 the British agency similar to our CIA?"

"It's sort of like the FBI." Luke heard Henry sipping something—coffee? "Just the MI5 Director General's identity is made public. All other MI5 employee identities are secret."

Luke scratched his hair. "Sounds like a domestic CIA."

"MI5 is different from both the CIA and the FBI. MI5 has extra leeway compared to the FBI." He took a breath. "MI5 may break the law if doing so would do less harm than terrorists or foreign spies could cause."

"Should I tell Rory I know he's in MI5?"

"Sure. Tell him his MI5 boss, Ashton Boxman, okayed it. He'll call Rory soon."

"Okay." Luke kicked a pebble off the stoop in front of the manor house. "Layla is suspicious of Sonja."

"Our CIA folks are trying to figure out what you're up to. Sonja's been asked to find out what she can from Layla."

Luke rubbed his eyelids. "CIA's investigating the FBI?"

"Not for long." Henry's brow wrinkled. "MI5 is setting up a baroness murder and battle tank task force." He exhaled. "You're a talented investigator. It's the reason why Rita and the FBI still want to hire you."

"I like my deputy sheriff job." Luke glanced at Estrella's open front door. "I gotta hang up and catch up with Rory."

"Okay."

FIFTEEN

WHEN LUKE ENTERED Estrella's luxurious manor house, he smelled tobacco smoke. Ten feet past the foyer to his right, he saw Rory talking with Estrella in a front room. Sitting on a couch next to Rory, she puffed a cigarette.

Rory spoke. "You're the president of the London Readers Book Club. Anne had been a member. When did you see her last?"

Estrella smashed her cigarette butt in an ashtray and lit another cigarette. She blew smoke in Rory's direction off to his left side. "I saw her Friday evening at our club meeting."

Luke felt as if he were intruding when he walked into the front room. "I had to take the call."

Estrella glanced at Luke and then stood. "I have a dinner date at the Striped Badger Pub." For a moment, she pressed her lips together. "I must leave. But if you can give me a ride to the pub, I can answer queries en route. I'll take a cab home."

Rory stood. "Fine, but first I'm required to take a DNA sample from you."

Estrella crossed her arms. "Don't I have to give my permission?"

Rory reached into his sports jacket pocket and pulled out his portable DNA collection kit. "In this case, we are authorized to collect samples. It's routine." He slipped on a pair of nitrile evidence gloves and took a swab from his kit.

Estrella bared her teeth and glared. "I'll ask my solicitor about this. You'd better have the right to do this, or I'll see you in court."

Rory extended the swab in front of him. "Please open your mouth. I must brush the inside of your cheek. It's painless."

Estrella stared at Rory and opened her mouth.

After he stored the sample in a vial, Rory sighed. "Let's go. We don't want to keep your dinner partner waiting."

SIXTEEN

THE SUN HAD SET. The headlight beams of Rory's undercover police car bobbed up and down, lighting the rough road ahead. Rory drove fast. He, Luke, and Estrella arrived at the Striped Badger Pub in less than a quarter hour. The pub sat between stands of trees alongside the same country lane where Estrella's manor house stood.

Though Rory had asked Estrella questions during the brief ride, Luke noticed she had dodged Rory's queries.

As Estrella opened her passenger-side door, Luke glanced at her. *This ride didn't yield any important info, but if we eat here, that could change.* Luke tapped Rory's shoulder. "My stomach's growling. Wanna have dinner here?"

Rory shifted in his car seat. "Sure. I'm hungry."

Estrella turned toward Rory as he exited the driver-side door. "You've been persistent. Why not sit with me and my friend, Phoebe Hackle?"

Rory smiled. "Thank you for inviting us to join you and Ms. Hackle."

Estrella shifted on her feet. "Of course, I should inform you she's recently been released from the hospital after a mental breakdown. I'm trying to help her reintegrate into society. She's still a bit out of touch with reality."

Rory shrugged. "That's good of you."

Estrella stared at Rory and Luke for a second. Luke felt like her eyes were burning holes in his jacket. "You're going to find out sooner or later." She paused. "I'm a lesbian. Anne Thorpe and I had one or two dates, but our relationship was platonic."

To Luke, Rory appeared gob struck. Rory rubbed his lips. "Thank you for being honest. No worries. I won't broadcast your status."

A chilly breeze blew a cold mist against Luke's face as Luke and the others neared the pub entrance. When Rory pulled its front door open, heated air rushed out, warming Luke as he entered. Though dim inside, warm, indirect lighting made the building seem cozy.

Estrella waved, and a well-dressed woman with graying hair waved back. "Estrella, how are you?"

"Fine." Estrella gestured at Rory and Luke. "I've brought two men to join us for dinner, DCI Rory Calvin and his associate, Mr. Luke Ryder." Estrella glanced at Rory and Luke. "Gentlemen, please meet my friend, Phoebe Hackle."

Luke estimated Phoebe to be in her early fifties. Of average height and overweight, she seemed friendly at first glance.

After everyone sat, a waitress came to their table. Glancing at a nearby dinner party, Luke saw a man eating a jumbo bowl of lamb stew. It smelled great. "I'd like lamb stew, a side order of mixed vegetables, and your biggest lime cordial."

The young waitress smiled. "Yes, sir." She took the rest of the orders.

Estrella stared at the waitress. "Also please bring me my usual whiskey on the rocks."

"Yes, ma'am."

Luke lifted his chin. *Estrella's tongue may loosen after she has had a shot or two.*

* * *

8:10 P.M., SATURDAY, THE STRIPED BADGER PUB

Luke watched Estrella as she ate fish and chips and sipped scotch. After two whiskeys, she slurred her words. While Estrella turned her head toward Phoebe to speak with her, Luke glanced at Rory and tilted his head toward Estrella. Luke wondered if Rory got his unspoken message, *Since Estrella is drunk, now's a great time to ask her questions.*

Rory winked and dipped his head as if he understood. He sat up straight and made eye contact with Estrella. "Who do you think killed Anne?"

Estrella rubbed the back of her neck. "Could've been a number of people. Anne handed keys to her flat to some of her acquaintances."

"Why?"

"I'd call her place a clubhouse. She often hosted our reading club in her flat."

Rory raised his eyebrows. "Why didn't you hold those meetings in your manor house?" Rory spoke in a soft voice.

Estrella shrugged. "Anne's flat is in London, closer to where many members live. Her husband, Lord Thorpe, objected to having meetings in his house." Estrella's words were indistinct.

"Wouldn't the baron be irked if she had rented a flat for the sole purpose of staging meetings?"

Estrella wavered in her chair, plastered. She mumbled, "Rumor has it Anne had male friends visit her apartment, too."

Rory displayed a wide grin. Luke figured Rory wouldn't make a decent poker player. Rory leaned forward. "How about women?"

Estrella broke eye contact with Rory and then glanced back at him. "Anne was curious about female-female relationships. But I assure you she was heterosexual. I returned her key."

Rory tilted his head sideways. "Did Anne and the baron get along well?"

"I believe his infertility led them to drift apart." Estrella sighed. "Also, Anne wanted a baby."

Rory zeroed in on Estrella's eyes. "How would you describe Anne?"

"Easygoing. She shied away from arguments or conflicts." Estrella studied the ceiling for a second. "I believe she watched the telly in excess because she lived in a fantasy world, not in the real one."

"Did you dislike her?"

"No, but she didn't like me."

Rory sighed. "Thank you for your cooperation." He'd cleaned his plate. "I think we'll leave soon."

Luke set his spoon on the table, surprised at how filling the lamb stew was. A quarter of it remained in his bowl. "I'm done. But the stew tasted great."

Phoebe's cheeks turned a light pink. "If you can't finish it, I will." She had spoken loud enough that people at an adjoining table glanced at her.

Luke felt warmth spread across his face.

Estrella laughed. "Phoebe and I often share a meal, but tonight I was hungry and ate all my fish." Estrella glanced at Luke. "I'm glad Phoebe will be able to eat the rest of your lamb stew, if you don't mind. No point in wasting good food."

Luke raised his eyebrows. *Strange.* He shoved his bowl of lamb stew across the table. Phoebe took a spoon and began to eat the rest of the stew.

Rory's phone chimed, and he stared at its display. Though he couldn't read it, Luke saw Rory had received a text message.

* * *

LUKE SAW Rory's eyes dart back and forth as he read the

text. Rory peered at Luke. "We have a lot of work to do tomorrow. We'd better leave and get plenty of sleep."

"Okay."

Rory addressed Estrella and Phoebe. "We've had a nice visit, ladies. But Luke and I must go."

Estrella sipped her third scotch on the rocks. "Thank you for having dinner with us." Her words were more indistinct than before.

As Luke and Rory exited the pub, Rory stopped outside the building. "I'm authorized to tell you I work with MI5 as well as with the Metropolitan Police Service. Also, SIS has informed MI5 that Lord Thorpe has called his British Army procurement office and assigned an assistant to attend the robotic tank demonstration on Tuesday. Lord Thorpe said he wishes to continue to mourn at home."

"Henry told me you work for MI5. Your DG said Henry could tell me."

Rory's eyes lit up. "Our several organizations are forming a task force. We're the point men."

Luke rubbed his hand through his hair. "What's our marchin' orders for tomorrow?"

"Thames House sent me the addresses for the golfer and his golf club. We'll visit Arnold Beeker tomorrow. As for the banker, we'll surprise him on Monday when his bank opens. I know a lot about Yegor Bulot and where he lives. We don't want him to flee the country. We'll keep him under surveillance."

When the two men stopped outside Rory's car, Luke pulled his satellite phone from his pocket. "I gotta call Layla. How long will it take to drive to my Airbnb?"

"We'll arrive by nine."

* * *

8:35 P.M., SATURDAY, THE RED FEATHER PUB

Although louder than earlier in the week, the noise in the Red Feather Pub this Saturday night didn't bother Layla. She glanced backward at two London construction workers who had challenged her and Sonja to a game of slop pool. Layla couldn't help smiling. *They won't like losing to two women.*

Layla rubbed chalk on the tip of her cue stick and then leaned down over the table covered with green felt to line up her shot.

An instant before she hit the white cue ball, her cell phone sounded. She tapped the cue ball. It struck the black eight ball. It took three rolls and dropped into a side pocket.

Sonja gave Layla a high five. "Nice shot, Layla."

The two men, who still had work clothes on, laughed and shook their heads. As they congratulated Sonja, Layla's phone continued to ring.

Layla grabbed her phone. "Hello, Luke."

"Where are you, hon?"

"At the Red Feather playing pool. You coming back soon?"

"I'll git there by nine."

"Give me a call when you get close."

"Okay. Does Sonja need a ride home? Rory said he can drive her."

"I'll check." Layla lowered her phone and glanced at Sonja. "If you need a ride, Rory can take you home."

Sonja nodded yes.

Layla put her phone against her ear. "She needs a ride. We'll meet you in front of the pub when you get here."

"Okay." Luke hung up.

SEVENTEEN

RORY GUIDED his vehicle toward the Red Feather Pub. London's traffic flowed more slowly than it would have on a normal Saturday night.

Two intersections from the pub, Luke caught sight of a dark sedan, with its front license plate covered by a brown paper bag. He glanced at Rory. "Y'all have toll roads in London?"

Rory turned a corner. "The new Silvertown Tunnel charges tolls. It connects the Greenwich Peninsula to the Royal Docks." Rory paused. "Why do you ask?"

"Before we turned the corner, I saw a parked, black car with its license plate covered. Do drivers cover their plates to evade tolls?"

"The driver could be trying to slip by CCTV cameras. At least a half million of them are in London."

Still 500 yards from the Red Feather Pub, Rory slowed and pulled to a stop. "I'm going to call in your sighting." He touched his cell phone display. "This is DCI Calvin. We saw a black sedan near 45 Kingston Road with its number plate covered. Send an ARV to investigate."

"What's an ARV?"

Rory pulled away from the curb. "An armed response vehicle. Most police don't carry firearms, but ARVs do."

In a minute, Luke spotted Sonja's bright, blond hair illuminated by a streetlight. Layla waited next to her.

Rory stopped at the curb and turned to Luke. "I'll meet you here tomorrow morning at eleven. If my arrival time changes, I'll ring."

"See you then." Luke exited the car and held the door open for Sonja. "Thanks fur watchin' Layla."

"My pleasure. We had a great time." Sonja got in the passenger's seat and waved.

Luke moved close to Layla. He gave her a long kiss and glanced upward. Tilting his head, he peered into a darker place in the sky. "For a change no clouds are in the sky. I see stars."

Layla caressed him, and then glanced at a park bench near the sidewalk. "Let's sit out here for a few minutes." She held Luke's hand and squeezed it.

Luke guided Layla to the bench. "What are you plannin' for tomorrow?"

"Sonja will meet me for breakfast. We'll plan our day then." Layla wrapped an arm around him.

They sat and kissed again. Layla gazed into his eyes. "Let's go upstairs and make love. It won't be long and my baby bump will show."

* * *

9:10 P.M., SATURDAY, NEAR THE RED FEATHER PUB

As Layla and Luke rose from the park bench, Layla saw a movement in the dark shadows of a bush twenty feet from them. She squinted. The dim figure of a man stepped into a pool of dim light. Layla felt a chill run through her body. She pointed and clung to Luke. "A man with a knife."

"Get behind me. Then run."

Layla scooted behind Luke as he got into a balanced, fighting position. He backed toward the locked iron gate behind them.

Like a cheetah, the man bounded toward them. His flashing eyes made him appear fierce and determined. Layla felt in her purse for the key to the black iron gate behind them, but her bag was jam-packed with all kinds of items.

Damn, our backs are against the fence.

* * *

LUKE'S EYES focused on the shiny combat knife the Latino-looking man held as he gained forward speed. Luke felt Layla sheltering behind him, her hands on his hips. *I gotta give Layla a chance.*

Luke shoved Layla to his right along the Red Feather Pub's side brick wall. She began to run toward the street in front of the pub. When he'd pushed her, his right foot had stomped on a rake propped against the pub's wall. As the garden tool fell toward the pavement, he grabbed its wooden handle and raised it skyward. *Goddamned lucky I leaned it there this morning.*

The attacker leaped forward, bringing his knife down in a slashing motion. At the same time, Luke stepped toward the street and slammed the rake's head on the man's wrist.

The assailant screamed. His knife tumbled from his hand. The razor-sharp weapon fell through a grate and into a street drain. His olive skin and black hair lit by a streetlight, the attacker scampered backward. He turned and sprinted across the street like Usain Bolt running the hundred-meter dash.

Luke ran after the man as he neared a dark sedan. *It's the same one with the paper bag tied around its license plate.*

The car's back door swung open, and the attacker dove into the vehicle's rear seat. Its tires squealing, the black automobile began to move.

A fraction of a second later, Luke heard his rake whistle

through the air as he smashed the fleeing car's rear trunk lid. The smell of burning rubber lingered in a mini cloud of pollution. *Is Matéo, the Mexican drug lord, behind this? He ain't forgot I killed one of his guys.*

Two pub patrons emerged from the Red Feather's front doorway. A tall man with a beer belly watched as the accelerating, black car slid around the corner and disappeared. He stared at Luke, who held the rake. Its wooden handle had snapped. "Do you need help?"

"No, I'm gonna call the police. A man tried to rob me." Luke smiled, pulling his phone from his hip pocket with his free hand. "Thanks though, sir." After setting the broken rake down, Luke touched Rory's name on his contact list.

The heavy man waved. "Best of luck with the coppers."

After a third ring, Rory answered. "We're on the way. Layla called Sonja." His words were rushed. "You hurt?"

"No. I hit the perp with a rake."

"See you soon." Rory disconnected.

Luke glanced at the pub's side wall. A CCTV surveillance camera was aimed at the black iron gate. *I reckon it got a sharp pic of the bastard.*

* * *

FOUR MINUTES after Luke had called Rory about the knife attack, Detective Sergeant Boutwell arrived at the Red Feather Pub. Luke still held the broken rake while he talked to Layla on his satellite phone. "You can come back. The police are here."

Layla had entered a pharmacy at the next intersection after running from the attacker. Luke figured he still felt jumpy because adrenaline hadn't stopped shooting through his body.

Boutwell studied Luke. "You okay?"

"Yep."

"Do you think this incident is connected to the murder of the baroness?"

"No." Luke paused. "It wasn't a mugging, either. The perp didn't ask for money. He tried to kill me."

Boutwell stepped closer to Luke. "Call me Rick. Rory told me you're helping with the baroness investigation." He paused. "Why do you think the man attacked you?"

"A Mexican drug lord wants me dead. I worked undercover on a task force. We busted up his operation in Lexington, Kentucky."

Rick stiffened his posture. "Why do you suspect the attacker is connected to the drug cartel?"

"He appeared to be Mexican. Minutes ago, when me and my wife were talkin' on the phone, she told me she spotted the same guy two times today during her tour."

Rick wrote in his detective's notebook. "You say the black getaway car had its number plate covered by a paper bag?"

"Correct. I hit the trunk lid with the rake. It's gotta have a dent."

Rick's cell phone sounded. "Hello, Mal. Excellent." He listened. "Keep patrolling the area." He disconnected his phone. "They found the car three streets away."

Luke raised an eyebrow. "I bet the perps stole the black sedan, and they had a getaway vehicle waiting where they left the black one."

Rick seemed to relax, and a smile formed on his lips. "Criminal *modus operandi* is similar across the globe."

Luke pointed at the street drain. "The attacker's knife fell through the grating."

Rick peered at the grate in the street near the curb. "We'll open it and find the weapon."

A dozen people had gathered in front of the Red Feather Pub. They pointed and mumbled. Rick held up his hand. "The situation is under control. Go back inside."

Alexander, the Red Feather bartender, approached. "My CCTV camera must've gotten pictures of the attack on Luke." He pointed to his camera on the outside wall of the pub, above the iron gate.

Rick lifted his chin. "I'll meet you inside in a moment."

Alexander went back into his pub.

Rick turned to Luke. "I'll station an undercover crew to keep an eye on the pub and your Airbnb until you and Layla leave tomorrow."

Rory's car pulled to the curb near Luke and Rick. Both Rory and Sonja got out. Rory opened his mouth as if to speak, seemed to be thinking, and then said, "We heard everything on the two-way radio." He scanned Luke. "I'm glad you're okay."

"Thanks."

"I talked with Henry. He wants all of us including Layla and Sonja to meet at the Red Feather at nine tomorrow morning to coordinate."

Luke glanced at the pub. "A private room's in the back."

Rory's eyes glistened in the light from the streetlamp. "I called and reserved it." He turned to DS Boutwell. "Log this as an attempted mugging, Rick. Have the pub's surveillance pics sent to the techs."

"Yes, sir."

Rory turned his gaze to Luke, "We'll see you at nine tomorrow morning."

"See you then."

* * *

10:45 P.M., SATURDAY, RORY'S OFFICE, SCOTLAND YARD, LONDON

Rory turned on his desktop computer and opened his email. He saw a message marked urgent from Art Granger, the young MI5 man in charge of tracking Yegor.

The email read, "See the attached video file from a CCTV camera placed over the side entrance of Anne's apartment building. We've identified Yegor entering the building the night of her murder."

From his plump glass container, Rory grabbed a mini candy bar, opened its wrapper, and smiled. He clicked on the video icon and saw its time stamp, *10:05 p.m., Sept.13,*

2030, Crows End, East London. Yegor walked to the building's side door, staying in dark shadows. Even so, the picture of his face was sharp, enhanced by the surveillance camera's night vision capability. The video ended. It did not show Yegor leaving.

Rory raised his eyebrows and sat up straight. *Yegor must have left through the rear entrance where there's no camera.*

Rory tapped his fingers on his desktop. *Because we don't know the exact time of Anne's death, we can't be sure Yegor's the killer. But this puts him at the scene of the crime close to the time she died. Plus we can't be sure the scream Luke heard was Anne's. Another woman could've been screaming.*

Rory's desk phone rang. "Hello?"

"Rory, I have a request." Rory recognized the speaker as Ashton Boxman, the Director General of MI5, its top man.

"Yes, Ashton?" Rory figured Ashton had been working unusually long hours in recent days. He was hell-bent on nabbing spies who might be after the autonomous, US robotic battle tank's secrets.

"I want to address your task force meeting tomorrow morning."

Rory flexed his fingers. *Ashton is micromanaging.* Rory pressed his ear against his telephone handset as Ashton continued to speak. "I need the task force to understand the importance of the mission."

Rory touched his parted lips. "Do you plan to attend our meeting in the Red Feather Pub in person?"

"No, I'll call your satellite phone. Put me on speaker-phone when you answer." He paused. "Be sure to have Layla Ryder sign a nondisclosure document. Both the CIA and the FBI require this."

"I'll ask Henry, the FBI's legal attaché, to get her to sign one. I'm sure he'll take care of it before the meeting."

Rory heard Ashton fumble with his telephone. "I'll call fifteen minutes after you begin." Ashton took a moment before he continued. "Do you have news to report?"

"Yes. We have surveillance footage showing the

suspected KGB RB operative, Yegor Bulot, entering Anne's apartment building the evening she died. He's a strong suspect in her murder. We believe he tried to get robotic tank intel from her."

Rory could hear Ashton take a deep breath. "Will you pick him up and charge him with Anne's murder?"

"No. We can't be sure whether or not he entered the building before or after the murder. Also, we've identified four persons of interest we need to continue to investigate."

"Excellent work."

"Thank you, sir." Ashton hung up. Rory wondered if Ashton would ask SIS to send one or two of its agents to join the new Alphabet Soup Task Force, which he'd just named.

Though MI5's role was to protect UK citizens from national security threats both at home and abroad, SIS gathered intelligence overseas. Therefore, Rory figured SIS could share what it knew about Yegor, the Belarusian secret agent.

Maybe Henry has some intel about Yegor as well. Rory tapped Henry's phone number on his keypad.

* * *

11:02 P.M., SATURDAY, LUKE AND LAYLA'S AIRBNB ROOM ABOVE THE RED FEATHER PUB

Layla heard the patter of raindrops hitting their bedroom window overlooking the road in front of the Red Feather Pub. She glanced outside across the street and saw the much larger Golden Sword Pub. A pair of focused spotlights lit it. Two unsteady men exited its front door. One unfolded an umbrella. The rain fell faster and harder. Layla pulled the drapes across the window and felt protected from prying eyes.

Luke stepped from the shower stall into the bedroom and dried himself with a man-sized towel.

Layla smiled and felt her temperature increase. *He's handsome.* "Hon, don't put anything on."

"Yur wish is my command." Luke focused on her.

I know what he likes. Layla raised her sheer negligee over her head and dropped the garment onto the carpet. She took her time approaching him. Feeling her breasts against his chest, she said, "Take me." Her tongue probed his mouth.

She liked how his muscles tensed as he picked her up and carried her to their bed. Her back on the white sheet, she peered up into his brown eyes.

He opened his mouth to speak, but then closed it, and stayed mum.

She felt his bare body on hers. "You're my hero." She touched his strong shoulders. "We could've been killed if you hadn't fought off the man."

When he kissed her forehead, she rubbed his back. She paused and asked, "Who was he?"

Luke peered into her eyes. "We'll learn about him tomorrow during the nine o'clock meeting." He pulled a sheet over them both. "I need you."

* * *

11:03 P.M., SATURDAY, RORY'S OFFICE, SCOTLAND YARD, LONDON

Rory composed an email to Art, the blond MI5 man supervising the surveillance of Yegor. "Double the men following Yegor. He's our number one suspect in Anne's murder."

Rory thought for a moment, and then typed, "Take care not to alert him. He may depart the country." Rory continued to tap his keyboard. "Bug the phones of all suspects in Anne's murder." Rory clicked "send." The message sped into cyberspace.

Rory scratched the stubble on his chin. *It's doubtful Yegor has robotic tank secrets to pass to his handler, or Yegor would've left the country. We have time to stop him.*

* * *

11:04 P.M., SATURDAY, SOMEWHERE IN LONDON

A man with olive skin and black hair stood in a London hotel room. With a trembling hand, the Mexican assassin, a *sicario*, tapped a Tijuana, Mexico, phone number onto his satellite phone's keypad.

Matéo Guerra, head of the Mexican drug cartel, *Nuestro Club*, answered. "Holá, amigo. Any news?" Matéo's voice sounded upbeat, hopeful.

The Latino man felt sudden nausea. "Boss—*Jefe*, Lucas Ryder is working with the London police. We tried to get him, but he broke José's hand with a garden rake two hours ago."

The assassin heard Matéo puff out a heavy sigh. "I thought Ryder was on his honeymoon."

Wiping a clammy hand on his shirt, the hired killer struggled to respond. "Someone murdered a baroness, chopped her head off. We've learned from the Latin Mob gang the police asked Ryder to help with their investigation of the killing. Coppers are with him most of the time. They follow him, too."

The assassin heard Matéo take a deep breath and then release it. "Are you telling me you can't get him?"

The paid killer lowered his chin to his chest. "It would be better to wait until he returns to the US. Cops won't be watching him all the time."

"Okay." Matéo's voice shook. "While José's hand heals, I'll assign a new associate to assist you when you get back." He paused. "I'm not irritated with you. But Luke Ryder is getting me super irate."

"I understand, *jefe*."

"Fly back after you hire someone to treat José's hand. We will make fresh plans for Ryder after you two return." Matéo's words seemed calmer to the *sicario*. "Ask around. See if you can find out why the cops are following Ryder even though he's working for them. It's weird."

"I'll check with the Latin Mob."

"Give me their top man's number."

"Sí, *jefe*. I'll text it to you. Their leader goes solely by his first name, Carlos."

Matéo paused for three long seconds as he was prone to do when thinking. "I'll find out what's going on. The Latin Mob could take care of Ryder for us. They know London better than we do."

"Sí, *jefe*."

"I've changed my mind. Fly back to California as soon as possible. Get pills to numb José's pain. We'll treat him in San Diego."

"Sí, señor."

Matéo disconnected his phone.

EIGHTEEN

FINISHING BREAKFAST, Luke sat at a long table in the Red Feather Pub's private meeting room with Layla. He pinched his lips together as he thought about red tape. Moving his gaze from his over-easy eggs to Layla's eyes, he said, "When government agencies try to work together, they get tangled like a bunch of extension cords."

Layla leaned close to Luke. "The meeting with the MI5 chief this morning should cut the red tape."

Luke heard the door open behind him. He turned to see Henry enter the room, carrying a leather briefcase. The barrel-chested black man moved like an agile, heavyweight boxer.

Henry patted Luke on the back. "I heard about the knife attack. You attract trouble." Henry laughed.

"The Mexican cartel won't leave me alone."

"Rita, me, and others are working on a plan for when you return stateside." Henry sat at the large dinner table. "We'll nail the Mexican bad guys."

Luke saw Layla begin to shake a trifle. *She's gotta be scared the Mexicans won't quit comin' after me.*

Henry placed his briefcase on the tabletop. "Before the

meeting gets started, I need to ask Layla to keep everything she learns about this operation to herself. We'd like her to sign a secrecy nondisclosure document." He unsnapped the case and took out a paper.

Layla peered at Henry. "Do you have a pen? I'll sign it. Does Luke need to sign one, too?"

"No. He signed one when he went undercover at NASA."

Henry handed Layla a pen. "Are you going to read it?"

Layla sighed. "Nope. I can't change it." She scanned the document and then signed and dated it.

Luke heard the door snap shut behind him. "Hello, Henry." Rory's low voice boomed across the room. Luke saw Rory and Sonja carrying steaming cups of tea and coffee.

Rory set a cup of coffee in front of Henry. "Thanks, Rory." Henry smiled and glanced at Layla. "Layla signed a US government nondisclosure agreement. You can speak freely."

Luke studied Layla's face. She seemed to be on high alert. He recalled he'd promised to tell her about Sonja. He turned toward Layla. "Sonja's a CIA agent."

Layla glanced at Sonja. "No wonder you're excellent at martial arts."

A flush spread across Sonja's face. "I'll be glad to teach you one or two moves."

Layla sat straight up and showed a wide grin. She seemed less nervous.

Rory scanned the people around the table. "Since we represent or will coordinate with MI5, SIS, FBI, and CIA, let's call this the Alphabet Soup Task Force."

Henry exhibited a rare smile.

Rory glanced down at a piece of paper. "From the Red Feather's CCTV camera footage, we identified Luke's attacker as José Ramirez of Tijuana, Mexico. We were lucky to get DNA from his knife we recovered from inside the sewer. We passed this info to the FBI. We believe Ramirez and a companion left the UK by private jet early this morning."

Rory's mobile phone rang. He glanced at the device and then caught Henry's attention. "It's Ashton Boxman, the MI5 Director General. He said he'd call and give us a pep talk." Rory pushed the speaker button on his phone and set the device on the table.

* * *

THE SOUND of MI5 Director General Ashton Boxman's baritone voice came out loud and clear from Rory's satellite phone. "Rory, thank you for arranging this Alphabet Soup Task Force meeting."

Rory pictured Ashton, a thirty-eight-year-old man who looked too young to lead a secret agency of 5,000 employees. Ashton was clean-shaven, well-groomed, smart, and brainy in a nerd-like way. His clear, blue eyes appeared to delve into the minds of the people he met.

Rory rubbed his chin. *This task force must succeed. He's giving us a motivational talk.*

Ashton's voice boomed from the speakerphone. "I've studied each of your backgrounds. I have no doubt your team will solve Baroness Anne Thorpe's murder. And I have faith you will do your utmost to stop foreign spies from learning how the US robotic battle tank's artificial brain works."

Ashton took a deep breath. "For many decades, computer scientists have dreamed of making a synthetic computer brain modeled on the human brain. But only in the last two years have the Americans been able to create a neural net brain that is conscious. It can reason and make its own choices. I personally define it as a living machine."

Rory noticed both Luke and Henry leaned forward, concentrating on the satellite phone on the table. Henry's eyes widened.

Ashton continued, "Scientists are working to improve the

tank's neural net brain. Its artificial intelligence is imperfect. Though the mammoth tank can make battlefield decisions without human consent, it would be folly to let it have free rein until it is improved." Ashton paused for a long moment. "If this tank were armed with tactical nuclear weapons, an out-of-control, synthetic brain could trigger world war. Even after perfecting this tank's AI, we'd be fools to arm it with nukes. On the other hand, I think our enemies would do it. We must keep the details of this intelligent machine top secret to avoid calamity."

Rory saw Layla's chin tremble. *Did she envision a nuclear war?*

Ashton spoke in a strong voice. "Best of luck. MI5 and your respective organizations will provide the people and funds you need to complete your mission. I thank you all. Rory will keep me up to date on your progress. Goodbye, and may history be on our side."

A click sounded, and Ashton's call ended.

Rory wondered if the call was needed, but it did stress the importance of the team's task.

Rory smiled and scanned the faces of the people around the table. "Ashton is the sole member of MI5 whose identity should be revealed to the public." Rory caught Luke's and Layla's attention. "My job at MI5 should be kept secret. The news media are aware of our police investigation of Anne's murder, but we will keep our mouths shut about our secret robotic tank inquiry."

Luke blinked.

Rory touched his fingertips together, forming a steeple. "Because we're in the UK, de facto I am in command of the Alphabet Soup Task Force. Of course, we're partners who will work as equals to solve the murder and to block foreign actors from stealing US robotic tank secrets." Rory paused. "A security camera photographed the suspected Belarus KGB spy, Yegor Bulot, entering Anne Thorpe's apartment building the night she died."

Henry leaned forward. "Is he our best suspect?"

"Not necessarily. Anne mentions additional persons of interest in her handwritten exposé. They include her husband and Estrella Bach, the president of the London Readers Book Club. Luke and I have interviewed them." Rory smiled at Luke. "The other two persons Anne noted are banker Robert Rothstein and professional golfer Arnold Beeker. Today, Luke and I will surprise Arnold at his Green Valley Golf Course, and Monday we'll visit Robert at his bank when it opens."

Henry cocked his head. "What about Yegor?"

"We doubled the surveillance on him after we obtained the video of him entering Anne's building. If we were to interview him and not detain him, I'm sure he would flee the country."

Luke glanced at Layla and then at Rory. "What will Layla's and Sonja's roles be?"

Rory remained mute for a moment. "Layla will be herself, a wife on her honeymoon. Sonja and an MI5 detail will continue to watch over Layla in case the Mexican cartel decides to strike again. A robotic tank demonstration will take place Tuesday at Poppins Proving Ground. We'll devise a reason for Luke and Sonja to attend. MI5 has learned the baron decided not to attend the demo because he continues to mourn Anne's death. Yegor may go."

Luke made strong eye contact with Rory. "When are we going to leave for the golf course?"

"Let's shoot for ten twenty-five. Sonja and I will grab breakfast."

* * *

LUKE AND LAYLA sat at their favorite table twenty feet away from the dartboard at the back of the Red Feather's barroom. They were drinking their after-breakfast coffees.

Rory, Sonja, and Henry approached the table. Henry smiled. "Our breakfast should be coming soon." The trio sat down.

Though Luke was studying a dessert menu, out of the corner of his eye he caught sight of a man with swarthy skin and black hair. The stranger picked up a blue dart and tossed it. The projectile hit the cork target's bull's-eye with a plop-like sound. Luke tilted his head and made eye contact with the dart thrower. The dark-complected man fingered a second, red dart and wound up as if he were throwing a fastball. Luke glanced away from the man.

With his side vision, Luke then saw the swarthy man twist his torso toward Luke's table.

A ripple of caution sped down Luke's backbone. The man hurled the dart. In a fraction of a second, Luke raised his cardboard menu like a shield. To Luke, time and the dart seemed to travel in slow motion. Still holding the menu in front of him, he ducked. The sharp projectile struck the menu, punching a hole in it. But the improvised armor stopped the sharp-pointed missile. Still holding the menu, Luke pulled Layla under the table with him.

The man threw another red dart. It also hit the menu. A third red dart stuck in a table leg. Luke rolled away from the table. Pushing up to his feet, he barreled toward his assailant. The swarthy attacker leaped at the pub's front door. Luke dove. He grabbed the olive-skinned man's ankle, and the man crashed to the floor.

Rolling aside, the aggressor got to his knees, pulled a switchblade from his rear pocket, and flicked the blade open. He lunged at Luke, who also had risen to his knees. Dodging the shiny knife, Luke swung the edge of his left hand down on the man's right wrist. The weapon clattered to the floor. Luke threw a right hook. The blow hit the wrongdoer on the left side of his chin. He fell like a bag of rocks.

A slim hand holding a pair of handcuffs thrust past Luke. Sonja's short, blond hair bounced behind her as she cuffed the defeated assailant.

Luke glanced at the petite, blond woman. "Where'd you git the cuffs from?"

Sonja shrugged. "I keep a pair in my purse."

A microsecond later, Henry and Rory stood over the unconscious man. Rory entered a number on his mobile phone. "Code Zeta. Send Team A and crime scene techs to the Red Feather Pub in Crows End." He disconnected and peered at Sonja. "You're quick as a cheetah. If you want a job with us, apply."

Sonja grinned. Pub customers mumbled among themselves. Rory raised his hand, holding his badge. "The situation is under control. Feel free to finish your breakfast. After an investigator arrives, he'll ask you to describe what you saw during the incident."

Henry raised his eyebrows. He spoke in a quiet voice. "Why'd this happen, Luke?"

"I figure the Mexican cartel took another shot at me. But why use a dart?"

Sonja pointed at Luke's menu on the floor under the table. "I'd check the darts for poison."

Rory's eyes didn't waver. "She's right." He frowned. "Is this bloke a foreign agent or a cartel thug?" He paused. "We'll find out."

* * *

RORY HAD ASKED the Red Feather's customers to move into the pub's private room where an undercover MI5 investigator, posing as a policeman, began taking witness statements.

Rory paced back and forth across the barroom. All of a sudden, he heard the pub's front door swing open. Turning, he saw Sergeant Rick Boutwell arrive with a special MI5 interrogation team. "Thanks for getting here fast, Rick." Rory spoke in a whisper. "Where are you going to question the offender?" Rory pointed at the man who'd attacked Luke with three darts. Conscious, the handcuffed man sat with his back against the pub wall.

Rick stared at the prisoner. "In the van."

Rory scratched his scalp, and then he leaned close to

Rick's ear. "This case is a matter of national security. Use chemicals." Rory knew MI5 was permitted to break the law to gather intelligence. Though iffy and dangerous, using truth serum was acceptable in this case in Rory's opinion.

His eyes steady, Rick said, "If he provides useful info, I'll let you know at once."

Minutes after Rick and his men escorted the prisoner from the pub, three MI5 crime scene techs in white jumpsuits arrived. They put on shoe coverings and nitrile crime scene gloves. A tall, lanky man came forward. "What do you need us to do here, Rory?"

Rory pointed at the menu Luke had used to shield himself from the darts. "Check the darts for poison, Jerry." Rory had kept his voice down. He glanced at Luke, Layla, and Sonja, who sat in a far corner. "Luke, can you show the team where the other dart is?"

Luke got up and led the forensics team to the table in the back of the room near the dartboard.

Jerry and his colleagues photographed the darts, the table, and the barroom. They measured the room and estimated the flight paths of the little missiles. Then Jerry picked up the menu, removed the two darts stuck in it, and placed them in an evidence bag. He pulled a third dart from the table leg. Turning to Rory, he said, "We'll do a preliminary check of these items in the evidence van."

As Jerry and his men exited the pub, he added, "I'll ring you after we get our initial findings."

Rory focused on Luke. "We'll leave for the golf course in a minute. Layla and Sonja, you're coming, too."

NINETEEN

STANDING NEXT to Rory's unmarked police car, Luke peered at the sky above the Crows End neighborhood. He glanced at Layla. "At least it's sunny, and it ain't raining."

As Luke opened a rear door of Rory's vehicle for Layla, she smiled. She glimpsed at him. "If it were drizzling, we wouldn't have a decent reason to pose as golfers."

Luke watched ahead as Henry's car pulled away. The FBI agent had begun his drive to the US Embassy to arrange an investigation of the Mexican *Nuestro Club* drug cartel and its leader, Matéo Guerra. Luke flared his nostrils. *The FBI better get those bastards before Layla and me fly home.*

Rory had assigned MI5 undercover agents to guard Layla and Sonja and watch for more potential Mexican cartel assassins. But the MI5 detail had not yet arrived. Therefore, Luke felt happy Layla and Sonja would stay with him and Rory for the time being.

Her bright blond hair bobbing, Sonja walked with Rory, who opened the other rear car door for her.

As he got into the front passenger's seat, Luke guessed

the outside Fahrenheit temperature had reached the mid-fifties.

Rory settled in the driver's seat and pulled out his cell phone. After tapping an icon on the device's display, he showed a picture of a man to Luke. "This is golfer, Arnold Beeker. He's the pro at the Green Valley Golf Course." Rory tilted his phone, enabling Layla and Sonja to see the golfer's image, too. "On weekends he's often in the pro shop." Rory clicked through a series of pictures of Arnold.

Tall and thin, the golfer appeared to be in excellent physical shape. His hair was short and blond, and he had a freckled face and blue eyes. In every picture, Arnold smiled.

Rory continued to stare at the last image of the golfer. "He's unmarried. May play around with women." Rory turned off the picture on his phone. "I've put my golf clubs in the boot." Rory pointed backward at the car's trunk. "We'll go to the pro shop and find Arnold if we're lucky. We'll start by renting clubs for the three of you and surprise him with questions about Anne."

Layla shifted in her seat. "I don't know how to play golf."

Luke threw his shoulders back. "No problem. I'll give you a lesson."

Sonja smiled at Layla. "I love golf. I could teach you how to swing if the men are busy asking Arnold questions."

Rory started the car and pressed the accelerator pedal, and the tires squealed.

* * *

10:45 A.M., SUNDAY, INSIDE THE POLICE CRIME SCENE VAN BY THE RED FEATHER PUB

Jerry put the evidence bag containing a dart on the mini workbench inside his van. "Tommy, hand me the Geiger counter, please."

Tommy watched as Jerry turned the instrument on and

held its probe near the tip of the dart. A needle in the Geiger counter display swung, indicating the dart's sharp point was emitting radiation.

A wide grin formed on Jerry's face. "The dart tip is radiating alpha particles."

Tommy appeared puzzled. "How do you know?"

"Alpha particles don't go far through the air, at most ten millimeters. If I pull the probe farther away from the dart tip, I get no reading."

"What does it tell you?"

"I think the tip contains polonium-210 because polonium emits alpha particles. It's a lethal radioactive poison if it gets inside someone's body."

Tommy took a step backward, and his eyes bulged out. "Should we shield it?"

"It's not dangerous unless it gets into your body. Even a piece of paper will block alpha particles."

Tommy pressed his lips into a fine line. "Then how can it kill?"

"You remember Alexander Litvinenko, the ex-Russian spy who was killed by polonium twenty-five years ago? His assassin spiked Litvinenko's tea with polonium-210. Once it gets into the victim's organs, it damages them and leads to death." Jerry paused. "A few milligrams can kill a man."

"Are you sure this is polonium?"

"No, not yet. We'll confirm it in the lab." Jerry grabbed his mobile phone and touched Sergeant Rick Boutwell's number. "Hello, Rick. This is Jerry. I believe polonium-210 is in the dart tips."

Jerry listened and then answered. "We'll confirm with laboratory tests, but I'm ninety percent sure I'm right." He sealed his phone against his ear. "I'll ring you back after we confirm the results. Then you can update Rory." Jerry disconnected his device.

Tommy pointed at a pile of evidence bags and notebooks related to the dart attack. "Are we done here?"

"Yes." Jerry moved to the front passenger's seat of the

evidence van. "You drive, Tommy. Let's see how fast you can get us to Thames House."

* * *

10:50 A.M., SUNDAY, INSIDE AN MI5 PADDY WAGON NEAR THE RED FEATHER PUB

Ginger Graham, a thirty-eight-year-old MI5 agent, reminded Rick of a British Roller Derby queen of yesteryear. Rick viewed her tough body. *She likes to intimidate people, men in particular.*

Her short red hair, Ginger glared at the handcuffed dart thrower. She shoved him onto a steel-legged kitchen chair inside the back of the heavy-duty paddy wagon. "I know how to make you talk, turd." She squeezed her fingers together as if she were crushing an egg in her hand. "You'll talk, or I'll burst your bollocks."

Rick wondered if Ginger would indeed squish the man's testicles, if she had a chance. Rick sighed. "Take it easy, Ginger. Violence doesn't work." *She knows how to play good cop, bad cop.* Rick stepped forward with a can of cola he'd spiked with scopolamine, the original truth serum made from the dark seeds of a Colombian tree. This drug has the benefit of causing interrogated persons to forget they'd been questioned.

Rick unlocked the perp's cuffs and gave him the cold soda can. As he drank, the man kept his eyes on Rick. After the potion took effect, the mystery thug appeared to get drunk. Rick leaned forward. "What's your name?"

His head wavering, the man mumbled, "Roberto Avila."

"Why did you throw darts at the man in the Red Feather Pub?"

"To kill him." Roberto slurred his words.

"How can a dart kill a man?"

"It's poisoned. Carlos told me."

"Who is Carlos?"

"Top man in the Latin Mob." Roberto's head flopped sideways and his eyes half-closed.

Grasping Roberto's longish hair, Rick held up the man's head and stared at his face. "Why'd Carlos order you to do this?"

"The *Nuestro Club* Mexican cartel's paying us big money…" Roberto closed his eyes and began to snore.

Rick stood and glanced at Ginger. "Put the cuffs back on Roberto."

Ginger grinned.

Rick thought, *She enjoys wielding power.* He watched Ginger tighten the cuffs on Roberto's wrists.

* * *

11:35 A.M., SUNDAY, EN ROUTE TO THE GREEN VALLEY GOLF COURSE

As Rory drove along a country road bounded by a rock fence, Luke saw a golf course come into view. The lush grass of a long fairway had been cut short like a well-groomed lawn. Rory's undercover police car slowed, and Luke felt it bump over shallow potholes on the pavement.

Trees lined both sides of the fairway, while two sand traps sat halfway to a distant green. A red flag marked the middle of the green's carpet-like surface.

Rory glanced at Luke. "We're here."

As the car skimmed over a smoother part of the road skirting the fairway, Luke saw four players who were pulling golf carts toward the green. Two white balls sat on its surface, while a third yellow ball had landed in a sand trap near the green. A fourth ball perched on long grass three yards short of the putting surface. Beyond the green, a massive clubhouse sat on a hill. Luke thought the building could've been a manor house, if he hadn't known better.

Rory put on his right turn signal, guided his vehicle up a

long, steep driveway toward the clubhouse, and pulled into a parking area.

Layla peered through her backseat window. "It's gorgeous, like a park."

Sonja stroked her blond hair. "I'd like to come back later and play eighteen holes."

Luke heard Rory's phone ring. The London policeman unbuckled his seat belt, grabbed his phone, and peered at it. "It's Sergeant Boutwell." Rory tapped his phone's touch screen. "Hello, Rick." Rory listened. "Fine work. I'll tell him." Rory continued to listen. "Is it confirmed? Okay. Bye."

Staring at Luke, Rory began to speak. "The darts are infused with poison, polonium-210."

Luke felt a rush of concern. "What is it?"

"A radioactive substance. Two or three milligrams can kill a man."

Layla appeared concerned. Luke opened his mouth to speak, but thought for a moment, and then asked, "Who's the perp?"

"A gangster. The Mexican *Nuestro Club* cartel paid a London gang, the Latin Mob, to do the deed."

Luke closed his eyes for a moment. "The damned dart could of did me in." *I gotta figure how to protect Layla when we get back home. She needs shootin' lessons.*

Rory turned to Sonja and Layla in the back seat. "It'll be safer if the ladies stay with us until Sergeant Boutwell raids the Latin Mob's headquarters." Luke saw Rory frown. "Rick will make sure the Latin Mob leaves you alone."

Luke focused on Rory's face. *I got to deal with Matéo Guerra and his Nuestro Club when I git back, even if I gotta go to Tijuana.* Luke gazed at Layla and wondered if she felt terrified. An artery in her throat pulsed, and she blinked.

TWENTY

MILES FROM BARON THORPE'S country estate, two MI5 agents following Rory's orders stood near a pile of metal in a recycling center. Clad in soiled and stinky blue overalls, Reginald and Marshall sat on a splintery plank of wood balanced on top of the junk.

Reginald took off his work gloves, stroked his bald head, felt its smooth surface, and lowered his chin to his chest. "We've been searching for the bloody hard drive from last night until dark, and this morning, too. I don't think it's here."

Marshall, a stocky, compact man, stared at the dirty gloves he wore. "The baron lied about recycling it."

Reginald reached into his overalls pocket and pulled out his mobile phone. "I'll call Art to report we haven't found the drive."

Marshall's shoulders curled forward. "I agree."

Reginald touched Art Granger's MI5 number. He heard Art answer in his unique tenor voice. "Reg, you find the computer drive?"

"No."

Reginald heard Art sighing. "Did you examine the correct piles of recycled metal?"

"Yes. The recycling center manager pointed out the two lorry tips from the baron's neighborhood."

"Thanks. I'll text Rory." Art hung up.

TWENTY-ONE

ART GRANGER SAT in his Thames House office and stared at a video playback on his computer screen. Labeled at the movie's bottom as "Crows End Camera 15," the high-definition video showed a tall, thin man carrying a shopping bag. He entered Anne's apartment building at 4:00 p.m., Thursday, September 12, according to the video's time stamp.

Art crossed and uncrossed his legs. *It's time to try the latest software.* Art clicked on the icon for the new, in-house MI5 facial recognition app he'd downloaded minutes ago. First, he linked images of the suspects in Anne's murder to the program as well as a database of people who had interacted with her.

Next, Art clicked on the app's icon to start an analysis of the image of the mystery man who carried the shopping bag.

The CCTV video camera that had taken the movie of the unknown man had shot thirty frames each second. Art's program combined unique bits from hundreds of those video frames to create a sharp, enhanced still image of the suspect.

The software flashed a message on Art's computer screen, "Positive ID, Arnold Beeker."

Rory needs to know this at once. Art picked up the handset of his secure desk phone. He clicked "Rory" in its speed dial list.

TWENTY-TWO

SLUNG OVER HIS RIGHT SHOULDER, Rory lugged his golf bag as he, Luke, Layla, and Sonja trudged uphill across the golf course's car park. Rory saw a pro shop sign pointing to the back of the clubhouse. His secure satellite phone rang. He set his bag down on the pavement and drew the phone from his jacket pocket. Everyone else stopped.

Peering at his phone, Rory saw that Art, his man in charge of MI5 surveillance, was calling. "Hello, Art."

"Rory, I have two new bits of info. From CCTV footage, I identified the golf pro, Arnold Beeker, going into Anne's apartment building at 4:00 p.m. last Thursday. He carried a shopping bag. Second, Reginald and Marshall searched the piles of recycled metal tipped by the lorry from the baron's neighborhood. They found no four-by-six-inch hard drive."

"Top-notch work, Art. We'll speak with Arnold within the next ten minutes. I'll talk with you more about this later." Rory hung up. He turned to Luke. "I have news about Arnold."

TWENTY-THREE

PRO GOLFER, Arnold Beeker, age thirty-four, stood behind the counter in the Green Valley Golf Course's pro shop. He glanced up at a telly mounted on the wall across from him. He didn't watch television except for sports broadcasts and an occasional movie. He didn't read newspapers or listen to news on the radio, either.

A spontaneous extrovert, Arnold was the life of any party or get-together. He figured he wouldn't marry any time soon. He'd been having plenty of fun dating a variety of women.

At the moment, the shop wasn't crowded. Arnold began to visualize Anne, nude in the bed in her Crows End flat. *She had been a great lay until recent days when she'd become more distant, and her behavior had turned him off.*

The bell on the shop door sounded. Arnold glanced away from the telly screen and saw four people enter. A short, wiry man with hairy arms set a golf bag in a rack near the doorway, while an attractive, petite blond; a tall, muscular man; and a young, buxom, black woman neared the counter. The hairy man held a windbreaker in his left hand.

The tall man with the two attractive women stopped at the counter. Arnold figured the man had Italian or Spanish blood because of his strong, thin build, black hair and mustache, and brown eyes. The man leaned on the counter. "I'd like to rent three sets of clubs, two for the ladies and one for me. Can we git a tee time soon?"

Arnold heard himself say, "You're in luck, sir. A foursome canceled five minutes ago." He paused as he watched the shorter, second man with hairy arms and tanned, leathery skin approach. Arnold caught his attention. "I take it you're with the two ladies and this gentleman."

"Yes."

"As I told your colleague, a foursome rang to cancel minutes ago. You could have a 12:20 p.m. tee time, if you'd like."

Rory's lips formed a wide smile.

"We may play nine holes after we speak." The wiry man flashed his Metropolitan Police badge. "First, we'd like to speak with you about the murder of Baroness Anne Thorpe."

Arnold stepped backward. "She's dead?"

The policeman lifted one eyebrow and nodded.

Arnold realized his voice had been shaky. *Do I look guilty?* He gulped. *Why'd I ever get involved with Anne?*

TWENTY-FOUR

LUKE STUDIED Layla and Sonja as they began to rummage through sports clothes in the pro shop. Speaking in low tones, they pulled items from the racks and held them in front of themselves.

Rory stared at Arnold. "It is better we speak in private."

"Let's step into my office." Arnold gestured across the shop to a medium-sized, glassed-in space which included a small desk and folding chairs.

Rory and Luke followed Arnold toward his office.

Feeling Rory tap his shoulder, Luke stopped six feet from the office doorway.

Rory whispered, "You question him." Luke asked himself why Rory would hand off the interrogation to him. *Is it cuz I'm not as threatening as Rory? Rory had flashed his badge. As a result, Arnold could become defensive and not give Rory useful info. I'm American, and I don't seem like a cop.*

Luke recalled interrogation tips Kentucky Sheriff Jim Pike had once shared with him. He'd said it's best for a suspect to sit with his back eighteen inches from the wall. The interrogator should sit in a chair facing the person of interest. The investigator can then move closer and closer to the suspect to increase the interviewee's tension as questioning continues.

When he went into Arnold's office, Luke saw two folding chairs along a bare wall fifteen feet from the desk. Arnold stood near his desk, biting his lips.

As Luke neared Arnold, the man rubbed his hands along his trouser legs as if he were drying sweat from his palms. *He's jumpy.*

Luke unfolded one of the chairs and sat. He gestured at the second chair, already open with its back near the wall but not touching it. "Have a seat. I'm gonna ask questions while DCI Rory Calvin takes notes."

Rory pulled his petite, spiral notebook and a pen from his pocket.

Arnold sat and began to bounce his foot on the carpet.

Luke gazed at Arnold and decided to speak with simple words in an exaggerated Southern drawl. *I gotta make him think I'm a dumb cop.* "I'm Luke Ryder, and I'm a deputy sheriff in the US. I'm helping DCI Calvin investigate the death of Anne Thorpe. Bear with me cuz DCI Calvin's teachin' me how the London police work." Luke smiled. "Please tell me yur name." Luke spoke with a soft voice. He knew asking the man neutral, nonthreatening questions would show him Arnold's "innocent face."

"Arnold Beeker." The man appeared to relax.

I gotta observe him to see what his innocent face is. "What's yur job?"

"Pro golfer." Luke studied Arnold's body language. *He's calmer. The artery in his throat's not pulsing.*

I gotta search for signs of deception. Luke scooted his chair forward an inch. "Do you know why we came to see you, Arnold?"

"You just told me when you got here." Arnold replied in a muted, forceful shout.

"Why would someone murder Anne?"

Arnold appeared nervous, and he shrugged. "I don't know."

Luke wondered if the man knew more than he was saying. Was he a good liar?

"How could you not know about it before we told you she was murdered? All the papers and TV stations have been carrying the story for two days."

"I'm out on the course most of the time…"

"When's the last time you saw Anne?"

"A week and a half ago." Arnold answered with clipped words and shifted his rear end in his chair.

Luke squinted. *Liars often move their butts in the same way.*

Luke shoved his chair closer to Arnold, whose chair now bit into the wall behind him. "We got a CCTV movie of you on Thursday, not a week ago, goin' into Anne's building carrying a shoppin' bag."

"Carrying a shopping bag is legal."

Luke stared at Arnold. "What was in the bag?"

"A bottle of wine and cheese. She's one of my golf students."

"Did you get together with her anywhere else besides the golf course and her flat?"

"I saw her at parties."

Luke leaned closer to Arnold. "You saw her only at her apartment, the golf course, and parties?"

"Yes."

"Why did you go to her apartment last Thursday?"

Arnold let out a breath. "I needed someone to talk to, and I thought she'd enjoy my company."

Luke glared at Arnold. "We got papers Anne handwrote describin' how you had lots of sex with her. You didn't mention it."

The artery in Arnold's throat pounded. "If you go to bed with a married baroness, you need to keep quiet about it." He rubbed the back of his neck.

Luke stared at Arnold for three solid seconds. "Did you kill Anne?"

"Hell no." Arnold's face and neck flushed deep red. His nostrils flared. He stood and peered downward. His breathing became noisy, and then he pounded the wall with his fist. "If you think I killed her, charge me. I'll sue you for false arrest and win."

Rory cleared his throat. "Arnold, we aren't going to arrest you, but I'm required to take a DNA sample from your inner cheek." He took his handy DNA sampling kit from his jacket pocket.

Arnold glared at Rory. "If I find it's not legal for you to take a sample, I'll take you to court."

Holding a swab on a stick, Rory neared Arnold. "Open your mouth, please. This will take a moment, and it won't hurt."

Arnold opened his mouth, and Rory rubbed the inside of the man's cheek. "Thank you, Arnold. You can give the twelve twenty tee time to someone else."

Luke stood and followed Rory from the office. Luke could feel Arnold's eyeballs staring at his back.

As Luke left the building with Rory, Layla, and Sonja, he spoke in a low voice. "Unless he's a pathological liar, he's tellin' the truth."

Rory glanced at Luke. "We'll discuss it in the car."

Luke pulled at his collar and shuffled toward Rory's automobile. *I won't use the hostile method of interrogation again fur a while.* Luke shook his head. *Feels wrong.*

TWENTY-FIVE

LUKE SETTLED in the front seat of the unmarked police car and turned to face Rory. "We didn't learn anything useful from Arnold." Luke paused. "I pushed him too hard."

Rory swallowed and then blinked. "When you asked Arnold if he had killed Anne, his denial was forceful. It's a sign he may be innocent. Then again, he lied about how well he knew her and the last time he saw her."

Luke lowered his gaze.

Rory's phone rang. "Hello." He shot a glance at Luke and kept listening. "Anything else?" He squinted. "Thank you." Rory disconnected, focused on Layla and Sonja in the back seat, and then cast his gaze at Luke. "The medical examiner says Anne was pregnant. He's sent the baby's DNA out for analysis."

A tear trickled down Layla's face. She wiped the drop away. "It's sad." She glanced at Luke and touched her belly. Luke knew she was thinking of their unborn baby. *Them Mexican drug cartel guys better not go after Layla, or else…* Luke raised his chin and blinked. *She's extra sensitive cuz she's pregnant.*

Sonja patted Layla's back and gave her a brief hug.

Luke examined the two women. *Sonja's a little warrior and caring, too.*

Rory's voice cut into Luke's thoughts. "Would a man kill his mistress if he learned she was pregnant?"

Sonja crossed her arms. "If he did, he's a sorry excuse for a man."

Luke heard himself start to talk, and wondered if his guts were guiding his tongue. "The baron is infertile. Didn't Anne say Yegor, the Belarus guy, had sex with her? What about the banker, Robert Rothstein? Also, Arnold coulda made Anne pregnant."

Rory stared out the car window. "If she had relations with at least three men, it's possible she had no idea which one impregnated her."

Luke decided to speculate. "The baron coulda killed his wife if he found out she slept around." Luke tapped his fingers on the dashboard. "Anne spurned Estrella's advances. Estrella may have hired a hitman to kill Anne."

Layla leaned forward, and took a deep breath. "Why would Arnold kill Anne?"

Luke made strong eye contact with Layla. "My gut tells me no. If he knew he'd made her pregnant, he might've asked her to keep the baby."

Rory cleared his throat. "But Arnold lied. He saw Anne Thursday. Yet he said he hadn't seen her for a week and a half." Rory narrowed his eyes. "Right now we can't rule out any of our persons of interest. There could be further suspects, too."

Luke turned to Rory. "What about Yegor? Would he kill his source of info about the robotic tank?"

Rory's forehead wrinkled. "If Anne threatened to reveal Yegor had been spying, he may have decided to do her in."

Luke scratched his scalp. "We still need to talk to the banker."

Rory nodded. "Surprising him at his bank tomorrow morning may yield useful evidence." Rory's phone rang and he tapped it to answer. "Hello, Art." Rory listened, peering out the windshield and into the trees along the first fairway. "Old Stone Cemetery...yes, we passed it on the way to the golf course. Thank you." Rory hung up.

Rory glanced at Luke. "Our men saw the baron approaching his family mausoleum in the Old Stone Cemetery not too far from here."

Luke tilted his head to the side. "He could be hiding something inside the tomb."

Rory started his car. "We need to check it out right away."

* * *

12:26 P.M., SUNDAY, THE THORPE FAMILY MAUSOLEUM

Under a thick canopy of branches and leaves, dim light seeped into the Old Stone Cemetery's gloom. The ancient, aboveground Thorpe family tomb had stood in the semidarkness of the graveyard for centuries. A building made of gray stones and crumbling mortar, the mausoleum was covered in green, lush moss on its north side.

Unsteady on his feet, the baron trudged at a slow pace over the moist, moldy turf toward the tomb. He touched his painful throat and exhaled. His breath smelled of whiskey. The scotch he'd just drunk made him feel warmer despite the damp, bone-chilling air.

Reaching in the left pocket of his windbreaker, he felt a computer thumb drive, which weighed less than an ounce and was the size of a small piece of chalk. *Which crypt should I hide it in?*

If anyone found the stubby, chalk-sized thumb drive and learned what had happened between Anne and him, he'd be ruined. He'd no longer be admired. After a period of embarrassment—weeks or months—he'd become a nobody. Never mind he'd been born into a higher class than the average British bloke. A flush of shame crossed his cheeks.

If no one uncovered his secrets about Anne, he would remain inconspicuous. He regretted that being an SIS official did not give him the acclaim he craved. Regulations barred him from revealing anything about his top secret, SIS work. It might never become public except perhaps long after his death. He sighed.

He stood by the rusty, iron gate, which guarded the tomb's entryway. Reaching into his hip pocket, he grabbed a skeleton key. Hands shaking, he slipped the key into the lock. It clicked as he opened it. As he pulled the gate toward himself, it creaked. A tingling feeling crawled up his spine.

Stooping, he stepped through the stone doorway, and closed the gate behind him. As the iron door impacted stone, a clanking noise echoed inside the stone building. He sat on a cold, marble bench inside the entrance, took out his hip flask, and sipped whiskey. As his eyes adjusted to the dim interior, he spied the sealed crypts protecting the coffins of his ancestors.

It wouldn't be easy to open a crypt, though he had a screwdriver and a chisel in his jacket pocket. Concrete encased his brother's coffin. Cemetery workers had caulked the edges of the crypt's opening, placed a steel sheet over it, and screwed it shut. Later, they'd installed a marble panel over the steel barrier and attached a faceplate with Josh's name and dates of birth and death inscribed on it.

The baron figured the oldest crypts were not as well sealed and would be easier to open. Then again, he'd have to chip away at one of them to open it. The damage he'd cause would be easy to spot. He stood, pulled his cell phone from his pocket, and turned on its light. He shuffled toward the far wall of the building.

Most of the mortar around one of the stones in the wall had crumbled away. Lord Thorpe felt in his pocket for his mini screwdriver. Jabbing at the remaining loose mortar, he chipped it away from the rock. Then he pried the stone out and set it on the floor. Shining his cell phone's light into the hole, he saw ample room for the stubby, chalk-stick-sized thumb drive. Careful not to crush the device, he slid the rock back into place. He then closed his eyes and slumped. After taking two deep breaths, he smiled and reopened his eyes. *I can come back here to retrieve the drive in case I need to prove Anne cheated on me.*

The baron went back to the marble bench and sat. *I should have a nip of whiskey to celebrate.* He held his flask to his lips and tilted it back. Whiskey flowed down his throat and felt warm, even toasty. His eyelids felt heavy. Leaning against the stone wall, he relaxed. Soothing darkness enveloped him. He saw Anne floating through the air in the nude. Like a graceful bird, she landed on the grass near a bed of tulips, and stared into his eyes. "Come with me, darling." She grabbed his hand and pulled him into the air, and they flew over the countryside.

Then the baron felt something irritate his cheek. He awoke when he brushed a spider from his face. *How long have I been sleeping? I better get out of here.*

TWENTY-SIX

SERGEANT RICK BOUTWELL, like the rest of Rory's men, worked for both the Metropolitan Police and secretly for MI5. Now dressed in civilian clothes, Rick led five MI5 men into an ancient, ramshackle brick building on Robin Wharf Lane, in a seedy East London neighborhood. He stared at a cheap, wooden door spray-painted with the words "Latin Mob HQ."

Rick scowled. *We need to scare the piss out of these blokes.* As he knocked on the door, he noticed a peephole. Then he heard a sound like a scratchy beard rubbing against the door's interior.

A low, accented male voice boomed behind the door. "Yes?"

"Police. Open up."

"Let me see your warrant."

Rick nodded at his biggest man. "Kick it in, Tony."

The sturdy man, who wore heavy-duty boots, gave the flimsy door a swift blow with his heel and shattered the weak wood. The four other MI5 agents pulled Uzi submachine guns equipped with silencers from under their jackets. They rushed through the doorway.

The first MI5 man into the spacious, dirty room shouted, "Everybody lie flat on your bellies, or you die."

Five Latin Mob thugs froze where they stood, bug-eyed. Next, they fell to their knees one by one and flattened their stomachs against the filthy, worn rug.

A black-bearded, stocky man asked, "Where's your warrant?" He'd spoken in a deep baritone voice as he knelt on the dirty carpet.

Rick walked to the olive-skinned man. "We don't need one."

"You're not police, then?"

Rick peered at the man. "Where's Carlos?" A ruthless gangster, Carlos led the Latin Mob.

The stocky man who'd asked to see a warrant smiled, shrugged, and got in a prone position. "I don't know him."

Rick turned to Tony and a second MI5 man. "Find Carlos."

In two minutes, Tony shoved Carlos in front of him toward Rick. "I got him." Tony glanced aside. "I found a room where you can speak in private."

Rick grinned. "That's helpful."

After Tony had tied Carlos to a heavy-duty chair in the sleazy, little office, Rick dragged a garden chair close to the gangster and sat, holding his chin high. "Don't fool yourself, Carlos. We don't have to follow the law, if it's in the best interest of the country. Leave Luke Ryder alone, or they'll find your body floating in the Thames. We know the Mexican *Nuestro Club* cartel paid you." Rick took his time to pull a hunting knife from his belt. He held the weapon at Carlos's throat and nicked it with the razor-sharp blade. A trickle of blood ran down Carlos's throat onto his chest. "Get my message, Carlos?"

Carlos gulped. "Yeah." The crotch of his trousers turned wet.

Rick pulled his knife away from the mobster's throat, and smelled the man's urine. *Carlos shouldn't be a problem for Luke Ryder in the future.*

TWENTY-SEVEN

AS RORY GUIDED his undercover police car along the country lane, Luke felt his stomach growl. He glanced at Layla. *She's gotta be hungry, too, cuz she's eatin' for two.* Luke studied the sky. It had clouded up earlier and had turned darker. The trees along the road swayed in gusts of chilly wind. *I wonder how long it'll take to check out the baron and his family tomb.*

Drops of rain hit the windshield. Rory turned on his wipers at their slowest, intermittent setting.

Luke saw Rory scan the left side of the road. "The cemetery's around the next bend." Rory cracked his driver-side window. Luke figured Rory wanted to hear and smell, as well as see, his surroundings. Luke recalled a retired Kentucky deputy sheriff who had given him a tip: "Roll down your cruiser's windows. Hearing will give you extra situational awareness."

A rancid, rotten-hay odor blew into the car's cabin through the open window.

Luke squinted and peered leftward. As the car followed the curving road, a thick grove of beech trees came into view.

It was as murky as dusk under its canopy. A bolt of lightning flashed, brightening the darkness under the trees for a fragment of a second. A rumble of thunder followed.

On the left side of the road, a giant boulder popped into Luke's view. Rory lifted his foot from the accelerator pedal. A sign behind the big rock read "Old Stone Cemetery." As Rory turned left onto the cemetery's main driveway, his car tires crunched its crushed gravel. Huge tree branches arched over the cemetery's main lane. Luke felt like he was traveling through a dark, green tunnel.

Rory flicked on his headlights and peered to his right. "I see my agent, Nigel, near his vehicle in the closer car park." A second parking lot stood three hundred yards farther down the gravel drive.

Rory stopped next to Nigel, a man in his sixties. A pair of binoculars dangled from the tall, thin man's neck over his tan trench coat. As the agent walked toward Rory's open window, Luke studied the older gentleman. He sported gray hair in need of a trim. *Is he wearing the coat to play the part of a modern 007?*

Nigel leaned down toward Rory's open window. "The baron's still in the mausoleum." Luke thought Nigel sounded like an Oxford professor who smiled when he spoke. He pointed at a massive, aboveground tomb standing a hundred yards farther along the gravel roadway on its right side.

Rory nodded. "Did he spot you?"

Nigel stuck his chest out. "No. I've been drawing birds whilst also watching the baron." The ancient spy held up a vest-pocket-sized sketchbook. Luke thought the agent had drawn a dove with the skill of a well-trained artist.

Luke noticed a small digital camera hanging under the agent's left arm. Rory glanced at it. "Did you get pictures?"

"Yes." The gray-haired agent fingered his tiny camera. "Don't be fooled by its size." Nigel kept his eyes on the distant burial chamber, though he continued to speak. "This camera has our best experimental chip and captures ultra-sharp images."

Luke noticed movement by the entrance of the tomb. The old-fashioned agent stood taller and put his binoculars to his eyes. "The baron's on the move."

* * *

12:38 P.M., SUNDAY, THE GREEN VALLEY GOLF COURSE

What can I do to clear my head? Arnold had taken the canceled 12:20 p.m. tee time for himself, but the players ahead of him were slow. *After I play a hole in the fresh air, I'll feel better.*

Arnold pulled his driver from his golf bag, which was strapped on the back end of his electric cart. The memory of Anne on her mattress in the nude made him feel guilty. *How the hell am I going to survive this? I gotta plan to leave, change my name. Where should I go? Overseas.*

Carrying his driver, Arnold walked to the tee box of the first hole, and stood between two black markers. He stared along the fairway. *The fairway grass needs to be mown. I should speak with the groundskeeper.*

Pushing a wooden tee into the short grass, he set his golf ball on top of it. He sucked air through his nostrils and exhaled. He did this again. *I'm calmer.*

Standing up straight with his club in his hands, he took aim at the ball. He guided his club backward and up. At the top of his swing, a vivid image of Anne smiling and in the nude flashed into his mind's eye. He mis-hit the ball, and it skittered 150 yards into the fairway.

He gulped. *How the hell am I going to play Thursday?* He'd planned to play in the Brightdale Open. *I'm not going to make the cut if the coppers hound me. If they toss me in jail, I'll have to withdraw before I start. It would ruin my life. But gambling's already caused me huge problems. Sammy wants his money now.*

The rumble of distant thunder pulled him from his thoughts of a dire future back to the equally bleak present.

Peering at the distant sky, he saw a black cloud. A cold wind rustled his sports shirt. It's going to pour. He pulled his umbrella from his golf bag.

* * *

HOLDING HIS UMBRELLA OVER HIM, Arnold sat on a bench next to the second tee. Thoughts of his large gambling debt gave him a headache, and his pulse pounded his temples.

After leaning his opened umbrella against the bench, he rubbed his head and then withdrew his mobile phone from his hip pocket.

He took three deep breaths. Sighing, he touched "Bookie" on his phone's contact list.

The phone on the far end of the call rang four times. "Hello, Arnold, you have the five grand you owe me?"

Arnold drew air into his lungs. "I'm ringing you because the person who had planned to loan me the money has died."

"You better find an alternate money source by noon tomorrow. It's hard to play golf with broken fingers."

"For Christ's sake, Sammy, give me a week. The coppers are questioning me."

"What for?"

"The person who died was murdered, a baroness, one of my student golfers."

Arnold heard Sammy gasp. "You mean Anne Thorpe?"

"Yeah. I found out less than a half hour ago."

"Don't you read a paper or watch the telly? The goddamned story's all over."

"I'm playing in a tournament starting Thursday. The purse is large. You of all people know my odds of scoring well are excellent." Arnold gulped.

"Okay, okay. I'll give you one extra week." Sammy hung up.

TWENTY-EIGHT

A MISTY DRIZZLE fell on the cemetery, drifting among the trees. Rory rolled up his driver-side window, squinted, and felt upbeat. The investigation had been going well.

Still sitting in the driver's seat next to Luke, Rory took his compact binoculars from the unmarked police car's glove box. Peering through them, he saw the baron locking the Thorpe family tomb's iron gate. "The baron's placing a bouquet at the bottom of the gate. He's slow as a snail."

Rory lowered his undersized field glasses and glanced out of his car at his gray-haired, MI5 surveillance man, Nigel. The old agent used a collapsible, petite telescope to watch the baron.

"Nigel, better start your car. He'll go soon. "

"I won't lose him. I put a tracker on his vehicle."

Rory noticed Luke squinting as he stared at the distant mausoleum.

Luke turned to Rory. "He spent a long time in the tomb. Can we git inside?"

Rory placed his binoculars back in the glove box. "I'll pick the gate's lock." He turned to face Layla and Sonja.

"You two can stand outside the mausoleum and keep watch whilst Luke and I are inside."

After the baron's car left the car park nearest the old tomb, Rory started his car. He drove toward the lot nearest the creepy, stone building.

* * *

BARON THORPE STEERED HIS POWERFUL, luxury automobile along the rain-soaked, gravel driveway toward the exit of the Old Stone Cemetery. Two pieces of broken stone propped a rusty nail in an upward position, its tip pointed at the sky. The back right tire of the car rolled over the nail's sharp point. Impaled in the wet tire between two treads, the spike-like piece of steel still kept most of the air from leaking out. But some air slowly escaped as the car traveled toward the Thorpe manor house.

TWENTY-NINE

LUKE WATCHED as Rory tinkered with the centuries-old lock on the Thorpe tomb's iron gate. The mechanism clicked open, and Rory stuck his picklock in his jacket pocket. The rain had stopped, but random drips fell from the trees, dampening the men's jackets.

Luke saw that both Sonja and Layla had opened compact umbrellas they'd stowed in their purses. Sonja knelt to examine the bouquet of flowers the baron had put near the gate. "They're gorgeous." She glanced at Layla. "Too bad he left them to hide his reason for visiting the crypts."

Luke scratched his scalp, thinking. *Sure as hell the baron put something in the tomb.*

Rory tapped Luke on the shoulder. "We'll do a quick check. I'll send a team here tonight to do a proper search."

Luke followed Rory into the timeworn stone tomb. He switched on the flashlight Rory had given him. The MI5 man also clicked his on. A dank smell permeated the stone enclosure.

Scanning the rows of crypts, Luke noted the newest ones were made of concrete. But in the rear of the building, the oldest of the burial chambers were fashioned of stone and brick. Luke caught Rory's attention. "Even the old crypts would be hard to open."

Rory directed his torch beam over the crypts. "Yep. They're sealed."

As Luke moved toward the rear of the tomb, he spied crumbled mortar on the floor. Aiming his flashlight beam higher, he saw a stone in the wall with no mortar around its edges. Leaning close to the rock, he noticed scratches on its edges. He turned to Rory. "I found something."

Rory neared him. "I bet the baron scraped the stone."

"Do you have a jimmy I can borrow?"

Rory handed Luke his small pry bar. Then Rory took his phone from his pocket. "I'll take photos."

After Rory snapped three images of the stone, Luke pried at the edges of the plum-sized rock. Rory shot a dozen extra pictures as Luke poked around the stone. It finally came loose and tumbled to the floor. Rory peered into the hole. "I see a computer thumb drive." He donned nitrile evidence gloves, grabbed the stubby thumb drive, put the device in an evidence bag, and labeled it. "Let's see what's on it. In the car, I have a laptop computer that has a USB port where I can plug in this drive."

* * *

RAIN BEGAN to pound the automobile a minute after Rory, Luke, Layla, and Sonja had settled in their car seats. Luke watched Rory pull a mini laptop computer from under the driver's seat. After putting on a fresh pair of nitrile gloves, Rory took the lightweight thumb drive from its evidence bag. The MI5 man glanced at Luke. "I can't wait to see this."

Rory inserted the small, stumpy drive into a slot in his police computer and clicked on a movie icon.

As a video began to play, Luke at once recognized the Thorpe country mansion's library. Baron Thomas Thorpe stomped into the room, his steps audible. Standing in front of a couch, he frowned and pressed his lips together.

Within a second, Anne followed him. Her face flushing, she said, "I don't love him. But I want to keep the baby." Her voice sounded high-pitched. She plopped onto the couch and then crossed her arms.

Even in the laptop's smaller video picture, Luke could see the baron's eyes flash. "Get an abortion." Lord Thorpe sat down on an easy chair across from Anne and the sofa. She scraped her hair back with her fingers.

"I shall keep the baby."

"Why should I raise this child as my own?" The baron's face flushed, and he coughed. "Who's the father?"

"It's not important."

"I'll divorce you. A paternity test will ensure I prevail."

Anne frowned. "Since you are unable to father a child, be grateful the Thorpe line will live on."

Muttering, Anne shook her head. Luke couldn't hear what she'd said under her breath. In an abrupt, sudden motion, she stood. "You won't divorce me. You couldn't stand the bad publicity, the scandal, and the rumors." Her voice had risen to a shout. Turning her back to her husband, she left, stamping from the room.

The video ended. Luke stared at Rory. "Is this a smokin' gun?"

Rory cocked his head to the side. "It's a clue, but inconclusive."

Luke leaned forward. "Should we question the baron today?"

Rory started the car. "Soon, but not necessarily today. I'll think about the timing."

Sonja tapped Rory's shoulder. "When Layla and I were standing watch outside, we decided we were in the way."

Layla nodded. "Could you take us to the Red Feather? We could eat a late lunch or have tea and make plans for tomorrow in London."

Sonja smiled. "Afterward, I'll take a cab to my place."

She sighed. "My boyfriend needs to know I'm still alive." Sonja's cheeks colored.

Rory put his car in park. "May I make a suggestion?"

Sonja wet her lips and showed a nervous smile. "Of course."

"My men have already been assigned to watch Layla. So, I could drop you at your flat."

Sonja leaned back in her seat and appeared to relax. "Thank you, if it's not out of your way."

"Since your place is near Thames House, I'll take the thumb drive to forensics after I drop you off."

Catching Rory's attention, Layla drew her eyebrows together. "Won't you need to eat?"

"I'll grab something on the way." Rory aimed his eyes at Luke. "MI5 agents are already watching the Red Feather. Relax and have tea with Layla."

Luke turned to Rory. "Thanks, I'm as hungry as a bear after it finished hibernating." *Layla will be safe, but I gotta have a plan for when we git back to the States. The Mexican cartel ain't gonna stop coming after me 'til I stop 'em.*

Layla rubbed Luke's shoulder. Her eyes appeared softer to Luke. "I'm tired. After we eat, I'll take a nap."

Rory placed his foot on the brake and put his car in drive.

* * *

1:35 P.M., SUNDAY, NEAR THE RED FEATHER PUB

Rory braked to a stop near the Red Feather Pub. Except for a light mist, the rain had stopped, though clouds dimmed the sky.

When Luke exited the car, he crossed his arms to ward off the chilly breeze. As Layla unfolded her umbrella, Luke waited. *Women are sensitive about their hairdos.*

Rory had also stepped from the car to open a rear door for Sonja, who headed to the front passenger's seat where

Luke had been sitting. Rory turned to Luke. "I'll be back later to pick you up, and we'll go question the baron."

"Okay."

"Nigel's watching the Thorpe mansion to see if Lord Thorpe stays put. If the baron leaves, I'll let you know what our next steps will be."

Luke rubbed his jaw. "I agree with what you were hinting before about Anne and the baron. Just cuz they argued, don't mean he killed her."

Rory took a step closer to Luke. "You're right not to jump to judgment." Rory slapped Luke on his shoulder and then got into his car.

After Rory's automobile went around the corner, Luke took hold of Layla's hand and turned toward the pub's front door. He saw a fit, stocky man with close-cropped, black hair, dressed in a blue suit and white shirt. *He may be Yegor.* Luke felt a tingle run down his backbone.

Luke leaned close to Layla. "I think Yegor, the guy from Belarus, just went into the pub."

Layla's eyes flickered. "You going to call Rory?"

"Not yet. I gotta be sure. Play along with me."

Layla aimed her eyes at the pub's front door. "Okay."

* * *

PEOPLE DRINKING beer jammed the Red Feather Pub. Luke estimated at least thirty patrons sat in booths and around tables. Peering to his left, he noticed Yegor had sat at a small, round table near the front window. *Yep, it's him. Lucky that Rory showed me Yegor's file and pictures.*

Leading Layla toward the table where they often sat at the back wall near the dartboard, Luke saw Alexander, the bartender. He was polishing a glass with a towel. The heavy man turned his head and beamed when he recognized Luke. After grabbing two menus, Alex came from behind the bar and stopped by Luke and Layla. "This place was ho-hum until the bloke threw darts at you. Did the coppers learn why he did it?"

"They said he's a nut job."

"Fortunate a dart didn't hit your eye. I hope they put him in the madhouse." Alexander paused. "Would you like to have tea, biscuits, and sandwiches?"

"Yes, that would be great." Luke paused. "Kin I start with green tea?"

Layla smiled. "I'd like to try green tea, too."

The bartender smiled and set the menus on the table. "It's good to see you try tea instead of lime cordials for a change." Alexander left to get the tea.

Luke leaned close to Layla. "The guy I saw go into the pub is Yegor fur sure. I'm gonna get a DNA sample from him."

"How?"

"Remember how I acted drunk on the Alaska cruise ship?"

"Yeah."

"As a recoverin' alcoholic, I know how to look drunk."

After the waitress brought a hamburger, fries, and a cola to Yegor, Luke stood. Shuffling and unsteady, he walked toward the front window and paused near Yegor's oval table. Luke squinted, peering out the window. "Where the hell is he?" Luke slurred. Turning toward the bar, he swung his arm in a clumsy motion, knocking Yegor's soda can to the floor.

Yegor glanced up from his phone and glared at him.

Luke wavered as he opened his eyes wider. "Sorry, sir. I'll pay for a replacement." Luke spoke with a loud, but slurred voice. He stooped, and with an unsteady hand, he picked up the can.

Yegor appeared surprised. "Thank you." He spoke with a thick accent.

Luke went to the bar, holding the can low near his trouser leg. "Alexander. I knocked a man's cola can on the floor." Luke showed Alexander a five-pound note. "Could you give him a fresh one?"

"No problem. Keep your money. It's on the house." Alexander signaled the waitress. "Suzy, please mop up the spill near the front window and provide a free fizzy drink to the man at the round table."

"Thanks."

Holding the cola can underneath his windbreaker, Luke returned to his table. He sat and smiled at Layla. "Do you still have quart-size plastic bags in your purse?"

Layla dug into her handbag and handed Luke a plastic sack.

Without touching the top of the can where its tab had been removed, Luke dropped the container into the bag and sealed it. "Put it in yur purse."

Layla stuffed the plastic bag in her pocketbook. She peered into Luke's eyes. "First-rate work, darling."

Luke winked, reached into his hip pocket, and pulled out his satellite phone. He touched Rory's name on its contact list. The man answered after two rings. "Hello, Luke." His voice sounded upbeat to Luke.

"Yegor walked into the Red Feather, and I snagged his DNA."

"How?"

"Faked being drunk and bumped a cola can from his table."

"Where's the can?"

"In a plastic bag in Layla's purse."

"Where's Yegor?"

"He's still here, eating."

"Stay put. See you soon. I'll park on the next street and ring." He paused. "Yegor must've evaded our surveillance again. I'll call Art Granger and update him with Yegor's location. Let me know if he leaves."

"Okay." Rory hung up.

Luke didn't notice Yegor raise his phone and snap a picture.

* * *

AS RORY NEARED the Red Feather Pub, he slowed and stopped in a parking lot by a mini market. Pulling his mobile phone from his jacket pocket, he touched Luke's name on the device's display.

Rory heard Luke's voice. "You close, Rory?"

"One street east of you in Marco Market's car park." Rory stared at his phone. "Is Yegor still in the pub?"

"Yep." Luke sounded calm to Rory. "He ordered dessert."

"You better walk here." Rory leaned forward in his car seat. "What about Layla?"

"She'll go upstairs and take a nap in our room."

"DS Boutwell has two men stationed at the pub to watch her. I have another team monitoring Yegor."

"Thank you. I didn't see them. They're on the ball."

Rory paused for a beat. "A courier will meet us here. He'll take the fizzy drink can to the lab."

"Okay." Rory tapped the disconnect icon on his phone.

THIRTY

IRRITATED his surveillance team had lost Yegor once again, Art Granger knew Rory would demand an explanation. But the young MI5 agent figured he could regain respect if he could uncover fresh evidence. Turning to his desktop computer, he decided to search a year further back in Anne Thorpe's credit card history.

Clicking on the oldest purchase link, Art saw an image of a special digital clock. It included a hidden camera. Art noticed the vendor had delivered the spy clock to Anne's secret flat in the Crows End neighborhood.

Art clicked his telephone's speed dial button marked "Rory."

"Art, anything to report?"

"Yes. I searched a further year back into Anne's online purchase history. She bought a clock equipped with a hidden camera. It was delivered to her Crows End flat." Art heard horns beeping as if Rory were in his car.

"The crime scene crew tore her flat apart. They found no such clock."

Without hesitating, Art said, "Anne had it sent to her flat

so the baron wouldn't open the parcel. I wager she placed it in their mansion."

"Excellent deduction, Art." More automobile horns blared and the sound of a distant siren interrupted the call. "I'm going to pick Luke up. We'll soon be on our way to visit the baron's manor house."

"I'll text a picture of the clock to both your phones."

"You're on the ball, my boy." Rory hung up.

Art's thin lips formed a grin. "Yes." Then he whooped in a tenor voice. His yell echoed in his bare, one-man MI5 office.

* * *

2:05 P.M., SUNDAY, NEAR THE RED FEATHER PUB

Layla stood, holding an umbrella to protect her hair from the misty rain. As Luke unlocked the iron gate alongside the Red Feather Pub, he glanced toward the street and saw Drake's familiar face. One of DS Boutwell's two undercover men, Drake had earlier waved goodbye to Luke and Layla at the Harrods luxury department store when he'd stopped tailing them. This afternoon, Drake stood next to a light pole watching the pub and Luke's Airbnb above it.

Drake shot a quick smile at Luke and winked.

Luke smiled. *He's gotta be one of the guys keepin' an eye on Layla.* Luke flashed a near imperceptible nod to the man, who showed a quick, subtle grin.

Luke held the gate open for Layla and kissed her. "Don't stare, but the guy by the streetlight is a part of the detail keeping an eye on you."

Layla glimpsed at the man. "I can sleep without worrying." She let go of Luke's hand, waved, and started along the dim alley leading to the stairs up to their second-floor, rented apartment.

Luke tightened his grip on a white plastic shopping bag. It held the smaller quart-size bag concealing Yegor's cola can. *I gotta power walk to Marco Market. Don't want to keep Rory and the courier waiting.*

* * *

2:11 P.M., SUNDAY, MARCO MARKET

A steady rain had begun to fall on Marco Market's parking lot. Rory opened his car's passenger-side door for Luke. Sliding into the car, Luke felt warm air from the heater bathe his face. He lowered his jacket's retractable hood and handed his white, plastic shopping bag to Rory. "The can's in a quart-size plastic bag inside this."

Rory set the shopping bag on the seat behind him. "Did you record the time and place where you got the evidence?"

"Yep. It's on a Red Feather dinner napkin. I signed it, too."

"Outstanding." Rory opened the bag, removed the napkin, wrote the time of transfer of the evidence to him, and signed the serviette.

Luke heard a loud engine outside the car. Turning backward, he saw a man in black leathers inching his motorcycle toward Rory's fogged, driver-side window. After rolling the window down, Rory said, "Quick response in the rain, Jarvis. Please get in and sign the chain of custody document."

Jarvis switched his motorcycle off and set its kickstand. After getting in the car's rear seat, he wiped his wet hands on his handkerchief.

Rory handed Jarvis a pen and the napkin. Jarvis paused and then chortled. "At first, I thought you wanted me to dry my hands with it." Smiling, he signed and dated the paper napkin.

Less than a minute later, Jarvis had stuffed the white shopping bag containing the chain of custody document and the cola can into his bike's saddlebag. He restarted the cycle and took off with a roar.

By the expression on Rory's face, Luke saw he was pleased. Rory's eyes sparkled. "We've learned Anne bought a digital clock with a spy cam hidden in it."

Luke tilted his head. "Where is it?"

"It wasn't in Anne's flat. It may be in the baron's manor house."

"How does it record pictures?"

Rory grinned. "On a flash memory card or a thumb drive. Either one of them can easily fit in a small clock."

"The clock cam could've recorded the video on the thumb drive we found in the tomb," Luke said.

Rory reached over his seat back and grasped two boxes. Luke saw one contained nitrile crime scene gloves, and the second held evidence bags. "Take two pairs and two bags, and put them in your pocket."

After returning the boxes to the car's rear seat, he started his vehicle. "Let's visit Lord Thorpe and see what we can find out."

* * *

2:30 P.M., SUNDAY, THE OLD STREET TUBE STATION

Yegor stroked his close-cropped, black hair and leaned against the wall in the Old Street Tube Station. Evading the tail he'd seen following him had been more difficult than he'd expected. He glanced at his watch. *Where's old man Viktor?* The elderly spy served as Yegor's KGB RB boss in the UK.

Yegor scanned the station, but still did not see Viktor. Yegor sighed. *We're mere pawns in the geopolitical chess game.*

As Yegor stared down at his hands, he felt a tap on his shoulder.

Viktor had approached from around a corner behind Yegor. In his sixties, the experienced, stealthy spy laughed. "Yegor, you must work on your tradecraft." Viktor spoke in

Russian. "I found it easy to surprise you." The aging man continued to grin, showing his bad teeth.

A train came to a noisy stop, and people got off and on it. Yegor glanced away from the nearest train car and then peered at Viktor. "Did you learn anything about the man who knocked my fizzy drink can down?"

Viktor displayed an amused expression. "You took a nice picture. Facial recognition identified him as Kentucky Deputy Sheriff Luke Ryder."

"I didn't see him discard the empty can, though he may have dropped it into a wastebasket near the bar. Many cans were in the rubbish."

Viktor's eyes gleamed from his wrinkled face. "I doubt he got your DNA. He's on his honeymoon, and he's an alcoholic. The FBI and CIA wouldn't hire a drunk, and it's rare for them to work with other law enforcement agencies."

"It's surprising how fast you found out about him."

Viktor shifted a shoulder. "Artificial intelligence is a fine tool. In seconds, it searches the web and dozens of other non-Internet, digital sources."

Yegor slipped his hands into his jacket pockets. "My gut tells me Ryder's not what he seems."

"Ah, but we also found out he's a part-time farmer." Viktor held onto the corner of the wall and leaned forward. "Ryder provides us with an opportunity."

Yegor stood straighter. "What?"

"The US is a signatory to the agricultural pact with the UK and Belarus. We want to begin operations in the US. Try to sell Mr. Ryder a tractor. If we get on the good side of local law enforcement, we can make inroads in US rural communities. Offer him the same deal you gave the two UK farmers."

"Yes, sir."

Viktor wrinkled his creased brow. "Since the baroness is no longer in the picture, you need to work fast."

"I will."

Viktor made steady eye contact with Yegor. "We'll set

you up with a new identity and send you to North America, if you uncover significant intel about the US robotic tank."

Yegor felt relief permeate his body. "Thank you for the great opportunity."

Viktor slapped Yegor's back. "I know why you're relieved. Have the police contacted you about Anne's death?"

"No."

"Let's hope your luck continues." Viktor raised his eyebrows. "On Tuesday do your best to secure intelligence about the tank at the proving ground show, as we discussed. If you do, we'll send you to Minsk for a debrief and preparation for the North American assignment."

THIRTY-ONE

THE RAIN HAD STOPPED, and the air felt humid and warmer. Rory pulled into the Thorpe mansion's driveway and stopped next to the baron's luxury automobile. Luke peered out the foggy, passenger-side window of the unmarked police car at the baron's auto. Its rear back tire appeared as flat as a flagstone.

Luke glanced at Rory. "I see a nail in the tire. It could have a slow leak, or someone would of fixed it by now."

Rory pulled in front of the fancy automobile and parked. Within a minute, he knocked on the baron's front door.

The heavy door swung open, and Baxter, the butler, peered out. "Gentlemen. I assume you're here to see the baron." Baxter's deep, bass voice sounded strong, though the tall, skinny man's old body wavered. His scarred, wrinkled face appeared serious to Luke.

Rory shot a pleasant expression at the butler. "We have follow-up questions."

"I'll tell the baron. Please wait in the foyer." Baxter nodded toward a marble bench.

Luke took a step closer to the butler. "One of the tires on the baron's car is flat."

"I called for roadside assistance." Baxter sighed. "I've misplaced the wheel brace."

Luke glanced at Rory with a puzzled expression.

Rory seemed amused. "In the US you'd perhaps call it a lug wrench."

The butler left. After Rory sat on the stone bench in the foyer, he glanced up at Luke. "I'll start by telling Lord Thorpe we've found his thumb drive and seen the video on it."

Luke shifted his weight from his left foot to his right. "How about I search for the spy clock before you dive into questions?"

"I'll give you a few minutes to scan the library before I begin asking questions."

Baxter returned. "The baron will see you in the library. Please follow me." His low-toned voice rumbled as if he were nervous.

Luke grinned and studied Rory's face. He, too, smiled. The spy clock could still be in the library.

* * *

2:50 P.M., SUNDAY, THE RED FEATHER PUB

Nursing a pint of beer, Drake sat in a booth on the far side of the barroom, away from the pool table. He watched as Layla racked up billiard balls on the game table's green, felt surface. When no one else faced him, he winked at her. Layla returned a quick, subtle nod. She wore a yellow cotton dress. It went well with her ebony skin.

Drake smiled. *She's practicing her game. Too bad I can't challenge her.*

A jingling from the pub's front doorbell caught Drake's attention, and he turned his head toward the noise.

Yegor entered the pub. Drake felt his body and mind go on high alert. *He's walking toward Layla.*

Drake rose and picked up his pint of ale. The bubbling, amber liquid sloshed in his glass as he moved to a table closer to the pool table. He sat and glanced aside at his partner, Ralph, a tall, bony man with dark hair. Seconds later, Ralph also stood and sat down near Layla and Yegor.

The man from Belarus had stopped near Layla. She leaned and sighted along her pool stick, ready to strike the cue ball.

"Excuse me, ma'am." Yegor spoke with an obvious Russian accent. He seemed to force himself to smile. "I think your husband knock my fizzy drink down today. He bought me a new one. I want thank him, but is not here. Instead, I thank you." Yegor made a short bow.

Layla's eyes shifted for a fraction of a second, catching Drake's attention. He sent her a brief smile. *Go ahead, Layla, speak to him. You may learn something important. You're under my protection.* Drake wondered if she'd picked up his vibes.

Layla straightened up from the edge of the pool table and held her cue stick at her side. "Thank you, but I should apologize for my husband. He had too much to drink." She sighed.

"Is okay. Drinking common in my country, too. Can happen anybody, me as well. Mrs....?"

"Layla Ryder."

"Pleased meet you. I, Yegor Bulot. I sell farm equipment, tractors, etc., etc." He paused and cocked his head. "I, too, like play pool. You want to shoot game with me?"

Layla grinned. "Sure."

Yegor grabbed a cue stick from a rack on the wall and rubbed its tip with blue chalk.

Using his side vision, Drake watched as Layla struck the cue ball, sending it at the rest of the billiard balls on the table. *Well done, Layla. Keep him talking.* Drake displayed a brief smile.

* * *

2:53 P.M., SUNDAY, THE THORPE MANSION

The baron sat on a brown, leather easy chair, smoking a pipe. The sweet, aromatic smell of tobacco greeted Luke as he followed the butler and Rory into the manor house library.

Luke noticed the aristocrat's nose and face were flushed as if he'd been drinking all day. Luke tilted his head sideways. *Heavy drinkin's not good for your health.*

Lord Thorpe stood. He swayed. "Gentlemen, please have a seat. I understand you have additional queries."

Rory made strong eye contact with the baron. "As our investigation goes forward, further questions come up." He sat down on a carved walnut chair near a coffee table.

Luke began to scan the library's shelves, tables, and nooks. *I gotta spot the spy clock.* Glancing behind him, he saw the clock between two volumes on a bookshelf. He heard himself say, "Excuse me, Rory, but I see the clock we thought we'd find." Luke pointed.

Rory threw his shoulders back and removed a folded document from his breast pocket. "I have a search warrant." He handed it to Lord Thorpe, who set his pipe on an end table.

As the baron unfolded the document, he wrinkled his brow. He scanned the warrant. "I already gave you permission to search."

Rory shrugged. "Thank you. We only wish to do things properly."

Luke caught Rory's attention. "I'll get the clock."

Rory nodded.

Luke slipped on a pair of nitrile gloves and picked up the timepiece. Luke held it close to his eyes. Peering into a hole drilled in the clock's decorative wooden frame, Luke noticed glass optics. "I see a lens inside a hole."

Rory stared at Lord Thorpe. "We learned Anne bought a clock with a spy cam hidden inside it."

The aristocrat pursed his lips.

Luke opened the back of the clock. "I found an empty USB slot for a flash memory card or a thumb drive."

His hands trembling, the baron tugged at his ear. "She must've taken it out. I had no knowledge of this."

Luke's eyes drilled into Lord Thorpe. "Rory, me, and a third man saw you go into your family tomb today."

The aristocrat bit at his lip, and he fidgeted.

Rory leaned forward. "We found the thumb drive we believe had been in this clock. We watched the video of you and Anne arguing. Why did you hide it in the back wall of the tomb?"

The baron breathed fast. He paused as if thinking. "Anne and I were not getting along well, to say the least." He peered out a window. The rain had started again. "Two weeks ago, I asked my solicitor to prepare divorce papers. I had no idea Anne had been recording our conversations until the day after she died. I found the clock and the thumb drive last night."

Luke sat across from the nobleman. "Why'd you withhold evidence?"

Lord Thorpe took a deep breath and exhaled. "I'd planned to ring the law firm I've employed for years for advice, but they're closed on the weekend. I decided to place the thumb drive in a safe place until I received proper legal advice."

Rory blinked. "Why not put the thumb drive in your pocket on a keyring?"

The baron sighed. "I could've been robbed."

Luke scoffed.

His nostrils flaring, Lord Thorpe opened his mouth, hesitated, and then spoke. "Unscrupulous reporters have been calling here. They'll do anything for a story, tap your phone...break and enter."

Rory nodded.

The baron appeared more than agitated, almost out of control. His head shook. "I thought the video would ruin my reputation, if tabloids got hold of it."

Rory sat straight up. "Did you kill Anne?"

Lord Thorpe seemed to shoot fire from his eyes. "Hell no. Why would I kill her, if I were going to divorce her?" He snatched his pipe from the end table near his chair. "I've been using the law firm Winchester and Malony for years. Nigel Winchester is my family's law solicitor and Joseph Malony is my barrister. I'll phone Nigel and instruct him to give you all the information you need about my preparations to divorce Anne. Until then, I'll say nothing to you unless Nigel and Joseph agree it is acceptable."

The aristocrat tapped his pipe on an ashtray, knocking the ashes out.

Rory stood. "We'll leave, Lord Thorpe." Rory held his chin high. "I believe your lawyers will suggest you continue to cooperate with us." He started to walk from the room and then turned to face the baron. "By the way, we know you're an SIS employee. I'm sure your superiors would like to be briefed about your situation."

Lord Thorpe glared at Rory.

* * *

FROM INSIDE THE foyer of the Thorpe mansion, Luke heard rain pound against the front door. He turned to Rory. "It's pouring." Luke pulled his jacket hood up and over his hair.

Rory draped his windbreaker atop his head. "I'll dash for the car and unlock it. Follow me after it's open."

"Okay."

Rory scampered to the car, slid into the auto, and waved at Luke to come.

Once inside the undercover police car, Luke lowered his hood, wiped rain from his face, and gazed at Rory. "Do you think the baron killed Anne?"

"I'm not sure. I'll ask his lawyers about his alleged divorce papers. Odds are it's true."

Luke thought Lord Thorpe had acted guilty as hell when he'd hidden the thumb drive. As Luke mulled over possibilities, he glanced at Rory. "The baron was angry when he denied killing Anne. Forceful denial is a hint he may be innocent." Luke paused. "And the thumb drive is proof she cheated on him. Why kill her when divorcing her would be easy?"

"Indeed, why would he?" Rory's slight smile wavered, and he sighed. "Each of our suspects, including Lord Thorpe, could be guilty."

Luke rubbed his elbow. "When you told the baron you know he works in the SIS, what did it mean to him?"

"He reckoned we work for SIS or MI5 as well as the Metropolitan Police Service. I believe he'll conclude ours is an MI5-led investigation."

Luke cocked his head to the side. "He's gotta be shook up."

"If he's guilty, he could take rash action."

Rory's encrypted mobile phone rang. He pulled it from his jacket pocket. "Hello, Jerry…"

* * *

3:09 P.M., SUNDAY, INSIDE RORY'S CAR IN FRONT OF THE THORPE MANSION

Rory pressed his phone against his ear. "Excellent." As he listened, he glanced at Luke, who sat next to him in the front passenger's seat. "Quick work, and an interesting development, Jerry. Anything else, call or text me. Thanks. Bye." Rory rubbed his hand through his hair.

Luke sat straighter. "What's up?"

Rory lifted his chin. "The lab got an excellent DNA sample from Yegor's fizzy drink can. Yegor is the father of Anne's unborn child." He leaned back in the driver's seat. "Terrific work by you to grab the can."

Rory stared at the pouring rain outside the car as if he

were trying to figure out how this fresh DNA evidence would affect the case.

Luke leaned toward Rory. "If she told Yegor he fathered her baby, is it a motive to kill her?"

Rory wound his arms around his torso. "If he's indeed a spy—and I believe he is—he could've thought Anne might tell the authorities about him."

Luke pressed his lips together and then spoke. "If Yegor's a spy, and killed her, wouldn't he have searched her flat and found her exposé? He would of burned it."

"What are you suggesting?"

"Yegor could be innocent."

Rory tapped his foot on the car's floor mat. "You're right. A spy wouldn't miss the hollowed-out book unless he panicked." Rory scratched his head. "The killer stayed long enough to decapitate Anne."

Luke sighed. "It's possible the killer cut her head off, heard a noise, and left."

"Good point, Luke."

"Anne wanted to keep the kid. Her baby would be great proof Yegor had been screwing her to get secret info. Would he kill her to get rid of the child?"

"He has a motive." Rory stopped speaking for a moment. "We have video of Yegor entering Anne's building the night she died. He's our prime suspect."

Luke peered downward. "Yegor appears guilty, but the baron's not always actin' like an innocent man. We gotta learn more details about the golfer, too. We don't know a lot about Estrella. And you said the banker's a big-time extortionist."

Rory rubbed his chin. "We still have to investigate the details of how the banker and the rest of the suspects interacted with Anne." Rory paused. "But we must be careful with Yegor. We don't have enough to charge him, and if we confront him, he'll get on the next plane for Minsk."

Luke began to speak, but stopped. "Would the robotic

tank live-fire demonstration give Yegor a chance to get secret intel?"

"Our agents will monitor the live-fire show." Rory started the car. "I'll drop you off at the Red Feather." He turned on his windshield wipers and guided his vehicle along the driveway toward the road. "Let's keep brainstorming."

THIRTY-TWO

HEAVY RAIN DRENCHED the countryside near the baron's manor house. Luke noticed Rory kept his eyes focused on the narrow lane as he drove toward Crows End.

As Rory guided the car, Luke glimpsed at the man's profile. "Tell me more about SIS and what the baron does there."

Rory's fingers twitched on the steering wheel. "Lord Thorpe secretly serves in the SIS. It's similar to your CIA. At the same time, he's chief of the British Army's procurement office in charge of acquiring advanced weapons."

"Buying arms is his cover?"

"Yes." Rory steered around a deep puddle in the left lane. "When making sales pitches to Lord Thorpe, Yegor got to know him. Yegor's selling cheap armored personnel carriers, which his company also produces. We think the Belarus KGB sent Yegor to the UK to compromise the lord and others who have secret or proprietary information."

"Belarus has KGB spies?"

"Yes." Rory paused. "When the USSR broke apart, Belarus declared independence from the Soviet Union in

1991. The branch of the Soviet KGB in Belarus became the KGB of the Republic of Belarus, or KGB RB."

"They kept the name and a lot of the same people?"

"Yep." Rory took a deep breath. "In recent years, the KGB RB has tortured political enemies."

"Is Yegor dangerous?"

Rory shrugged as he steered around a pothole. "We don't think he's a physical threat. Because he's selling tractors, he may be working in the KGB RB's Directorate of Economic Security and Anti-corruption."

Luke blinked. "Why didn't y'all expel Yegor from the UK?"

"Because we're watching him. We wish to learn who his contacts are. We want to know if he's compromised British citizens."

"But if you get proof he killed Anne, you'd have to arrest him, right?"

"We'd jail him in a microsecond." The pouring rain had morphed into a sprinkle, and Rory ventured a longer glance at Luke. "Yegor often eats and drinks at the Red Feather. If you see him, strike up a conversation. Mention you're a US farmer growing hemp."

"Y'all been checkin' on me?"

"We had to be sure about you." Rory glanced at Luke. "No hard feelings I hope. We like you."

Luke saw the Red Feather's sign come into view. In his mind's eye, he saw Layla. *By now she's awake from her nap. She could of decided to play a pool game or two in the pub.*

THIRTY-THREE

AS RORY'S car slowed to a stop at the curb close to the Red Feather Pub's entrance, his mobile phone chimed. He glanced at Luke. "I received a text."

Rory unsnapped his seatbelt and snatched his phone from his pocket. He began reading out loud. "Lab confirms DNA from Yegor Bulot, Arnold Beeker, and Robert Rothstein found at Anne Thorpe's flat. Robert Rothstein seen September 11 on CCTV footage entering Anne's apartment building."

Rory faced Luke. "Estrella's and Lord Thorpe's DNA weren't found in Anne's flat."

Luke frowned. "Estrella said she was in Anne's apartment," Luke said. "Weird her DNA wasn't there."

Rory glanced down at his phone. "The crime scene investigators also found a speck of Anne's blood on the inside of the hollowed-out book."

"She could've pricked her finger or had a bloody nose." Luke leaned back in his car seat. "If the killer read Anne's writings, why would he leave them in her place, if they mentioned his name?"

Rory frowned. "Someone else could've killed her and left the book in her flat to divert attention from himself."

"Could be."

Rory pushed a button and unlocked the car. "I'll pick you up here at eight tomorrow morning. We'll visit Robert Rothstein at Crows End Bank when it opens."

"See you then."

Rory's mobile phone chimed a second time. He tapped its display and glanced at it. "Drake texted me from inside the pub. He's watching Layla. Yegor's been playing pool with her."

Luke blinked and stared at the Red Feather's front door. His nostrils flared, and he unsnapped his seat belt in a rapid motion. He grabbed the car's door handle. "I'll find out what's happening. I'll call you." Luke stepped from the car.

Rory stared at him. "Don't blow your cover."

Luke leaned down and peered back inside the car. "Don't worry."

Rory nodded. "Call me when you can."

* * *

AS LUKE OPENED the front door of the pub, he heard pool balls smacking against one another. He peered at the back corner of the wide room and saw Layla straighten up. The billiard balls were still rolling on the table's green felt when Luke saw Yegor standing near Layla. He rubbed blue chalk on the tip of his cue stick.

Luke felt adrenaline surge throughout his body. He clenched his teeth, inhaled through his nose, and then let his breath ease out from his mouth. Feeling calmer, he walked toward the pool table, slowing as he neared Layla.

Catching sight of Luke, Layla smiled, and Yegor turned toward him. Out of Yegor's sight, Layla winked. Luke nodded. *Layla's up to something.*

At the corner of his eye, Luke saw Drake smile. Luke's heartbeat slowed to normal.

Yegor gestured at Layla. "Your wife is fine pool player." He spoke in what Luke thought had to be a thick, Russian-like accent. "She beat me four times in row."

Luke forced himself to grin. "She's the best pool player in the Greater Lexington, Kentucky area." Silent for a second, Luke shrugged. "Sorry about tippin' yur cola can over. I'd had a lot to drink."

Yegor flashed a grin. "No problem. In my country, many people drink much vodka." He shrugged. "Thanks for fizzy drink replacement."

Layla took a half step forward. "Luke, this is Yegor Bulot, and Yegor, this is Luke, my husband." Layla shifted her pool cue from her left hand to her right. "I told Yegor about our farm, and how we grow hemp."

Yegor extended his hand, and Luke shook it. The man had a firm grip. Luke shifted his weight. *Layla remembered Yegor's sellin' tractors made in Belarus. She's smart as a raccoon snatchin' food from a picnic table. Now I can chitchat with him.*

Yegor motioned toward a chair. "Layla beat me many times. I'm embarrassed." He set his cue on the pool table. "Let's take seat. Layla's told me about your farm. I have proposal for you."

Luke pulled a chair away from a dining table and gestured for Layla to sit. He turned to Yegor and asked, "What do you have in mind?"

Yegor sat. "Layla said your farm 300 acres. It is big for Kentucky farm. You need new tractor."

"How'd you find out?"

Yegor shrugged. "Layla said your tractor made in 1970s and underpowered." He glanced from Layla to Luke. "My company wish to export to US."

"How expensive are yur tractors?"

"We make farm machines reliable as US tractor makers do, but ours cost thirty percent less."

Luke leaned closer to Yegor. "How can you sell them cheaper than US companies do?"

"We have low labor and material cost."

Luke scratched his chin. *I gotta lead this guy on.* "I bin thinkin' of buyin' a tractor. You have a catalog?"

Yegor appeared eager to Luke. "Of course." He paused. "If you show to farmers, we loan you our midlevel model for year. Later, we sell it to you with deep discount, or you return to us no cost to you."

"Sounds great." *Does he know I'm workin' with the FBI and MI5?* Luke tucked in his upper lip. *I doubt it.*

"New US tractor costs thirty thousand dollars." Yegor scratched his black hair. "Our Model K is fifty horsepower, with four-wheel drive, and your EPA okay it. We sell in the US for twenty thousand."

Luke stared at Yegor. "Why would you let me use it for free for a year?"

"To show it in action. US farmers see it, and they will line up to buy."

"How would I git farmers to see it?"

"We bring farmers, farm co-op reps, farm machine dealers to your farm." He stared at Luke. "It will take your time, but you will not pay for new tractor right away. You get discount if you buy it."

Luke made strong eye contact with Yegor. *I gotta seem real interested, and it is a decent deal.* He smiled. Luke toyed with a bottle of mustard on the tabletop. "I'll do a deal with you."

Yegor's dark brown eyes flashed. "Let's meet for dinner here at seven, and I bring catalog and contract. You won't pay nothing for year unless you decide to buy Model K."

"Okay." Luke checked his watch. "Seven o'clock works for me."

"Good." Yegor rose.

Luke stood. Yegor grasped Luke's hand with a firm grip.

After Yegor opened the pub's front door and stepped onto the sidewalk, Layla leaned over and kissed Luke on his cheek.

Under the table, Luke held his hand against her waist. "Nice work, Layla. I'll call Rory and fill him in." Luke turned and winked at Drake. The MI5 man smiled.

Layla rubbed Luke's shoulder. "Better call from upstairs, hon." She peered deep into his brown eyes. "Afterward, I have an idea of what we can do before dinner. My baby bump could show soon."

Luke felt his body heat up.

* * *

3:55 P.M., SUNDAY, LUKE AND LAYLA'S AIRBNB SUITE

In his Airbnb room, Luke touched "Rory" on his phone's contact list. "Luke, did it go well?"

"Yep. Yegor wants to sell me a tractor and break into the US market."

Rory laughed. "Doesn't surprise me. I learned he's sold at least a dozen tractors to UK farmers."

"Do you think Yegor's onto me?"

"No." Rory paused. "Don't worry about Layla. Drake, my men, and Sonja will protect her."

"Thanks."

Luke noticed motion in his side vision. Layla took her time to unzip her dress, and he stepped closer to her. She smiled.

Rory brushed his phone against something, and it made a sound. "See you tomorrow morning." Rory hung up.

Layla began a slow dance. "I'm going to strip for my hubby." She removed her yellow dress and dropped it to the floor. "Come closer. Help me strip."

Luke felt like a stoked steam engine.

Layla dropped her panties to the floor. "Don't think about dinner with the spy. Let's have fun."

Luke unhooked her bra.

THIRTY-FOUR

AS LUKE ENTERED the Red Feather Pub's barroom with Layla, he saw Yegor sitting in a booth in a rear corner of the pub. He wore a blue suit, a red tie, and glossy shoes. Luke thought they'd been spit-shined. *He's acting like a regular salesman, dressin' to impress, or he's a perfectionist.*

Yegor was studying the menu. He glanced up and waved. Luke returned the gesture, smiling. Layla held his arm as they neared Yegor. The stocky man stood. "Feel free to try new dish. Dinner is on me." Yegor spoke with a thicker accent than before. He shook hands with Luke.

Luke flushed. "I ain't used to being treated. Thanks, Yegor."

As Luke and Layla settled themselves on the booth bench across from Yegor, Luke smelled whiskey on the Belarusian man's breath. Luke sighed. *I've got the self-control to skip alcohol, even if I'm an alcoholic.*

Yegor pulled a bottle of scotch close to himself. "Would you like drink?" He slurred his words, and his Russian-like accent became even stronger.

"Thanks, but no. I'm trying to cut back on my drinking, and Layla's with child."

Yegor smiled and appeared relaxed. "Layla said you're on honeymoon. Congrats on the news about your baby."

Alexander, the bartender, approached with two lime cordials. "I took the liberty of bringing your drinks." He set them in front of Luke and Layla.

Luke nodded. "Thanks, Alexander."

Yegor raised his whiskey glass. "To you both and healthy baby."

Luke and Layla clinked their glasses against Yegor's tumbler.

The waitress came to their table and took their orders.

Luke reckoned he should start fishing for facts about the alleged spy. "Yegor, you come here often?"

"Yes. Alexander is friend. There is excellent food, drink, and fun here. One friend used to live nearby." The man brushed a tear from one eye. "Allergies." He swallowed and showed a smile.

Luke reckoned Yegor still had feelings for Anne. *Does he know she had carried his child?*

Yegor gulped his whiskey, and then set his empty glass on the oak tabletop. "I want to visit USA. Specially big and little farms. My tractor company can help your farmers. They don't earn what they deserve for work. Belarus can help farmers 'round the world." He waved his arm across the table.

Luke sipped his cordial and then spoke. "If I sign the tractor deal, will you visit my farm in Kentucky?"

"Yes, I would be honored." He reached under the table and lifted a leather briefcase. He unsnapped it. "Here is brochure with Model K pictures."

Luke examined the tractor's picture while he chewed on a slice of fish. The machine appeared equal to a pricey American model. Scanning the specs, he heard himself speak. "Impressive."

Yegor fished a single page from his case and handed it to Luke. "Here's one-page contract in big print. Read and sign, or study it later and decide." He shrugged.

Luke read the contract as he sipped his lime cordial and helped himself to french fries. *It's simple, and I don't see show-stoppers.* "I'll sign."

His eyes glowing, Yegor handed Luke a ballpoint pen.

As Luke wrote his name, he felt a shot of excitement. *Yegor's drunk enough, he could say somethin' useful.*

"Thank you, Luke. You are friend of me and Belarus. Together, we can help US farmers get better life."

Yegor held his hand across the table and Luke shook it. *He's a salesman for Belarus. Plus he's idealistic—thinks he's doin' the right thing for his country. He ain't such a bad guy, even if he's a spy. Too bad he's on the wrong side.*

Luke released Yegor's firm grip. "You'll like visitin' my farm, Yegor."

"I can't wait to travel to your great country." Yegor had rushed his words, and then he reached into his briefcase again. "I have two extra tickets for special event, if you want to go." Yegor handed a brochure and an unsealed envelope to Luke.

Luke lifted the envelope flap and fingered the tickets. The brochure described the three-day, "International Battlefield Machine Show, a live-fire, multi-country demonstration of battlefield vehicles, including the US Raven Robotics' remote-controlled battle tank, to begin Tuesday, September 17, at Poppins Proving Ground in the UK."

I better not let on I know about the robotic tank. "How did you git tickets to see a robotic tank?" Luke handed the brochure to Layla, who was enjoying her shepherd's pie.

Yegor shifted his shoulders. "My tractor company also sells armored personnel carriers that we will show at demo. Smaller tanks, too." He paused. "It is like Paris Air Show, but for battlefield machines."

"Y'all make weapons of war?"

Yegor puffed his chest out. "Yes. Battle vehicles are like heavy-duty farm machines." He smiled. "I want to see the US robotic tank 'cause you can run its joystick from an office far away. We soon will add remote control to farm tractors."

Luke studied Yegor's face. "Could I plow my fields using a joystick from my porch?"

Yegor held his chin high. "Yes. I will try get my company to put prototype software on your Model K tractor."

"It'll be fun to try."

"For sure you will go with me to Battlefield Machine Show as guest of Belarus?"

Luke glanced at Layla, and she nodded yes. Luke turned to Yegor. "Yep, if it's nearby. We got one week left to spend honeymooning."

Yegor relaxed in his chair. "Proving ground is 125 miles away, northwest of here. We will give you free air or car transport. I will check with my boss when and where we leave. You have cell phone? I will text details."

Luke scratched his whiskers. *I better not give Yegor my satellite phone number.* He turned to Yegor. "I'll give you Layla's number. I forgit my phone once in a while." Luke grabbed a napkin, wrote Layla's number down, and shoved the serviette to Yegor.

Yegor stuffed the napkin in his shirt pocket and glanced at Luke. "In case I can get helicopter ride, I need take picture of your and Layla's passports. Okay?"

"Sure." Luke fished in his trousers pocket and nodded at Layla. She dug her passport from her purse.

Yegor set the passports on the tabletop next to his plate of food. Pulling his phone from his jacket pocket, he shot pictures of each passport. "Thanks." He handed the documents back to Luke.

Luke shoved his passport back into his pocket, and then sipped his lime cordial. "Would we leave Tuesday morning?"

Yegor waved his hand. "Some time in morning. It's all-day event." He smiled. "Even BBC and CNN will film. You could be on TV." The Belarusian man swayed in his seat, sipping his whiskey.

Luke leaned forward. *Yegor's drunk enough he could tell me what he knows about the robotic tank.* "Do you think you can learn something about the robotic tank you could use in the Model K?"

Yegor's dark eyes sparkled. "You smart. We got tractor remote control software, but the US tank app better. We will ask Raven Robotics to license software so we can use in our tractor. I hope we will do deal with the US company. Who knows?"

"Would Raven Robotics deal with you?"

"Slim chance. We will try to copy what the tank can do, if not get US software." He grinned. "I am ready for dessert." He motioned to the waitress. "Please bring dessert menu."

Luke couldn't stop himself from smiling. *After we're done eatin', I gotta call Rory. I better fill in Henry Dunbar, too.*

* * *

7:55 P.M., SUNDAY, LUKE AND LAYLA'S AIRBNB SUITE

Luke pulled his secure satellite phone from his jacket pocket and sat on a hassock in his Airbnb. He touched Rory's number on the phone's contact list.

Five ring tones sounded, and Rory answered. "Hello, Luke. How was dinner with Yegor?"

"He's gonna ship a loaner Belarus-made tractor to my Kentucky farm, if I show it to a bunch of US farmers."

"Interesting."

Luke nodded. "After a year I can buy it cheap."

"Surprising."

Luke crossed his legs. "Said he wants to break into the US market. I signed a contract."

"He did the same for two UK farmers. Sold a number of tractors here since then."

"Do you think he suspects I'm workin' with y'all and the FBI?"

"I doubt it."

Luke tapped his toe on the carpet. "A second big thing. He invited Layla and me to see the US robotic tank Tuesday during the Battlefield Machine Show at Poppins Proving Ground."

Rory coughed. "So, Yegor will go. He could've convinced a US contact to sell him robo tank intel. The show is a suitable place for a brush pass." Rory's voice sounded higher than he normally spoke.

"What's that?"

"To brush pass means to slip something from one person to someone else." He paused. "Did you accept the invitation to the show?"

"Yep. He gave us tickets as guests of Belarus. He's gonna either drive us or fly us to Poppins."

Rory cleared his throat. "We'll increase our surveillance at the show." He paused a second. "We'll have a team meeting at four o'clock tomorrow afternoon at MI5 headquarters to make sure everyone knows what their roles are."

Luke crossed his legs. "I'll call Henry. He and Sonja will want to go, 'specially if a US citizen could try to brush pass robo tank intel to Yegor."

"I've already contacted Henry and Sonja to invite them to the meeting. Tell Henry I'll ring him within a half hour to chat."

"Okay." Luke paused. "You know what the robo tank will do?"

"A Raven Robotics company engineer sitting thousands of meters away from the tank will use a joystick to drive it through an obstacle course with hills, rocks, and trees. He'll also fire the tank's weapons."

"How will we be able to see the tank driving through the course?"

"You'll sit on bleachers like those you see at a football match." Rory took a breath. "After the live-fire exercise, the spectators can walk to the tank and examine it."

"What about other battlefield weapons?"

Rory paused. "The bigger ones will be demonstrated on a schedule."

Luke scratched his arm. "There's something else. Yegor's gonna text more details to Layla's phone. She'll call me tomorrow if Yegor contacts her."

"Good. I'll see you at the pub tomorrow morning at eight."

THIRTY-FIVE

A BRISK WIND GUSTED, and clouds drifted across the sky. Luke stood behind the iron gate which guarded the steps to his second-floor Airbnb apartment. *No point Yegor showin' up and seein' me get in a car with Rory. Would Yegor recognize Rory?*

Three minutes late, Rory stopped near the Red Feather Pub. Luke scanned the area and didn't see Yegor. After a quick walk to the car, Luke slid into the front passenger's seat. He figured the Crows End Bank wouldn't be far from the pub. "Are you gonna give me a rundown on the banker?"

"Yes, but let's get to the bank first." Rory pushed his fingertips together into a steeple shape. "It's better to arrive early than late. We'll wait in the bank's car park and talk about Mr. Rothstein. He's cheating old people out of money."

Rory pulled into traffic.

* * *

AS HE HEADED toward the Crows End Bank, Rory stayed below the speed limit. The bank didn't open until nine. Luke peered at Rory. "You said Robert Rothstein cheated older bank customers."

"Yes. He's under investigation for embezzling funds. He stole a million pounds."

Luke raised his eyebrows. "How?"

"Identity theft. He withdrew a hundred thousand pounds from one man's retirement account."

Luke shook his head. "Robert must've been sucking money out of retirement accounts for a while."

Rory turned a corner. "Yep. Most withdrawals were trivial—not easy to spot. Old people he cheated didn't often check their accounts."

"Did he take out cash?"

Rory stopped at a traffic light. "He opened a fraudulent banking account in the name of an existing business. After writing cashier's checks payable to the business, he withdrew cash. At first, the company's owners had no idea this had happened. Then a document related to the bogus account showed up in their mail."

"They called the police?"

"Yes." Rory pulled into the bank's parking lot. "He doesn't know he's under investigation. We'll arrest him for his bank crimes after we determine whether or not he had a role in Anne's murder." Rory stopped the car in a parking place and took the vehicle out of gear. "We'll ask him about Anne and her death, nothing else for now."

A man dressed in a suit neared the bank's entrance. Rory tilted his head. "I see Rothstein. Let's go."

Luke and Rory exited the car. At a quick pace, they walked to Rothstein, who had reached into his trousers pocket and pulled out a key ring.

Rory held up his badge. "I'm DCI Rory Calvin, and this is Luke Ryder, who's assisting me. May we have a word with you inside before the bank opens?"

Rothstein's eyes widened, and he bit his lip. "Of course."

* * *

8:15 A.M., MONDAY, CROWS END BANK

Rothstein led Rory and Luke into his glassed-in office and shut the door. "Please sit down, gentlemen."

As Luke took a seat in one of the two chairs in front of Rothstein's desk, he saw the banker's Adam's apple move up and down three times as if he were nervous.

Rory took out his mini notebook and a pen. "Robert, are you aware Baroness Anne Thorpe is dead, murdered?"

Robert drew in a deep breath and exhaled. "I read it in the paper."

Rory leaned forward and stared at the banker. "Your name appears in documents she wrote. We know you've visited her flat not far from here."

Robert's chin quivered. His face turned ashen.

"She noted you gave her an expensive diamond necklace."

Robert bit his lip. "Yes."

"When's the last time you saw her?"

Robert blinked, stared at the ceiling for two seconds, and then returned his gaze to Rory. "Wednesday, September 11."

"Are you married?"

"No, I'm divorced."

"We found your DNA in Anne's flat." Luke figured the police who'd been investigating Robert for embezzlement had grabbed a DNA sample from his trash or a drink can.

Robert gulped and then shrugged. "It's not surprising my DNA's in her flat because we've been dating." To Luke, Robert appeared to be defiant. "By the way, I didn't submit a DNA sample."

"We have it on file." Rory paused. "Did you know she was married when you dated her?"

"Two consenting adults can do what they will. It's not against the law."

"How'd you meet her?"

Robert appeared nervous. "She asked for a loan which I arranged."

"Why would a wealthy woman want a loan?"

Sighing, Robert cocked his head to the side. "She wanted to keep her husband from learning about her rented flat."

Rory squinted, pressed his lips together, and then said, "We've spoken with tenants who have a flat close to Anne's. They heard a loud row with a lot of yelling in her flat on Wednesday the fourth. You were seen entering Anne's flat that day."

Robert rubbed the back of his neck. "We had words. She told me she had pawned the necklace I gave her. She said we were through. I left."

A fact popped into Luke's mind. *Anne wrote in her biography she'd pawned an expensive diamond necklace to get money to pay her flat's rent.*

Rory glared at Robert. "We'll be back in touch, Mr. Rothstein." Rory stood.

Robert clutched his arms against his chest. His face turned even paler. "Okay."

Luke got up. *I ought to tell Rory I saw a pawnshop on the way here. We should check it out.*

* * *

RORY LEFT through the bank's front doorway, followed by Luke.

When Rory halted by his car, his mobile phone chimed. Peering down at a text message, he seemed shocked.

Rory's eyes flashed. "The electronic forensics lab sent me a text Rothstein wrote to Anne. Quote, 'Why did you pawn the necklace? It cost a fortune. I should slit your throat.'" Rory exhaled. "It's damning."

As they got into Rory's car, Luke said, "On the way to the bank, I saw a pawnshop two streets from the Red Feather Pub. Would've Anne pawned the necklace at the shop?"

Rory started the car. "We'll stop there next."

* * *

BELLS on the shop door jingled as Rory and Luke entered Perry's Pawn Place. Luke heard its old wooden floor creak while he walked toward a worn counter. Standing behind it, a dark-complected, heavyset man chewed on an extinguished cigar. He pulled the stogie from his mouth when Rory displayed his badge. "Are you Perry?"

"Yup."

"I'd like to see a diamond necklace pawned by Anne Thorpe."

The obese man belched. "Do you have the ticket?" Luke smelled Perry's foul breath, and saw his teeth were brownish yellow.

Rory narrowed his eyes and stared at Perry. "No, but the necklace is evidence in an investigation regarding Anne Thorpe's death."

With a surly expression on his face, Perry blinked three times, and then opened a safe behind the counter. Within thirty seconds, he dangled a diamond necklace in front of Rory, and set it on the countertop.

Rory pointed at the expensive jewelry. "I must seize this as evidence. Anyway, by law you must keep it in your shop for six months after it was pawned."

Perry crossed his arms. "You'll give me a receipt before you walk away with it."

"Of course."

His fingers twitching, Perry pulled open a drawer under the counter. He took out a form and began to fill it out.

Luke noticed Rory relax as the pawnbroker completed his ticket. Rory spoke. "Please describe what happened when Anne pawned this. Surely you remember Baroness Thorpe."

Perry shoved the ticket toward Rory and handed him a pen. "It was a no-brainer to give her the loan. She's wealthy." Perry seemed a slight bit calmer to Luke. The pawnbroker took a breath and exhaled. "I asked her what she needed the money for. She surprised me when she said, 'I require money to pay for something I don't wish my husband to be aware of.' Strange, eh?"

Rory signed the receipt. Perry gave him a carbon copy. After slipping the necklace and ticket into an evidence bag, Rory noted the time and place, and signed the outside of the bag.

Rory gave Perry a business card. "Thank you for your cooperation. We will be in touch with you again."

As Rory and Luke left the shop, Rory's mobile phone chimed. He stopped and pulled it from his pocket. "This time it's a text from Jerry."

* * *

RORY REPLACED his phone in his pocket and peered at Luke, who stood on the opposite side of the unmarked police car parked outside of the pawnshop. "According to Jerry's text, Tommy found a key. It had fallen through a grating into a vent in Anne's flat. The lab detected Estrella's DNA on the key."

Luke nodded. "Estrella admitted Anne gave her a key." He rubbed his chin. "Didn't Estrella say she returned it to Anne?"

Rory stared at the sky for a moment. "Yes."

Luke wrinkled his brow. "We don't know fur sure if Anne or Estrella would have dropped the key down the vent."

"You're saying Estrella may have lied?"

"Yeah."

"Let's revisit Anne's flat." Rory got in the driver's seat. "We're just a short distance away from it."

* * *

9:10 A.M., MONDAY, CROWS END BANK

The manager of the Crows End Bank, Robert Rothstein, stood up from his desk in the middle of the banking room. Moving his head in a jerky motion, he caught sight of Jane Woo, his assistant manager, sitting at her desk fifteen feet away. "I don't feel well. I'm taking the morning off." He figured Jane was suspicious because it was as rare as snow in June for him to take time off after the workday had begun.

Jane, a thin woman with long, black hair, examined him with concern. "Your face is pale."

Jane's eyes seemed to burn into his body like death rays.

Robert loosened the top button on his dress shirt. *Did Jane see me with Anne when she asked for the loan?* "I'll see you after lunch if I feel better."

Robert's mind ran full speed ahead as he neared his luxury automobile. *Anne caused nothing but trouble. Good riddance. Is this nightmare never going to end?* His thoughts skipped on to an additional, dreadful worry. *Do the coppers suspect I've been embezzling? A whiskey or two will settle me down.*

He unlocked his car door. *The Red Feather isn't a long drive.*

Pulling away from the bank's car park, he headed for the pub. *DCI Rory Calvin's as trustworthy as a cold-call telemarketer.* Robert bit his lips and turned the steering wheel, his mind on what the coppers could do to him. An oncoming auto squealed to a stop, and its driver pressed down on his horn for at least three seconds.

His heart pounding, Robert turned left at the next corner, watching in his rearview mirror. The car that had come close to smashing into his did not follow him. Robert pulled into a parking space and turned off his vehicle. *What am I going to do if I lose my job? How would I survive in prison? What's the easiest way to commit suicide?* He held his hands against his temples.

I could seek a job overseas. Canada? New Zealand? Australia? For now, I better investigate programs to quit drinking and drugs.

* * *

9:10 A.M., MONDAY, NEAR ANNE'S APARTMENT BUILDING

Luke tapped Rory's shoulder and pointed to the entrance of an alley. "Let's park behind Anne's building. We could git a better idea what the killer did before murdering her."

Rory nodded. "It's worth checking the alley again." He parked close to a brick wall twenty feet from the building's back door.

When they neared the door, Luke saw the deadbolt was taped over, ensuring the door wouldn't lock when closed. He glimpsed at Rory. "According to your men's crime scene report, it wasn't taped over when they investigated the night of the murder."

Rory peered at the door. "Odds are the killer had easy access through this doorway because the deadbolt was likely taped over before Anne's murder."

"Yep. He took off the tape after he snuck in." Luke pulled on his earlobe. "As I recall, the CCTV camera didn't see anyone unusual go in the front door."

Rory nodded. "I'll ask a man to search the trash cans and alley for a piece of tape. It could have DNA on it." Rory pulled the tape off the deadlock, and Luke followed him into the building and along a corridor.

A policeman sat on guard in the hallway near Anne's apartment door. Without asking, he handed Rory and Luke nitrile crime scene gloves and shoe covers. Rory winked at the officer.

After donning the gloves and shoe covers, Rory and Luke sat on Anne's worn couch. Rory closed his eyes for five seconds. Luke wondered if he was relaxing or perhaps trying to visualize how the murder had happened. Luke studied Rory for a moment. "You tryin' to imagine the killing?"

"Aye. Whilst my eyes are closed, it helps me think outside the box."

"I'll try it." Luke closed his eyes. "Feels calming."

"Try to picture Anne entering her flat. Would she have been surprised, or would she have let the killer in?"

From the snapshots Rory had shown him, Luke recalled Anne's unique, yet attractive face. Then he pictured her entering her apartment. "My gut tells me he surprised her." Luke paused, and he remembered the crime scene photo of Anne's severed head. It seemed to stare in terror at him. Coldness ran through his body.

"Anything else?"

"Anne's cutoff head seemed to be frozen in fright." Luke paused. "But she would have been terrified whether or not the killer was waitin' for her, or she let him in."

Luke opened his eyes and noticed Rory had done the same.

Rory rubbed his eyes as if he'd awakened. "I saw her detached head, too. Why cut it off?"

"Last night I wondered the same thing. I got up at two in the mornin' and searched the web."

"Did it help?"

"Yep. I found an article by a psychiatrist." Luke recalled having read about five types of killings after which the murderers cut up all, or parts, of a body. "Murderers are either crazy or have a logical purpose for choppin' up a body."

Rory tilted his head to the side. "Makes sense."

"Madmen have nutty reasons to slice and dice. Sane ones do it to hide evidence or to send a message like in Mafia killings."

"Are any of our known suspects maniacs?"

"As best I can tell, no." Luke scratched his elbow. "The perp didn't do it to hide evidence. Would he be sending a message? It's possible. But to who and why?"

"If it had happened seventy years ago, the IRA could've done it to send a message. They wouldn't do that today."

Luke cocked his head. "The killer could of chopped off

her head to make him appear to be nuts—unless a crazy suspect unknown to us did the deed."

Rory touched his cheek. "Excellent points, Luke."

Luke's phone rang. "It's Layla. I better git this." He stood and stretched. "Hi, Layla."

"It's wonderful here at the changing of the guard, but I think Sonja's fishing to find out details about you. She's asking lots of questions. They're digging deeper to check you out…"

Luke glimpsed at Rory. "Yep, Rory's with me. Tell me all about yur tour tonight."

"Okay."

Luke turned away from Rory. He whispered, "I bet it's cuz we're goin' to the robotic tank demo tomorrow." He turned back to face Rory but spoke in a normal voice into his phone. "I can't wait until tonight, hon." He paused. "Okay, bye."

Rory smiled. "It'd be grand to be a newlywed again." He paused. "Let's go for a cup of tea at the Red Feather."

THIRTY-SIX

BANKER ROBERT ROTHSTEIN walked out of the Red Feather Pub's front entrance. Though unsteady on his feet, he felt warmth inside his chest. *Scotch whiskey has a healing effect, even if it's short-lived.*

Standing near his luxury automobile, he fumbled with the vehicle's key fob. Pressing the unlock button, he heard the driver-side door click. After settling into the front seat, he started his car. In his rearview mirror he saw two TV news remote trucks in front of Anne's apartment building. *I better leave the area.*

Then he saw a car turn the corner. *Damn, it's the two cops.* He pulled into traffic and sped away.

* * *

UNSEEN BY RORY AND LUKE, the banker's automobile turned the corner thirty seconds before Rory parallel parked his unmarked police car on the street near the Red Feather Pub. Luke kept his eyes on the two TV remote trucks parked across the street. "Two cameramen and reporters are headin' this way."

Rory turned his head toward the approaching news crews as they stopped near his car door window. Two reporters held microphones aimed at his open window. A woman reporter with bleached blond hair thrust her mike next to Rory's face. "DCI Calvin, can you confirm Baroness Anne Thorpe was beheaded?"

Luke turned his head away. *No way should I be shown on TV in a police car.*

Rory started his car and started to creep forward. "I'm sorry, but this is an ongoing investigation. We'll reveal details to the media when it's appropriate." Rory pulled away.

Luke heard the blond reporter yell. "Has anyone been arrested?" Her high voice lessened in intensity as Rory accelerated.

Rory rolled up his window and turned the corner. "Let's have tea at Brick Lane."

"Is it a neighborhood?"

"It's a street in Tower Hamlets with ethnic eateries, art galleries, and vendors."

THIRTY-SEVEN

RORY PARKED his automobile on a side street in Tower Hamlets, located between Crows End and Whitechapel.

After he left the car, Luke took a step toward colorful cartoon characters spray-painted on a brick wall and studied them. He glimpsed back at Rory. "It's like graffiti, but a lot better."

Rory snapped his car door shut. "Along Brick Lane, lots of murals are painted on buildings." He squinted down the street. "I need my tea. A-One Indian Restaurant serves excellent green tea." He nodded toward a street sign ahead that read "Brick Lane."

As they took their time strolling along the sidewalk, crowded with pedestrians, Luke saw eye-catching graffiti. "This is real art, not spray-paint scribbling." Luke took his phone from his hip pocket and stopped to photograph the urban art so he could later show Layla the murals.

Rory stared at a wall adorned with the image of a roaring lion. "Famous artists paint some of these." Rory gestured down the roadway. "The Brick Lane Gallery is here, too."

As Luke checked out both sides of the street, he saw a great number of apparel shops and clothing street vendors.

"They're selling a lot of clothes." Luke watched shoppers as they sorted through garments hanging on racks.

"The lane's famous for underground and international fashions."

As they made their way along the sidewalk, Luke saw peddlers selling paintings, photographs, pottery, sculptures, and items made of blown glass. He stopped to buy a small, beautiful, glass swan for his stepdaughter, Angela. *This'll show her I didn't forgit about her in London.* He scanned down the street. "I see A-One Indian Restaurant."

Within four minutes Rory led Luke into the eatery. A woman wearing East Indian garb approached. "DCI Calvin, welcome. Will you be having brunch?"

"My friend and I will talk and drink tea, and then we'll order." Rory motioned toward a corner away from the rest of the customers in the dining area. "Could we have the booth in the back?"

"Of course."

Her graceful hips swaying, she led the men to the rear wall of the restaurant. "Would you like your usual Himalayan green tea?"

Rory slid onto the booth's seat. "Yes. Thank you." He caught Luke's attention. "I recommend it."

"I'll try it." Luke figured the restaurant wouldn't have lime cordials or ginger ale.

Three minutes later, a waitress arrived with a pot of green tea and two cups. Rory poured the brew. "Tell me what you think of Yegor."

Luke glanced at the ceiling for a second, and then spoke. "He's impatient and proud of his country. If he's a spy, he's doin 'it cuz he's loyal to Belarus."

"What else?"

Luke didn't blink. "He's hardworking and idealistic." Luke paused. "I wonder if he believes in being honest, and the life of a spy is hard for him cuz he has to deceive people."

"How did you come to those conclusions?"

"Gut feelings." Luke shrugged.

"Would he kill a woman?"

"It would have tied him in knots, but if he thought she'd turn him in, he could'a decided to do her…"

Rory swished the tea in his cup and glanced at Luke. "He may've killed her for the greater good of Belarus."

"Maybe." Luke took a sip of tea and then asked, "When we go to the proving ground, what do you expect Yegor will do?"

"He could try to sell armored personnel carriers to the British Army representatives. Or someone may sell intelligence about the US tank to him."

"It's like a chess game, but you could die if you lose." Luke frowned. "Why'd he invite Layla and me to the show? He met us a short time ago. Is he onto me?"

"I doubt it." Rory pressed his lips together. "We're watching him. But we have no solid proof whether or not he knows you're working with us."

"Remind me exactly what'll happen at the tank demo."

Rory smiled. "The audience will be in a grandstand on the edge of a grassy field. A technician will sit at a table with a joystick. Everyone will be able to see him remotely run the tank from hundreds to thousands of meters away."

Luke cocked his head. "Will the artificial brain help the joystick operator control the tank?"

"I don't think so. Of course, the autonomous capability of the tank is top secret and won't be demonstrated."

"Anything else interestin' about the tank?"

"When it runs on batteries, you can't hear it if you're farther than eighty yards away. It can go 175 miles when running with its electric motor, excellent for a sixty-five-ton tank. It also has a diesel engine."

"Even if the tank's brain is secret, the electric motor's impressive."

Rory nodded. "The tank has other amazing capabilities, too. When you see it, the US company's reps can answer your questions."

Luke smiled. "Even if Yegor doesn't do anything illegal, it'll be interestin' to see the tank."

THIRTY-EIGHT

WHEN SONJA and Layla exited their taxi near 221B Baker Street, Layla saw Drake, her MI5 protector, park his car nearby. Sonja stepped up onto the sidewalk beside Layla. "Drake and his partner will keep a close watch on us."

Layla closed her eyes for a moment and laughed. "I'm glad. After the knife attack, I feel jitters whenever I see any Latino guy."

Sonja pointed up at a blue, circular sign high on the brick wall above a balcony. The placard read, "Sherlock Holmes, Consulting Detective, 1881-1904." Sonja smiled. "It'll be nice to visit Sherlock's fictional apartment and museum."

Sonja led Layla toward a wrought iron fence in front of the building.

Layla felt herself relax when she entered the museum. She smelled incense. In the dim, rear section of its gift shop, near the ticketing area, she saw wooden, mini filing cabinets. *They must simulate how Sherlock would've stored his notes in the late nineteenth century.* A candle lit a desk near the cabinets.

Sonja wandered close to an arrangement of touristy items

for sale—pens, toy-size Sherlock figurines, and other souvenirs. "Layla, come see this."

As Layla neared the display of knickknacks, she walked by a young man dressed in an old-style police uniform selling museum tickets. *I could buy a magnet for the fridge.*

While Layla examined a magnet in the shape of Sherlock's profile, she overheard a stocky, middle-aged man speaking to the young man in the police costume. She thought the brawny man spoke in what could be a Russian accent.

On the opposite side of the room, Layla saw Drake notice the man and then turn away to examine a picture of Sherlock Holmes on the wall. *Drake must be hiding his face from the burly guy.*

While Drake's partner kept watch of the man who spoke with a Russian-like intonation, Drake stepped into an alcove and pulled out his mobile phone. Typing with a finger on its screen, he appeared to be writing a text.

Sonja tapped Layla's shoulder. "Let's go."

Layla felt her heart skip a beat. *Must be something up. Could the tough guy be working with Yegor?*

Once outside, Sonja hailed a taxi. It stopped, and she motioned Layla to get in the back seat first.

The cab driver turned toward the women. "Where to, ladies?"

Sonja smiled. "The Churchill War Rooms."

"It's a super place to visit. Here from the States?"

"Yes. We're on vacation."

As the taxi merged into traffic, Layla leaned next to Sonja. "What's going on?"

Sonja whispered, "The tough guy you saw is a Belarus KGB operative. Tell you more after we get out."

* * *

10:38 A.M., MONDAY, A-ONE INDIAN RESTAURANT, BRICK LANE

Placing plates of East Indian food in front of Luke and Rory, the waitress smiled. "Enjoy." As the woman walked away, Rory's phone chimed. "Texts always come when I'm about to eat or do something important."

Rory set his fork down and snatched his phone.

Luke saw Rory's eyes move back and forth as he read the text. He handed the phone to Luke. "It's from Drake."

Luke furrowed his brow and read, "We ID'd a Belarus KGB man tailing Layla and Sonja at the Sherlock Holmes Museum. The two women left, and were not followed. Requested backup. We could have been made."

Luke thrust the phone back to Rory and whispered, "If the Belarus guy knows Sonja's CIA, my cover's blown."

"Don't worry. Henry said Sonja arrived just weeks ago. The Belarusians don't know who she is."

* * *

10:40 A.M., MONDAY, THE SHERLOCK HOLMES MUSEUM

The stocky Belarus KGB operative typed a text in Russian on his phone: "Black woman visiting tourist spots. I do NOT suspect she is with the agency."

He tapped send.

THIRTY-NINE

SITTING in a booth in the Red Feather's barroom, Yegor sipped from a pint of pale ale. He pulled his mobile phone from his pocket. The device was off. *Damn*. He powered it on and read a new text written in Russian.

He rubbed his chin and let out a slow breath. *There's no problem. Layla's touring. Where's Luke? Drinking? I bet he's having a shot or two.*

Yegor slipped his phone back into his hip pocket. He rubbed his chin.

Reaching into his suitcoat vest pocket, Yegor felt the envelope containing handwritten directions for Luke and Layla. He'd decided it would be best to send an embassy car to the Red Feather to pick them up at eight thirty tomorrow morning. The car would whisk them to the London Heliport at Battersea. There the three of them would board a chartered helicopter and fly to the proving ground for the battle tank's live-fire demonstration.

Yegor felt he'd made the right decision to hire the chopper. *I'll ask the pilot to fly over two or three London landmarks.*

Yegor believed he could chitchat with Luke and Layla

and win them over to his side. After careful finessing, he would convince them Belarus was respectable and noble despite Western propaganda. It painted a bleak picture of his beloved country.

Yegor recalled his days as a teacher before the KGB had recruited him. During his teaching years, he'd felt joy when he inspired promising students. He had convinced them not to strive for materialism, but to work to improve the world. He'd sacrificed his teaching career to elevate Belarus's standing on the world stage. To accomplish this, he realized at times he'd lied, cheated, and compromised his strong sense of right and wrong. *But does the end justify the means? At times it does. I'm a crusader.* He smiled.

A vision of Anne's face interrupted his train of thought. In recent days, he'd been obsessed with thinking about her. *Too bad she had to die, but you can't bring the dead back to life.*

His heart still ached for her. A tear leaked from his left eye. After wiping the drop away, he gulped a mouthful of ale. *I'm getting drunk again. I must rein in my emotions.* He filled his lungs with air.

After standing tall, he walked to the counter where Alexander, the bartender, stood gazing at a televised football match. "Excuse me, Alexander." Yegor forced himself to grin, showing his white teeth. "Luke Ryder told me he knows you. He said I can leave envelope with you. Luke and I will tour tomorrow. He will need these directions." Yegor held up the envelope.

Alexander winked. "No problem." The man reddened and took the envelope. "Luke texted me about it. I'll slip it under his apartment door."

"You rent Airbnb rooms?"

"Yep."

"One day, I think I will rent one."

A relaxed smile crossed the bartender's face. "When you're ready, tell me, and I'll show you a room. We have four flats above the pub."

"Thanks, Alexander." Yegor smiled, turned, and returned

to his booth. He forced himself not to think of Anne. Instead, he pictured Luke. *He's one American I like. There must be a workable strategy to get him to help Belarus after he returns home to Kentucky.*

Yegor picked up a menu and ordered lunch.

* * *

12:33 P.M., MONDAY, NEAR THE RED FEATHER PUB

An MI5 undercover man sat on a bench at the bus stop fifty feet from the Red Feather Pub. He whispered into his wrist-watch two-way radio, "Report." He listened through his earbud for a reply.

His partner's answer came from inside the Red Feather. "Target's leaving pub."

The undercover man stood up from the bench, waited, and began to follow Yegor. *Where's he going? I better stay back. He's usually as aware of his surroundings as a bat flying on a moonless night. But he seems unsteady on his feet. Has he been drinking?*

* * *

A BREEZE BLEW from the west, and the air smelled cleaner. Yegor took his time, strolling at an easy pace, as he headed for the Old Street Tube Station. Tipsy, he'd let his guard down. He didn't notice two MI5 agents following one intersection behind him.

Yegor breathed cool air. *The alcohol's wearing off. I must accomplish my mission at the proving ground tomorrow, or Viktor may not send me to North America. The coppers are bound to learn about me and Anne sooner or later.*

Yegor recalled Viktor's exact words: "We'll set you up with a new identity and send you to North America."

After his conversation with Viktor, Yegor had searched the Internet for pictures of places in the US. Envisioning himself in

Kentucky watching racehorses, he thought about visiting Luke's farm. *For an American, he's a fine man.* Yegor's instinct told him Luke could be trusted. He seemed to treat most people well. *He has an African American wife. He must have an open mind.*

Yegor imagined Luke on his Kentucky farm, doing honest work, toiling to help the whole world, not limiting himself to America. He raised fast-growing hemp, a crop factories had begun using to make building materials similar to plywood and even plastic. Millions of trees would be saved. Less oil would be needed to make petroleum-based items. Layla had explained how this worked.

If I go to America, I will be sure to visit Luke. He could be a friend. But how will I tell him I have a new name? I could Americanize it.

Yegor now felt damn near sober. He thought more about Luke. *It's a pity he has a drinking problem. He's a likeable man. He reminds me of our people who drink vodka often and are ensnared by it. I'll convince him to get into a program. I should, too.*

As he entered the Tube station, Yegor smiled and imagined the helicopter ride he'd take in the morning to Poppins Proving Ground with Luke and Layla. *If I get the robo tank's AI software, I'm home free.*

* * *

12:49 P.M., MONDAY, NEAR THE CHURCHILL WAR ROOMS

Near a wide set of steps and a statue, Layla and Sonja stepped onto the sidewalk after their leisurely tour of Churchill's underground headquarters. From there the British government had directed its World War II efforts.

Layla's phone rang. "Hello. This is Yegor. We need to talk about show at proving ground. Is Luke there?"

Sonja appeared to zero in on Layla's face.

Layla stood straighter. "No. I'll pass on details to him."

"I left envelope with Alexander. It has tickets in it for helicopter ride to proving ground. He will put envelope under your Airbnb door."

Layla felt a cool breeze rustle her hair and wash over her face. "It'll be fun."

Relaxing, Yegor sucked air into his lungs. "We will all enjoy the flight. To see London from the sky will be stunning. Then we will go northwest over farms and green hills to Poppins."

Layla smiled. *He's in a happy mood.* "Where do we take off?"

"London Heliport, Battersea." Yegor paused. "I will send Belarus embassy car at 8:30 a.m. to pick you up at the Red Feather Pub. You can wait in the pub. Driver will find you. You agree?"

"Yes. Luke will be excited."

"See you tomorrow. I need to go."

"Bye."

Yegor disconnected.

Sonja tilted her head to the side. "Who called?"

"Yegor. He arranged a helicopter ride for me and Luke to Poppins Proving Ground. A Belarus embassy car will pick us up and take us to a heliport."

"Fits right into our plans." Sonja checked her watch. "After we get a bite to eat, we should do just one more tour stop. Being early for the four o'clock meeting at Thames House would be a good idea."

"I better text Luke and tell him when we'll leave tomorrow." Layla started to compose a text.

* * *

3:30 P.M., MONDAY, NEAR MI5 HEADQUARTERS, LONDON

When Rory drove past MI5's headquarters in Westminster, Luke guessed the building towered seven stories high. It stood not far from the Houses of Parliament and the banks of the Thames River.

Covered by a light-hued Portland stone outer layer, workers had completed Thames House in 1930. Between the roadway and the building were black steel poles. Luke reckoned they'd been added since then to block terrorist car bomb attacks.

Rory pulled to a stop two streets away from the domestic intelligence agency's headquarters.

Luke glanced at Rory. "We gonna hoof it to the building?"

"Walking is healthful exercise." Rory smiled as he turned off his electric-powered car.

Luke's satellite phone rang. He grabbed it. "Layla's calling."

Rory unbuckled his seatbelt.

"Hi, Layla." Luke listened. "You just finished touring?" Luke paused.

"Sonja and I are having a grand time. We saw Churchill's wartime bunker, and then we looked around the British Museum." Layla's voice sounded loud and clear.

Luke nodded. "Nice."

The sound of an automobile horn blasted through the satellite phone's speaker. "I've got to hang up, Luke. A taxi just stopped to pick us up. We could be early for the meeting."

Luke peered at his phone. "See you soon. Bye, hon."

FORTY

RORY LED Luke along a long corridor on the fifth floor of Thames House. Their footsteps echoed, and Luke saw framed photographs on the walls of rural English scenes. *Seems out of place in a spy headquarters. But then again, folks here may need to calm down cuz they deal with tough situations.*

Rory pointed ahead to the end of the hallway where a gathering of people stood. "We'll meet in Situation Room 2. From its windows, you'll have a fine view of the river. Take a peek before we begin. The blinds are closed during sensitive meetings."

The building smelled as if a janitorial team had just mopped and waxed its floors.

Rory pulled the conference room door open. As Luke entered, he felt soft carpeting under his feet. Henry waved. He sat at a long, well-polished oak table. A thin man Luke hadn't met before stood in the room. He had blond, fine, straight hair and appeared to be in his early twenties.

Rory gestured toward the blond man. "Luke Ryder, this is Art Granger, who's coordinating the surveillance of Yegor Bulot."

Art stood and held his hand out. "I'm honored to meet you in person, Mr. Ryder." He spoke in a tenor voice.

Luke shook Art's hand. "Call me Luke."

"Of course, Luke." Art smiled, let go of Luke's hand, and sat. Luke eased onto a nearby seat, but left a chair vacant for Layla. Rory took the chair at the head of the table.

Luke studied the meeting place. In contrast to the typical, plain, government conference room, dark walnut paneling covered the walls. TV monitors showed views of London and other places in the world. Most of the images were labeled "Live."

The place exuded luxury, and everything appeared new and of the best quality. Luke also saw four TV cameras. One peered down from the ceiling with a view of the tabletop. He guessed the overhead camera could focus on documents. The other three cameras surveyed the table from their pan-tilt fixtures on the walls. When one of the cameras turned, panning across the table, Luke realized a projectionist was adjusting the television equipment from a control room behind and above the head of the table.

An eight-foot by ten-foot screen hung on the wall at the foot of the table. At three spots along the length of the table and in its middle were teleconference telephone sets. Luke had seen similar sets in a Kentucky district attorney's office.

The room door closed and the lockset snapped shut with a metallic click. Turning, Luke saw Layla, Sonja, Drake, Sergeant Rick Boutwell, and at least a dozen more people enter. A larger TV monitor along the right wall turned on, and the live image of FBI Agent Rita Reynolds popped onto it. She waved.

Luke waved back, and she smiled.

Five monitors displayed pictures of people attending the meeting from other remote locations.

Layla sat next to Luke and patted his arm. He blocked out the chatter of his colleagues as he remembered how life-changing meeting Layla had been. Afterward, he'd quit drinking, and she'd quit "the life." *We've changed for the better.* Luke smiled.

Layla focused on him. "You're happy, hon."

"I'm glad we met." He looked deep into her eyes.

"I'm grateful for it, too." She smiled, kept her focus on him, and whispered, "I love you."

Rory tapped the tabletop with his knuckles. He spoke into the teleconference microphone. "This meeting will come to order. I have good news about Luke and Layla Ryder..."

* * *

4:01 P.M., MONDAY, KENSINGTON GARDENS

Though he'd taken a taxi, Yegor arrived five minutes late for his meeting with his handler, Viktor. *I'm fortunate the old man is late, too.*

Yegor sat on a park bench in Kensington Gardens for three minutes before he saw Viktor. The old spy held a newspaper. Nearing the bench, he sat on the far end of it and set the paper in the space between himself and Yegor.

Viktor smiled, showing his well-worn, yellowed teeth. He began to tie his shoe. "The memory card is between sections one and two," the elderly spy said in a quiet voice. "Once inserted into the tank's computer slot, the program will download the robot brain's software and then upload a line of malicious code."

Yegor slipped his right hand between the two newspaper sections and grasped the memory card, a secret device with a thousand times more memory than the best card available to the public. "It has a virus?"

Viktor straightened up. "Yes. The tank will fail three minutes after you remove the card. It should start running in circles and cause a commotion. You will have an opportunity to leave the area unnoticed." After snatching the newspaper, the spy master began to walk away and said, "Best of luck."

* * *

4:05 P.M., MONDAY, MI5 SITUATION ROOM 2

Rory motioned at Luke and Layla. "Luke and Layla Ryder, please stand. Luke is a Kentucky deputy sheriff who's worked with the FBI and has been helping us with the Anne Thorpe murder investigation."

Luke felt his face turn deep red.

"The Belarus KGB agent, Yegor Bulot, has invited Luke and Layla to the International Battlefield Machine Show at Poppins Proving Ground tomorrow. We don't believe Yegor knows Luke's working with us." Rory's eyes scanned the people sitting around the table. "Yegor gave them tickets to enter Poppins. He's arranged a ride in a Belarus embassy automobile and a helicopter flight to the event for them. We'll discuss this and plans for tomorrow after everyone introduces themselves. I'll start."

"I'm Rory Calvin, and I'm in command of this task force." Then he pointed backward to the control room operator. "Please put the Kentucky feed on the big screen." A giant-size picture of Rita appeared on the wide TV display at the foot of the table. "Go ahead, Agent Reynolds."

"I'm Rita Reynolds, an agent with the Federal Bureau of Investigation in Louisville, Kentucky, in the US. I've worked with Luke Ryder as well as Henry Dunbar, the FBI legal attaché stationed in London. Hello, Henry." She waved. Henry nodded.

In short order, the rest of the people, including a US Army attaché, stated their names and positions. The large size of the task force surprised Luke.

Rory glimpsed at the control room. "Please put the Poppins Proving Ground map on the big screen."

Rory turned on a laser pointer and aimed it at the map. "This is a simple drawing of the setup." He guided the red laser dot onto a battle tank icon. "This is where the US robotic tank will begin and end its demonstration." Rory moved the red laser dot. "The joystick operator will sit at a table here at the base of the grandstand."

Rory scanned the people sitting around the table. "Of course, the tank will not reveal its autonomous capabilities, which are top secret." He swiped the red dot across the map as he went on. "Guided by the joystick operator, the tank will maneuver in this grassy field. It will use its cameras and radar to locate these junk automobiles, and fire at them with its cannon." He pointed to an area on the map. "The tank will also run through an obstacle course of trees, hills, and water hazards. It will then return to where it started, after which spectators can walk up to the tank to examine it."

Henry raised his hand. Rory glanced at him. "Yes? Please state your name, position, and question."

"Henry Dunbar, FBI legat in London. Because additional weapons, including mortars and rocket-propelled grenade launchers, will be shooting, how can we be sure spectators won't get in the line of fire?"

Rory aimed his laser beam at the map. "This dotted line indicates a temporary fence. It will block people from wandering past into the live-fire area. A gate will open to allow the tank to drive onto the field to begin its demo. At the end of the demonstration, the gate will again open, enabling the tank to return to its starting point."

Rory pointed the laser at the edge of the map. "Along the east side of the proving ground is a visitor center. This airplane icon is an old DC-3, which houses a walk-through display. It's being updated, and won't reopen until next year." He paused to point at buildings and hangar icons. "Here's the proving ground airfield. VIP aircraft will land on it, including Luke, Layla, and Yegor's helicopter. VIPs will ride electric golf carts to the grandstands. The proving ground has a fleet of these vehicles."

Rory peered at Art Granger, the thin, blond, MI5 agent in charge of surveillance. "Art, please explain team radio communications."

Art stood. "Everyone will be issued two-way wristwatch

radios and mini speakers to be concealed in your hair...
unless you're one of our bald members. If you are bald, see
me after the meeting."

The team members laughed.

Art, beet red, continued. "Most of us also will carry two-
way-radio-capable mobile phones for backup." He glanced
at Luke and Layla. "Luke and his wife will be supplied with
just wristwatches because the KGB won't suspect these
devices are two-way radios. I'll hand out this equipment
after the meeting and show you how it works." Art sat.

Rory gazed at the control room operator. "Please put a
picture of Yegor Bulot on the big screen."

The meeting attendees studied Yegor's image. "Most of
us are familiar with Yegor's appearance, but seeing his
picture as we discuss him will help you better remember his
face." Rory paused. "We believe someone will brush pass
secret intel to Yegor. This person most likely will be an
employee of Raven Robotics, the US manufacturer of the
robotic battle tank. Be on the outlook for this and any suspicious activity."

Rory turned and pointed at the control room operator.
"Please show the image of Baron Thomas Thorpe. I'm sure
you're all familiar with the baron. He had been scheduled to
attend but will not due to his wife's death. Yegor is the
prime suspect in her murder though we haven't ruled out
further suspects."

Rory switched off his laser pointer. "Let's go over your
individual assignments, schedules, and how you will travel
to the show. Art will provide detailed directions to each of
you. Please read them, and give them back to Art when you
leave the meeting." He glanced across the room at the attendees. "I'll go over highlights of each person's assignment..."

Luke leaned close to Layla while Art handed out instruc-
tion sheets. "I hope this ends soon." Luke paused. "Rory
wants us to take a cab back to the Red Feather."

Layla smiled, but she appeared jumpy and blinked more

than she normally did. Luke focused on her. *She must be nervous. I hope she'll do okay tomorrow.*

* * *

6:30 P.M., MONDAY, HOLLAND PARK, KENSINGTON

Lord Thorpe's chauffeur dropped him off near a restaurant and the Holland Park Orangery in Kensington. The embassies of Russia, Jordan, Lebanon, Ukraine, Greece, and Azerbaijan were near the fifty-six-acre public recreation areas, gardens, and arboretum.

The baron walked at a slow pace toward the park's formal gardens facing Holland House, a redbrick building. Range Man had instructed him to sit and wait on a bench near a pedestrian bridge leading toward Holland House's distinctive tower. It was topped with a sharp-pointed roof. The park would close today at 6:42 p.m., thirty minutes before dusk.

Lord Thorpe found an empty bench and sat. *I hope Range Man isn't late.*

The baron gazed at Holland House and saw its tall windows framed in white next to its tower. Now cloudless, the sky showed its natural blue color. He shifted his eyes to gaze at a labyrinth of hedges trimmed less than knee-high. They were squared off along their edges and enclosed flower gardens.

A statue on a stone or concrete pedestal stood in the middle of the maze of hedges.

Lord Thorpe's vision drifted toward the footbridge. He caught sight of Range Man. *I hope this brush pass goes well. I can't risk being seen receiving the item.*

FORTY-ONE

THE WAITRESS PLACED a plate with a thick steak, mixed vegetables, and mashed potatoes in front of Luke. The smell of the beef made his mouth water. Layla had already begun eating her cod dinner. Luke glanced at her. "How is it?"

"Excellent. I'm eating for two." Layla cut a piece from the fish. "Next, I'll order dessert." Luke noticed she tapped her foot once in a while.

Luke sliced his steak. "Ready for tomorrow?"

"I guess." She twisted her hair. "I don't know why I have to go except to play the part of a Kentucky farmer's wife."

"True, but it helps us not look like undercover FBI agents."

Layla rubbed her face and bit her lip. "I could lie and say I've got the flu, and stay here."

Luke set his fork on the edge of his plate and made eye contact with her. "It won't be dangerous. The rest of the folks on the team are supposed to make an arrest, if it happens." He shrugged. "It's something you can tell our kids about one day."

"If it doesn't stay top secret."

Luke smiled. *Layla's not stupid.* "True." He paused for a second. "Of course, you can tell everybody about the live-fire demos. It'll be like a fireworks show, but with real weapons."

Layla pressed her lips together and then spoke. "Will they give us earplugs?"

"I'm sure they'll hand 'em out."

Layla sipped her lime cordial. "If I see something like a—what did Rory call it? —a brush pass, should I mention it on the wristwatch radio?"

"You should mention it and where you saw it."

"We'll ride a helicopter with a Belarus KGB spy and a possible murderer." She exhaled. "I feel unsure about this."

Luke sat straighter. "Yep, Yegor's a spy, but he's takin' a liking to us. Rory and a bunch of MI5 folks checked out Yegor. He has no idea we're working with MI5."

"Didn't Rory say Yegor's the strongest suspect in Anne's killing?"

"I'm startin' to doubt Yegor did it." Luke pushed his mashed potatoes with his fork. "He got Anne pregnant. If he knew, would he kill her if he reckoned her unborn baby would be found with his DNA mixed with Anne's?"

Layla ate a french fry and then said, "You have a point." She picked up her glass of lime cordial. "And on the movie y'all found on the thumb drive, Anne told the baron about the baby. I bet she would've told Yegor, too."

Luke scratched his temple. "Seems like you think Yegor didn't kill her. Then you shouldn't be scared of riding in the chopper with him."

"Luke Ryder, you're as sharp as a Yale college professor. I feel better about going." She touched her fingertips together and grinned. "What about the baron? Did he kill Anne?"

Luke scanned the pub's dinner crowd. "Rory checked with the baron's lawyer. Lord Thorpe had been preparing to divorce her, as he claimed. Why would he kill her?"

"Jealousy, hate, rage. He could've asked for a divorce to cover up the motive."

"Yeah." Luke sighed. "I wish we knew more about the golfer. If we don't find conclusive evidence, we'll have to keep investigating him." Luke paused. "Estrella could've hired a hit man to kill Anne, too."

"And what about the banker? Didn't you say he's a big-time embezzler?"

"Yep." Luke scratched his scalp. "He could be a killer under certain circumstances. We gotta keep investigating him, too."

Layla smiled. "If you have to stay in the UK while you guys keep working on the case, it's fine. But I should fly home to take care of Angela soon."

"Agreed."

Layla finished her fish, and then ate the rest of her chips. "It's time for dessert, sticky toffee pudding with butterscotch sauce."

"I'll have some, too." Luke wiped up the gravy on his plate with a slice of bread.

Layla's eyes sparkled. "I feel pregnant. When we're done eating, let's go upstairs and cuddle."

"I like your plan."

FORTY-TWO

AFTER HIS CHAUFFEUR, Baxter, opened the car door, the baron got into the back seat of his luxury automobile. It sat in an oval drive in front of the Thorpe family's mansion, a manor house.

Lord Thorpe heard his bubbling fountain, surrounded by a short hedge, in the center of the oval.

Baxter shut the car door. It clicked with the sound of a well-made, solid machine.

The sky was still dark. Because the sun wouldn't rise for thirty-nine minutes, the fancy light on a pole near the front of the building lit the house's facade. The bright front of the impressive three-story edifice seemed to pop out from the inky black sky framing it.

The baron gazed at the front of his home with its six chimneys, five gables, and sizable, white-framed windows. *Doesn't seem important when your health begins to fail.*

Reaching under his coat, he patted his shirt breast pocket. He felt his British Army ID. *It's there.* He checked the breast pocket of his suit coat, too. Yes, he also had the entry ticket for the International Battlefield Machine Show at Poppins Proving Ground. He tapped the pocket and sighed.

It's not as if I would not be expected at all. Lord Thorpe closed his eyes for a moment and enjoyed the darkness behind their lids. *I'll tell anyone interested I changed my mind and decided to attend the show. I'll say I had to go to get my mind off Anne's death.*

Baxter put the automobile in gear and began the long drive to the proving ground.

* * *

7:45 A.M., TUESDAY, THE RED FEATHER PUB

Luke and Layla relaxed at their usual table in the Red Feather Pub. Luke scanned the breakfast menu and then heard footsteps.

Yegor stopped next to their table. "I will buy you breakfast."

The man appeared extra upbeat to Luke. "Thanks, Yegor. I figured you'd meet us at the heliport."

Yegor grinned and pulled out a chair. "I want make sure you did not oversleep. And I need to eat." He laughed. "You will like the show."

Luke didn't need to fake a smile. He felt like a kid on Christmas morning. "I ain't flown in a helicopter before and neither has Layla. We didn't fall asleep right away last night."

Yegor grinned. "It is like magic carpet. You see everything real clear. It is not like in jetliner. People, cars, houses, animals are like toys below you. You will love the ride even if it is shaky."

Luke tilted his head back. "I can't wait. The helicopter flight could be better than the show."

"I think you will enjoy the live-fire by tank, mortars, and RPG rockets even more. It will be like big firework show." Yegor sighed. "But I may not see you much after the show. In the next few days, I will transfer to America to sell tractors. I need to train and learn 'bout US. But I will visit your farm the month after you get demo tractor."

Luke glanced away from Yegor and then looked at him again. "Will the move to the US be helpful for you?"

Yegor's eyes danced. "Yes. Promotion. I get to see your Kentucky farm, racehorses, ranches, huge wheat fields. It is big country."

The waitress arrived, and Layla ordered ham, eggs, and rye toast.

While Yegor continued to talk about America, Luke half-listened. *Too bad he got mixed up with the wrong bunch back in Belarus. If he ain't the murderer, maybe the Brits could give him a light sentence for espionage.*

* * *

8:30 A.M., TUESDAY, THE RED FEATHER PUB

Twenty-five-year-old Maksim, a dark-haired Belarusian embassy driver, stopped the deluxe black sedan close to the Red Feather Pub.

Maksim often toured London in his spare time. He liked to eat and drink each week in at least one pub he hadn't entered before. He glanced up at the drinking establishment's sign and saw a vivid crimson feather painted on the wooden placard. *I should come back and have a drink here after work.* He thought in Russian. Although he spoke English well, he found it easier to think in his native tongue.

Traffic isn't too heavy. Maksim activated the car's flashers, exited the vehicle, and rushed to the pub's front door. He spotted Yegor sitting at a table with a man and a black woman. *They must be Luke and Layla Ryder.*

Maksim stepped to Yegor's table.

Maksim saw Yegor turn his head. "We're ready to go." Yegor glanced at Luke and Layla. "This is Maksim, our driver today. Maksim, meet Mr. and Mrs. Luke Ryder."

Maksim tilted his head down into a quick bow. "It is a pleasure to meet you both." He glanced through the pub's front window. "We should get in the car soon. I've stopped at a double yellow line."

Yegor stood and glanced at Luke. "No parking is in force all time at double yellow curbs."

Maksim held the front door open as they exited the pub. He felt his heart beat faster when he saw a policeman at the next intersection. Scampering ahead to the embassy car, Maksim opened the curbside back door for Luke and Layla. *Fortunate they're getting in fast.*

Yegor got in the front passenger's seat. After sliding into the driver's seat, Maksim stared in the rearview mirror. *The copper's talking with someone.* His hands trembling, Maksim started the car. As he pulled away, he realized the policeman hadn't seen the embassy car.

Yegor began to talk to his two guests. "On the way to London Heliport, Battersea, I'll point out famous places."

* * *

8:35 A.M., TUESDAY, EN ROUTE TO POPPINS PROVING GROUND

Rory guided the eight-passenger undercover police van through the English countryside. He drove northwest toward Poppins Proving Ground and the International Battlefield Machine Show. Glancing in his rearview mirror, he saw that the task force members—FBI Agent Henry Dunbar, CIA Agent Sonja Perko, and Sergeant Rick Boutwell —were all in high spirits. Drake slept, snorting as he snored. The team's MI5 surveillance specialist, Art Granger, studied the passing verdant landscape with obvious interest.

MI5 Agent Ginger Graham appeared to be in a gruff mood. Rory couldn't remember her ever being at ease during any operation.

Rory had decided to take a scenic route for part of the journey to the show. He reckoned the calming effect of rural scenery would help his team cope with the stress of their anti-espionage mission. Rory smiled. *The countryside is having the desired effect.*

The rest of his good-sized team traveled to the proving ground in separate vehicles to avoid arousing suspicion. Luke and Layla would fly to the International Battlefield Machine Show courtesy of Yegor, the Belarusian KGB spy.

The weather was better than normal. Blue skies and cotton-like clouds in animal shapes floated above their speeding vehicle. Rory hummed in a pleasant tone. As he followed a bridge over a river, his view of lush trees and vegetation along the alluvial shores of the watercourse elevated his mood.

Rory broke the silence. "Once at the proving ground, we'll leave the van and go our separate ways to our stations. We will pretend not to know one another and remain low profile until we make an arrest."

Rory saw Henry wink that he understood how the team would operate. Sonja nodded that she'd gotten Rory's message. Rick, Art, and Ginger had paid attention, too, but Drake continued to snore.

Peering along the roadside, Rory glanced at the narrow lanes he passed, which were lined by fences and trees. *I better get on the motorway soon. We're getting closer to the proving ground.*

Rory rolled down the window for a rush of fresh air. The cheery sounds of a robin's clear whistles greeted him. *I wonder if Luke and Layla have arrived at the heliport.*

* * *

8:45 A.M., TUESDAY, EN ROUTE TO THE LONDON HELIPORT, BATTERSEA

As the Belarus Embassy sedan sped along a road leading to the London Heliport, Luke glanced at the Thames River.

Statues faced the water on the vertical supports of the Vauxhall Bridge.

Layla grasped his hand, and Luke watched as she peered at the buildings along the wide, murky waterway. Puffy, cumulus clouds floated eastward against a deep blue sky. Luke squinted up at the bright sky. *Should be clear flyin' weather all the way.*

Luke saw Yegor staring at floating barges as a riverboat motored by with a crowd of tourists standing on its two decks.

Luke turned and peered backward along the south bank of the river at an enormous Ferris wheel, the London Eye, standing close to 450 feet tall. It seemed like a giant, spoked bicycle wheel.

Within minutes, the luxury car stopped near the heliport. Maksim opened the auto's doors. The odors of the Thames, marine diesel fuel, and pub food greeted Luke as he stepped onto the pavement.

Yegor said something in Russian to Maksim, and then turned to Luke. "Maksim will be here when we come back. The helicopter is waiting for us." He started for the terminal door, and Luke and Layla followed him inside.

Yegor stopped in front of a counter. A sign above it read "Harold's Helicopters." A thin, young woman stood behind the tall desk. Yegor reached into his jacket and showed her his passport.

The petite counter attendant smiled. "You are cleared." She glanced at Luke and Layla. "May I see your passports?"

While Luke handed her his passport, Layla opened her purse and grabbed hers. Thirty seconds later, the young lady handed the passports back to Luke. She grinned. "Have a nice flight." She motioned at a door to Luke's right. "You may go through Doorway 3. The pilot will meet you on the tarmac."

As Yegor neared Doorway 3, Luke heard a buzz, and the door unlocked after the lady at the desk pushed a button under the countertop.

The sound of a helicopter taking off from a landing pad assaulted Luke's ears. Yegor stopped and turned. "You are lucky. Passport pictures are all I needed to send to Harry's Helicopters."

A gray-haired man dressed in a blue uniform and pilot's cap stepped up to Yegor. "Nice to see you again, Yegor."

Yegor smiled and shook the pilot's hand. "Me too, George. This is Luke and Layla."

George tipped his cap. "Nice to meet you." He coughed. "It's procedure. Please show me your passports."

After glancing at the documents, he looked up. "Thanks. Let's get aboard. After a safety briefing, we'll take off." He pointed at a sleek, white helicopter. Luke noticed it had five rotor blades, an aerodynamic nose, and four side windows.

George opened the passenger door behind the pilot's seat. "This is an eight-passenger Wasp 99 electric helicopter. We received it a month ago. The motor is quiet. The rotor makes noise, but overall this aircraft is quieter than helicopters equipped with turboshaft engines."

After getting into the aircraft, George read a safety briefing out loud. Then he said, "Please put on your headsets. Push the button, and you may talk among yourselves. But refrain from speaking when I'm talking with air traffic control."

Luke saw George push a button, and then the fuselage shifted, the rotors gained speed, the flying machine vibrated, and it soared into the sky like a magic carpet.

A happy feeling filled Luke's chest. As he peered out his side window, he saw the helipad extended like a wide pier into the Thames River. "London" was painted on the pad as well as the giant letter "H." The building adjoining the heliport seemed to shrink to dollhouse-size as the whirlybird rose. Cars and people appeared the size of ants and gnats. Luke felt himself smile. *It's gonna be a fine flight, and watchin' a tank fire its cannon is gonna be even better.*

* * *

9:07 A.M., TUESDAY, THE LONDON HELIPORT, BATTERSEA

Her dark hair draping her shoulders, Carol had watched out the London Heliport terminal's window. She had seen Yegor, Luke, and Layla climb into the late model whirlybird. As the aircraft had disappeared into the northwest sky, she had opened her handbag and grabbed her MI5-issued satellite phone.

With two nimble fingers, she tapped a text message: "Rory, FYI George took off 9:05 hours with Yegor Bulot and Luke and Layla Ryder. ETA to proving ground 10:05 hours. Best, Carol."

She put her encrypted phone back into her pocketbook. Keeping an eye on foreign passengers and people of interest to MI5 earned her a bonus every month. And Rory had promised her a full-time job in the domestic intelligence agency after she completed special new-employee training. She began to speculate about what might happen at Poppins Proving Ground. *Must be something big.*

FORTY-THREE

A PETITE AMERICAN flag on a pole on top of the olive drab US robotic tank waved in the breeze. The sixty-five-ton vehicle sat on the grassy field close to the grandstand.

Dressed in an attractive blouse and tight-fitting slacks, Raven Robotics chief software engineer, Etta Jasek, neared the prototype battle tank. Her brunette ponytail moved up and down in short, quick movements behind her. *Mickey might be watching me.*

Joystick battle tank operator and eligible bachelor, Mickey Stark, sat at his card table fifteen yards from the scary killing machine.

Etta stroked her hair. *He's cute.* She shot a beaming smile at Mickey. "Dear, I have to update the remote control software again."

Mickey stood. "I wish they wouldn't have added the exterior card reader slot. Escorting you into the crew compartment used to be fun."

Etta flushed. "You'll have to wait until tonight, buster." She neared the slot on the rear end of the prototype battle tank. She'd asked the chief engineer to add it to make it easier and quicker to make frequent software updates.

Etta slipped a high-capacity flash memory card into the slot and pressed a button. In less than a minute, the update was complete, and she removed the card. "All done." She stared into Mickey's eyes. "See you after the sun sets."

Etta turned and paraded away toward the company's trailer, moving her hips in an exaggerated way. *I can't wait 'til the show starts.* She visualized what the steel monster would demonstrate as she surveyed the wide, grassy field. The odor of the grass and the damp soil reminded her that those smells would soon be mixed with the acrid scent of spent explosives. She'd had a whiff of the smoke and gases and had heard the loud noise when the tank had fired its weapons during a pre-demo rehearsal.

Reaching into her slacks hip pocket, she felt a vial. It held a pair of earplugs. *I'm going to need these when the shooting starts.*

* * *

12:18 P.M. (THREE HOURS AHEAD OF LONDON TIME), TUESDAY, KGB HEADQUARTERS, MINSK, BELARUS

Wearing jeans and a short-sleeved shirt, Alexei, a Belarus computer programmer and hacker, sat in a spacious room inside the KGB's Minsk headquarters. The expansive chamber housed rows of computers and monitors where people sat typing.

Alexei rubbed one of his bony elbows and leaned sideways, close to Mikhail. Speaking in a whisper, Alexei said, "The Brits and Yanks are going to get a big surprise today." He laughed.

Mikhail bit his lip. Staring across the room, he began to speak in a quiet voice. "What did you do?"

"I added twenty lines of code. They'll cause enough havoc to make the Raven Robotics battle tank computer engineers appear worse than unskilled." Alexei chortled and then belly laughed. Four men nearby stared at him. He felt his face get warm.

After he noticed that Mikhail pretended not to see his burst of merriment, Alexei stole a glance at the men and a woman working nearby. They no longer stared his way.

Mikhail kept focusing on his computer screen but said, "We were required to design the algorithm to steal the US tank's brain code and make the tank travel in circles, not to cause havoc. You're always acting like a strutting cock."

Alexei shrugged. "But we were to disable the tank and make it appear to be a failure." He showed a wicked grin. "Who cares if it acts crazy and stops two minutes later than the team planned?"

Mikhail shot an accusatory glimpse at Alexei. "You often go too far." He rubbed his eyebrow. "Let's hope we don't all get disciplined for your actions."

Alexei cocked his shoulder. "It should be okay. The higher-ups will like how embarrassed the Yankees will be."

* * *

9:25 A.M., TUESDAY, EN ROUTE TO POPPINS PROVING GROUND

The baron's chauffeur and butler, Baxter, a tall elderly man, guided the black luxury car along the road leading to the International Battlefield Machine Show at Poppins Proving Ground. As the car sped past fields and trees dressed in their autumnal foliage, the baron didn't view the scenery for the joy of it, but rather to take his mind off his suffering.

Breaking out in severe coughing fits every ten minutes, Lord Thorpe felt extreme throat pain. The plastic privacy barrier between Baxter and himself had a benefit the baron hadn't thought of before. It kept Baxter from becoming alarmed by his recurrent whooping.

Watching the trees, fields, walls, and buildings zip by, Lord Thorpe drew his eyebrows closer together. A friend, also an MI5 agent, had phoned the baron last night to report he'd heard an MI5 task force would be undercover at the International Battlefield Machine Show. *Why'd MI5 decide to monitor the machine show? They must be keeping a close watch on Yegor, and other foreign people of interest.*

The aristocrat shifted in his seat. *I must do what's necessary to protect the Thorpe name. This dreadful nightmare should be over by the end of today.* The baron's fitful thoughts plagued him. Even the beautiful blue sky and the vibrant fall colors of the countryside could not wrest him from his melancholy.

If I'm fortunate, I'll be famous for the good I've done in life. As he reached into a pocket of his business suit for his flask of vodka, he sighed. *Alcohol should kill germs and make my throat feel better.* He unscrewed the container's metal top.

Lord Thorpe sipped and then swallowed his vodka. It felt warm going down his throat. *Life is too short, and Anne had spoken the ugly truth. Without a baby, the Thorpe surname will not travel forward in time. My branch of the Thorpe Family will end with my death.*

After taking another sip of vodka, his thoughts went back to his mission. *How the hell am I going to do it with crowds milling about as well as an MI5 task force on scene?*

* * *

9:26 A.M., TUESDAY, POPPINS PROVING GROUND

Raven Robotics chief engineer, Jake Brass, stared at Mickey, who sat at the joystick table near the mammoth battle tank. "I heard you fire the machine gun." The olive drab tank sat idle on the verdant field fifteen yards away.

Mickey shrugged. "I got an all-clear to shoot into the safe zone. Had to be sure the gun won't jam like it did last week."

"What about the batteries?"

"Fully charged. Plugged in all night at the electric vehicle charger."

"I'm glad the electric motor's operating properly. It'd be a shame to have to fire up the diesel engine and create smoke and noise."

Mickey smiled. He'd tested switching from electric power to the tank's diesel engine, and the transition had been glitch-free. "Don't worry. Even if the wind's blowing toward the crowd, people won't hear the tank beyond seventy-five meters, if it's in electric mode. I tested it."

Jake lifted his chin. "I'm glad. The stealth option is a major selling point."

Mickey's eyes were unwavering.

Jake pursed his lips. "Are the onboard drone and mini robots working okay?"

"Yep."

Mickey recalled having awakened that morning, bleary-eyed, needing a cup of coffee. He pressed his hand against his cheek. "I've been checking and double-checking everything since dawn."

Jake squinted. "Sorry to give you the third degree, but this demo could mean we get a multimillion-dollar contract from the Brits." He moved closer to the tank and inspected the 360 degree camera and the night vision equipment. He noticed the lenses of the devices were spotless. "Did you clean the optics by hand?"

"No. The auto glass cleaner's working fine."

A compressor and a water sprayer washed the tank's visual equipment when sensors detected debris on the optical system. But Mickey knew this automatic lens cleaning system could fail. If it did, he could turn on the compressor and remotely spray water across the optics to wash off dust and debris.

* * *

JAKE STARED across the field at the water course. *Mud and water will come into play when the tank goes through the hazards. In a real war, mud, dirt, smoke, ice, and snow can mess up the optics.* Jake frowned. *Everything better work right, or the Brits will think the machine's not battlefield-ready.*

Jake took two deep breaths and sighed. *If this demo goes bad, I could be fired.*

* * *

10:05 A.M., TUESDAY, YEGOR'S CHOPPER APPROACHING POPPINS PROVING GROUND

As the helicopter carrying Luke, Layla, and Yegor flew over the expansive green carpet of fields and farms, Luke saw a long runway on the distant horizon. Sunlight glittered from what at first seemed like a giant field of broken glass. But as the chopper flew nearer to the airstrip, Luke realized at least a thousand cars sat parked on the left side of the airfield.

Glancing at Luke, the Belarusian spy pressed a button to activate the microphone on his headset. "We are near Poppins Proving Ground." His accent seemed extra guttural when it traveled through the aircraft's communication system.

Luke felt a tingle of excitement. "Appears it's big, judgin' from the long runway." The grounds looked to be as large as two expansive Illinois cornfields, covering 3,000 acres.

While the helicopter ate up the remaining distance to the proving ground, Luke saw the spread-out parking area to his far left. He figured it held enough cars to transport a Chicago Bears football crowd to Soldier Field stadium.

Yegor grinned, and Luke noticed the man's teeth were a light shade of tan. "It is the second biggest proving ground in Europe."

Luke peered downward as the chopper descended. On the right side of the runway, passenger jets, fighters, light planes, and helicopters sat near hangars. Taxiways led to the aircraft parking area, which reminded Luke of a terminal at a midsized airport.

Gazing at the edges of the premises, Luke saw a thick

barrier of trees at least a hundred feet across surrounding the proving ground. From the air, the trees could've been a giant's hedge encircling his yard. Luke scratched his whiskers. *Must make it hard for people to shoot pictures of equipment bein' tested at Poppins. I bet they've got an electronic sensor system guarding the perimeter, too.*

Luke felt like he was a passenger aboard a hovering flying saucer. Then the whirlybird began to descend on a spot marked with a large "H" painted on the concrete. A mix of standard and two-man helicopters sat parked nearby.

Chatter between his pilot and Poppins air traffic control grabbed Luke's attention for a brief moment. Then glimpsing aside at a field close to the many idle aircraft, Luke saw military trucks, cars, armored personnel carriers, medium-sized battle tanks, and jeeps.

Yegor's voice roared into Luke's ears through his headset. "See obstacle course for tank on far field?"

Luke nodded. "Is that the US tank sittin' by the grandstand?" Luke saw a man perched on a chair by a folding table in the grass near a battle tank. All of a sudden, the massive machine began to crawl forward.

Yegor cocked his head. "Yes, US Raven Robotics tank is moving. Maybe they test it before demo."

Luke stared at the tank as it crept across the field and pivoted. "When's the tank demo begin?"

"At 2:00 p.m."

Kicking up dust, the chopper landed.

* * *

AFTER THE WHIRLYBIRD LANDED, its rotor blades slowed and stopped. The pilot stepped from his aircraft and opened the passengers' doors.

After he hopped from the chopper, Luke felt warmth radiate from the concrete under his feet. Reaching up, he grasped Layla's arm and helped her from the helicopter. He smiled at her. "It's warmer here than in London."

Layla straightened as she stood next to Luke. "I've missed warm Kentucky weather. It's nice here. The sun's shining."

Birds sang, and the smell of cut grass drifted their way.

Yegor moved closer to Luke. "Before lunch, we will explore." He grinned like a child ready to play. "First, we will go to the edge of the vehicle test track. The Belarus Embassy rented me golf cart. We will ride." He pointed to a line of electric carts close to their helicopter.

Luke noticed an old, propeller-driven, passenger airplane sitting on the grass alongside a medium-sized, one-story building. A sign over its entrance read "Visitor Center." Luke turned to Yegor. "Do we have time to go into the visitor center to see displays about Poppins and the old DC-3 airplane?"

"We can see them after the tank demo." Yegor turned his gaze toward the ancient DC-3 passenger plane. "The DC-3 also has displays inside it. It is almost hundred years old. But the plane is closed for updates."

Yegor began to walk toward a row of electric carts. One had a placard, which read "Belarus Embassy," dangling above its front windshield." Yegor got into the driver's seat, and Luke took a seat next to him, while Layla sat on a rear, forward-facing bench seat. Luke figured the cart's layout had been modified for transportation across the proving ground. The vehicle had no place to stow golf bags. He also noticed a Belarus flag, the size of a playing card, flying from one of the cart's roof supports.

As Yegor steered the electric cart toward a chain-link fence, Luke saw a sign bolted to its top metal rail that read "Military Vehicle Test Course."

After guiding the cart to the top of a hill overlooking the military test circuit, Yegor stopped the vehicle. "The US battle tank will go into different zones. See the little lake?" He pointed at a long, oval body of water, two or three acres in area.

Luke peered at it. "Looks man-made to me." He stared

farther to his right. "I bet the tank's gonna go up the big hill and down into the grove of trees."

"Plus it will fire at old cars." Yegor aimed a finger at junked, gasoline-era automobiles. Luke noticed most had severe accident damage.

Yegor pressed down on the cart's accelerator. "Let's go see the tank close-up." He drove toward the massive US war machine. It had returned to the grassy area where the tank's joystick operator sat at his folding table.

FORTY-FOUR

YEGOR PARKED the electric cart by the grandstand. Then he led Luke and Layla to a pathway covered with round, pea-sized stones. It ran the length of the crowd's wide seating area.

Standing seventy-five yards from the US robotic battle tank, Luke stared at the prototype killing machine. A patch-work of random darker and lighter swaths of olive drab paint camouflaged the tank.

As Yegor, Luke, and Layla moved closer to the tank, its cannon on a turret swerved with a soft, electric motor sound and aimed at one of the junk cars. Luke glanced at the tank's machine gun. It seemed just as menacing as the cannon.

To Luke, the scary, tracked vehicle appeared ready to go into battle at a moment's notice. He turned to Yegor. "It's a metal pit bull, itchin' to attack enemy machines and soldiers."

Yegor cocked his head to the side. "Yeah, but my tractor company would like to buy the tank's joystick software for peaceful uses, here and in America. I can't wait to go to US." His grin was contagious.

Luke figured Yegor, the spy, had more interest in touring the United States than in doing his cloak-and-dagger work.

Peeking at Layla, Luke noticed she had erupted in a smile as she watched Yegor. Luke stuck his right hand in his hip pocket. *Yep, Yegor's got appeal. It makes him a better spy.*

Turning to his left, Luke saw the joystick operator peering at a computer screen. A black, plastic hood shaded it from the brilliant sunlight bathing the green field. Luke stepped up to the man whose hand rested on the joystick. Luke grinned. "Excuse me. Is it easy to run the tank with your control?"

The operator scrutinized Luke. "A teenager could do it." The young man spoke in a strong Southern drawl. "Are you from the South?"

"Sort of. Kentucky was a border state durin' the Civil War."

The joystick man offered his hand. "I'm Mickey Stark from Tennessee."

Luke shook Mickey's hand. "I'm from the Lexington area. I farm hemp."

"I heard it's getting to be a big crop because it's legal now."

Luke nodded. "Yep. It's a raw material you can use for makin' rope, plywood, plastic, and a bunch of other products."

Yegor stood next to Luke. "Hello, Mickey. I am friend of Luke's. I am rep for Belarus Tractor Company. We are interested in your joystick software. It could run our tractors."

"You'll have to ask Ms. Etta Jasek, our chief computer engineer, about that." Mickey glanced behind Luke and Yegor. "Here she comes. She can answer your questions after she does a quick update of the tank's software."

Luke watched as Etta stopped at the tank's rear and slipped what appeared to be an SD flash memory card into a slot in the machine's armor. The card was larger than the SD cards Luke used to store his cell phone pictures. He squinted as he watched Etta. *Must be a newfangled version of a computer memory card.*

When Etta pressed a button, an LED light next to the slot in the tank's armor blinked with an amber hue and then dimmed. Within ten seconds, another LED bulb glowed bright green. Etta pushed a button, and the SD-like computer card popped out from the slot.

As Etta removed the card, Mickey said, "The slot is on this prototype machine, but it won't be on production models. We installed it for convenience, so Etta doesn't have to climb into the crew compartment to do updates." Mickey stood.

Etta turned and walked to the three men and Layla. "What's up, Mickey?"

Mickey gestured toward Yegor. "This man from Belarus wants to explore acquiring the joystick software to use in farm tractors."

Etta raised her eyebrows as she inspected Yegor. "I'm not sure. Please give me your business card. I'll ask our spin-off officer to contact you."

Yegor smiled, fished in his pocket, and handed a card to Etta. "Here."

Etta's eyes flickered as she read the card. "Thank you, Mr. Bulot. I'm sure our spin-off guy will call or email you." She smiled and left.

Luke wondered if Yegor's business card handoff had been a signal for one of the Raven Robotics employees to sneak secret robotic tank computer code to him. Or had Yegor just been playing his role as salesman and representative of his Belarus agricultural machinery company?

Turning to Mickey, Yegor passed a business card to him. "I can't wait to watch your joystick tank demo."

"You'll like it." Mickey glanced at the joystick on the table. "But now, I have to test the software update."

Yegor snatched Mickey's hand and shook it vigorously. Mickey released his hand, nodded, and reached for his joystick.

As Yegor, Luke, and Layla walked back to their golf cart to park it, Yegor checked his watch. "It is early, but we can get box lunch and eat."

Luke eyeballed groups of people carrying cardboard food containers and drink cups. Clusters of show attendees stopped by the US battle tank and examined it. Spectators also sat in the grandstand and began to eat as they waited for the weapons show to begin.

A man's voice boomed across the field from three loud-speakers high up on steel poles near the gathering throng seated in the audience observation area. "At this time, no one should go past the fence into the weapons demonstration field. At one o'clock the live-fire will begin with the mortars and 75 mm howitzers demos. Pick up your free ear-protection plugs at the stations in the center of the grandstand."

* * *

11:45 A.M., TUESDAY, POPPINS PROVING GROUND

The baron seldom felt hungry after his throat had begun to bother him six months ago. During the last three months, he often had skipped meals.

As his chauffeur, Baxter, held a rear door of Lord Thorpe's luxury car open, the baron got out of his vehicle and stood. His body shook, so he steadied himself. *I must've been sitting too long during the ride. Should've asked Baxter to stop halfway along the journey.*

The aristocrat turned to Baxter. "Thank you. You can pick up your box lunch at the tent." Lord Thorpe nodded at a canvas shelter. "I'll ring you when it's time to leave. Enjoy the show."

Baxter displayed a rare smile. "Yes, sir. Should be fun to watch live firing. I haven't been near anything military since I served in the Royal Marines."

Lord Thorpe watched as Baxter melted into the growing crowd. *He never told me he'd been a marine.*

A sudden coughing fit pulled the nobleman from his thoughts of the enigmatic Baxter. Pain coursed down the baron's esophagus and into his chest. *With a crowd of people about, my task will be extra difficult.* He sighed and held a hand against his painful throat.

Turning his head, he spotted the sign for the VIP dining room on the east wall of the visitor center. Outside, near the eatery's door, stood the baron's SIS colleague, Cecil Billings. The man waved.

Lord Thorpe forced himself to grin and then held out his hand as he approached Cecil. "I didn't know you'd be here, Cecil."

"I couldn't miss the live-fire exercise. Lots of noise, smoke, and a bunch of military men."

The two colleagues neared the VIP dining room's entrance. Cecil smiled, and the baron glanced away and frowned in pain.

* * *

AFTER LORD THORPE and his SIS coworker, Cecil, had sat down at a dining room table covered in a white, starched tablecloth, the baron noticed Cecil seemed nervous.

"Anything bothering you, Cecil?"

Cecil shifted in his chair and set his menu aside. "A spy ring may be here, focused on the US robotic tank. I shouldn't tell you this, but a UK-US task force is here monitoring the situation."

Lord Thorpe felt his heartbeat increase. He figured he'd have to be on high alert. He sighed. *My tradecraft's rusty.* "Who's under surveillance?"

"I've heard the Belarus KGB may have a man or two here."

The baron smiled, revealing his teeth. "Well, let's hope a

cloak-and-dagger operation doesn't interfere with the live-fire displays."

Cecil cocked his head. "Indeed. I plan to eat fast and leave early to get an early peek at the weapons. The long-range mortars are scheduled to fire at quarter past one." Cecil placed a thick, white napkin on his lap.

Lord Thorpe put on his best act, pretending to anticipate an exciting afternoon. "Should be a bloody fine show. A lot of fire and brimstone, if you will." He turned aside, glanced away, and sighed. *If I don't complete my mission, I'll be going to hell and see real fire and brimstone.*

FORTY-FIVE

POPPINS SHOW officials had expected 2,500 people to attend the International Battlefield Machine Show. Three-quarters of the crowd had arrived before lunch, according to a preliminary computer tally. Minutes before the first live-fire exercise, the audience milled around the grandstand like a herd of cattle.

Luke watched the spectators from his seat in the third row near the center of the stands, a prime viewing spot Yegor had arranged. Seated beside Luke, Layla wore a base-ball cap she'd gotten free of charge from the Raven Robotics company display near the east side of the grandstand.

A man stood on the grass facing the crowd of spectators, some of whom sat in the grandstand. He moved a microphone to his lips. "Ladies and gentlemen, please find your seats. The RPG, or rocket-propelled grenade firing event, will begin in fifteen minutes."

Luke saw Yegor drop something on the grandstand steps and stamp on the object before it could fall through a crack between the structure's boards. *What did he drop?* Luke squinted.

Yegor stooped and picked up the thing he'd let fall and slipped it into his trousers pocket. He wiped sweat from his brow. *He's lucky whatever it is didn't fall between the slats and onto the ground.*

Yegor took notice of Luke, smiled, and sat next to him. "I dropped my lucky coin. I stepped on it before it fell in crack."

After Yegor had settled in his seat, the loudspeakers hissed. "The advanced rocket-propelled grenade live-fire event will begin in seconds. Please focus your attention on Gerald, who will fire a computer-guided round at the tank decoy 1,075 meters away at the two o'clock position."

Dressed in army fatigues and a helmet, Gerald slid an RPG round into his launcher.

The noise of static bathed the crowd in an electric hiss. It ceased, and the announcer said, "Gerald is pushing a button on his launcher to lock onto the target." The announcer turned to view Gerald. "Even if he's unsteady with his aim, the round will self-correct and hit the decoy."

A sudden flash and a bang made Luke jump as the RPG projectile streaked toward the dummy tank. Smoke trailed behind the speeding round. In a fraction of a second, the fake tank scooted right. The round veered, struck the imitation armored vehicle, and blew it to smithereens.

"Ladies and gentlemen, please give a round of applause to Gerald and UK Arms Limited, the maker of the advanced rocket-propelled grenade launcher system."

The crowd clapped for a polite five seconds.

"The Raven Robotics tank demonstration will begin at 2:15 p.m. Feel free to move close to the US tank. You can examine it, and speak to its joystick operator. He's sitting at the folding table in the grass at the center of the grandstand. But please be back in your seats by 1:55 p.m."

Voices in the crowd began to murmur, and then the spectators began to speak louder as they descended the grandstand to walk up to the fence separating them from the lethal, sixty-five-ton steel monster.

* * *

FROM THE THIRD row of bleacher seats, Luke gawked at the US robotic tank, which was sitting idly on the grassy field. He turned to his right to focus on Yegor and said, "Let's go down and ask questions about the tank." Luke scratched his ear. *I gotta keep a sharp eye on Yegor. It's possible the joystick operator or the lady computer engineer will pass somethin' to him.*

Yegor stood. "You are mind reader. I have questions."

Layla followed the two men as they climbed down the grandstand steps. In a few moments, they blended into a group of spectators who massed around Mickey, the joystick operator. The tank stood on the turf on the opposite side of a wire fence.

Yegor raised his hand and caught Mickey's attention. "What weapons does the tank have?"

Mickey bumped his lavalier microphone, and a thumping noise echoed across the crowd. He waved at the tracked vehicle with a laser pointer. "A machine gun and a turret-mounted, 76 mm cannon are on its rooftop." Mickey paused. "We also can add weapons such as rocket launchers and lethal lasers."

A man in a British Army uniform spoke up. "Can you operate all the tank's weapons with the joystick?"

Mickey grinned. "I can use the joystick, along with the mouse and software, to fire every weapon mounted on this vehicle. Our demo today will highlight how easy it is to run the tank and its arms from a safe distance. I can guide this tracked vehicle from hundreds of miles away from the battlefield. Tank crews are not necessary."

A woman who carried a clipboard slipped to the front of the crowd. "What is the slot on the back of the tank for?"

Mickey pointed his laser beam at the slit in the armor. "We've installed an external slot for a flash-cubed memory card, enabling researchers to update the tank's software without wasting time going inside the vehicle. The advanced flash card has a thousand times the memory of the best consumer card its size." Mickey focused on the woman with the clipboard, who took notes. "On the operational vehicle, there won't be an external slot, enhancing security."

A small number of spectators moved forward for a closer view of the metallic beast. A man in a gray business suit stepped closer to Mickey. "How is this battle tank powered?"

Mickey moved his microphone closer to his mouth. "It can run on battery power in silent mode for 150 miles, and switch to its diesel power at my command. The batteries can even recharge at electric vehicle charging stations."

A man dressed in a sports coat who wore no tie waved his arm. "Sinclair Maris, *Military Industry News Magazine*. I noticed a lake and a water-filled ditch across the field. Can this machine ford water?"

Mickey nodded. "Yes, it's amphibious and can even swim across a mile-wide river." He paused. "Also this tank can track the enemy with radar. It has a 360 degree camera and sensors with night vision equipment, too."

The reporter shouted. "How do you keep the lenses clean in the dirty battlefield environment?"

Mickey said, "I like your question. Air compressors squirt water to clean glass surfaces. It's vital to keep the lenses clean. But in case fog, smoke, or rain partly blinds camera views, the tank's radar system will fill in the gaps in the video. Also—and this is awesome—the tank has a photo library of enemy fighting machines and soldiers. These images are used to enhance blurred or incomplete images."

Mickey moved to his joystick. "Now I'll show you something else." He pushed a button, and his computer monitor lit up. He used a mouse to click on the icon of a helicopter drone on the computer screen.

A metal door opened in the top of the tank, revealing a helicopter drone the size of a drip coffeepot. "I can fly this drone to scout ahead. Its camera sends a picture to this monitor."

The reporter nodded. "Cool."

Mickey smiled. "Watch this." He tapped an icon on the screen, and two eight-inch-wide retractable ramps on the tank's rear extended. Then two mini robotic tanks, each the size of a shoebox, rolled down their slanting, steel ramps to the ground.

"These little guys can find improvised explosive devices (IEDs), explore damaged buildings, carry messages, and even place explosives."

Mickey paused.

Many of the spectators smiled, and looked at each other, nodding. Others clapped.

Mickey grinned, and then spoke. "Sorry to say, folks, our time is up. Please move to your seats. We'll begin the live-fire demonstration at 2:15 p.m." He turned off his microphone as he directed the tiny tanks back up their ramps.

Luke focused on Yegor, and the spy appeared to be stunned. He said, "Impressive."

Luke rubbed his chin. *If they let this metal beast go loose without human supervision on a battlefield, the tank could knock off a company of soldiers.*

* * *

2:13 P.M., TUESDAY, POPPINS PROVING GROUND

The proving ground's announcer, dressed in a nice suit, faced the grandstand. He grasped a handheld microphone.

The presenter reminded Luke of a circus ringmaster about to introduce a trapeze act. "Next, ladies and gentlemen, please direct your attention to the Raven Robotics remote-controlled battle tank, sitting near the large card table on the lawn."

With a sweeping motion, the announcer pointed. "The joystick operator, Mickey, will use an off-the-shelf, computer-game joystick to control this sixty-five-ton, steel killing machine. He'll drive it, fire its many weapons, run it through a large-vehicle obstacle course, swim it across a lake, and punch it through a thick forest." The announcer gestured toward three giant TV screens, the types often used at football arenas to show instant replays. "Watch the big screens for images from onboard the tank as well as video from its hawk-sized, scout drone. Let the show begin."

From his seat in the grandstand, Luke held his hands against the plugs in his ears when the US robotic tank fired its first round. Even so, the boom of the tank firing its main gun sounded loud. An orange fireball erupted from the tank's barrel, and gases and smoke lingered in the air as the projectile sped 3,600 miles per hour toward a junked car.

In an instant, the tank's round hit the car body, which disintegrated. Flames burned what remained of the wreckage while thick, black smoke bellowed skyward. The spectators cheered. Luke reckoned the old automobile's fuel tank still had contained gallons of gasoline. *Do Raven Robotic's salesmen want to make the show dramatic with fire and smoke?*

Yegor yelled, "It like Hollywood. Raven Robotics sure wants to sell the tank. It's fine show." He grinned.

Luke squinted to view Mickey, the joystick operator. The man's fingers wiggled the joystick, and the tank raced toward a car body 200 yards distant. The tank hurried forward and shifted directions like an agile Los Angeles Rams halfback. From his position, Luke couldn't hear the tank's engine. *It must be using its electric motor.*

The robotic tank skidded to a sudden stop, tearing up the sod a hundred yards from the second car body. Luke heard a faint hissing sound and saw a stream of liquid spraying from the tank. Luke smelled diesel oil drifting on the breeze. In a blink, the liquid ignited. *It must be a tank-mounted flamethrower.*

Yegor tapped Luke's shoulder. "This tank has lot of weapons. Mickey is pro, doing it all from far away."

Luke nodded. He glanced at Layla. She appeared to be horrified. Her body shook, and then she peered down between the bleacher's wooden slats.

Luke strained to see what Mickey, the joystick operator, was doing next. After a quick motion of Mickey's wrist, the lethal machine backed up. It turned ninety degrees to its right at the same moment a dozen man-shaped targets flipped up from their hidden positions. The tank's machine gun fired in staccato bursts. One out of every five bullets was a tracer, and red streaks marked their paths. The targets, each the silhouette of a soldier, went down.

Yegor glanced at Luke. "The tracers look like fireworks."

Luke wondered if Yegor would try to contact one of the US robotic tank's employees right after the demonstration. *Makes sense. If he makes a move to receive intel, he'll wait until after the motorized howitzer demo, which is next.*

Yegor caught Luke's attention. "When howitzer is done firing, I want talk to Mickey, the joystick man, again."

Luke noticed the three large-scale TV screens facing the audience had turned on, revealing the tank's view of the field. The tank traveled up a steep hill. Then the mammoth, tracked vehicle raced toward the oval lake. *The tank's gonna cross the pond. If the tank sinks, it'll be hard as hell to drag it out.*

Within thirty seconds, the heavy, steel-clad vehicle splashed into the water, floated, and began to move across the lake to its far shore. The joystick operator stood up by his table and studied his computer screen. Luke reckoned Mickey had activated a water-crossing computer routine. Luke squinted. *I wonder if motorboat-like propellers are on the tank's tail end.*

Mickey spoke. "Retractable propellers have been deployed from their waterproof enclosures and are driving the tank across the water."

The audience cheered as they watched a televised tank's-eye view when the tracked giant climbed the opposite shore of the lake onto dry ground. Next, the heavy vehicle approached the water-filled ditch and stopped. A helicopter drone soared up from the tank and hovered over the ditch. A TV picture from the mini aircraft showed a view of the long, skinny waterway from above. Mickey moved the joystick forward, and the tank lumbered toward the ditch and crossed it at an oblique angle.

As the Raven Robotics battle tank drove back to its home position in front of the grandstand, a self-propelled, 155 mm howitzer moved into position.

Luke leaned close to Yegor. "It's hard to believe Mickey used a joystick and a computer to make the tank do everything it did."

Yegor smiled. "It is why we want joystick software to run farm tractors. No farmer needs to sit in the tractor."

Luke pointed to the huge, lumbering howitzer. "What is it?"

"Artillery. Howitzer can go fast and far. It is new model made for the European Union."

Luke scratched his head. *How's anybody gonna get secret info to Yegor? Did one of the Raven Robotics employees already pass somethin' to him?*

Mickey took two steps toward the grandstand. "The demonstration of the joystick operation of our Raven Robotics battle tank has ended. Please visit us again after the final live-fire event of the afternoon, the self-propelled howitzer demo, which is next."

The crowd applauded Mickey. He bowed.

Yegor stood. "I need to stretch. I can't wait to see Mickey again." He paused. "The howitzer is big gun. Should be loud. Make sure you use earplugs when it shoots."

From afar, Luke strained to view the huge howitzer as it inched forward.

Even larger than the US robotic tank, the wheeled, self-propelled howitzer drove at the pace of a slow-walking man, its heavy, long gun pointing forward. The mobile weapon stopped in the field of lush grass close to the grandstand.

Layla turned to Luke. "I'd never join the army. It'd be too loud and dangerous." She frowned.

Luke smiled. "Dear, I'm glad you ain't plannin' to join."

Layla grinned and kissed his cheek.

Yegor glanced at his watch. "This demo will be done after two shots."

Within minutes, the huge gun fired a round with a loud "whoomp" sound, and the vibrating ground shook the grandstands. Blackish smoke rose, and then the gun crew fired again. Luke rubbed the whiskers on his cheek. *Sure's a powerful weapon.*

Yegor got up right away after the second shot. "Let's see Mickey, the joystick man." Yegor moved toward the grandstand steps.

* * *

USING HIS COMPACT BINOCULARS, Rory saw Yegor rise from his seat next to Luke and take a step down the grandstand stairs toward the robotic tank.

* * *

A STEP BEHIND YEGOR, Luke stood and led Layla down the steps toward the Raven Robotics battle tank. *I gotta keep a close watch on Yegor.*

The jumbo speakers high above the stands buzzed, and then the announcer spoke in a clear voice. "This concludes the live-fire portion of today's activities. Please feel free to move into the field to examine the hardware after the fence gate is open."

* * *

RORY SHIFTED his binocular view to Mickey, the youthful joystick operator. The young man stood and waved to a Raven Robotics representative, summoning the older man. Rory recognized the senior man as the firm's sales manager.

FORTY-SIX

3:10 P.M., TUESDAY, SEPTEMBER 17, 2030, POPPINS PROVING GROUND

THE POPPINS ANNOUNCER continued to speak after he had told the spectators the live-fire part of the show had ended for the day. His voice echoed across the grandstand. "Be sure to take a close look at the rocket-propelled grenade launchers, the mortars, the self-propelled howitzer, and the joystick-controlled battle tank. Tomorrow's live-fire demonstration will begin at 9:00 a.m."

Luke felt pea-sized stones underfoot after he, Yegor, and Layla had stepped down from the jam-packed grandstand to ground level. They moved along a path toward the Raven Robotics battle tank.

Luke figured he had to be extra observant. Glancing around, he caught sight of Rory and Henry. He knew that Sonja, Ginger, Drake, and Sergeant Rick Boutwell were also mixed into the throng flowing around the US prototype tank.

Luke relaxed. *They have plenty of people. If anything goes down, someone's sure to see it happen.* With care, he surveyed his environs, viewing 360 degrees around him. *The tank's gettin' lots of interest. Plenty of spectators are skipping the rest of the weapon displays.*

Luke spotted the baron and locked eyes with him. Luke felt his senses go on high alert. *I thought he had skipped the show. Bein' in SIS, he must know we're watching over the US tank.*

Luke noticed Lord Thorpe shift his gaze and catch sight of Rory. In less than a second, the baron blinked and, with a quick side step, turned away from Rory.

* * *

RORY AND HIS AGENT, Ginger, had not seen the baron. Instead, they watched Yegor. They took their time to get closer to the Belarusian spy.

Rory quickened his pace and bit his lip as he neared Ginger. *She's as hard to control as a lioness.*

Rory grabbed Ginger's arm. She stopped and bristled. For a split second, she glared at him. But in less than two heartbeats, she exhaled and smiled at the man she now recognized as her MI5 boss.

Rory leaned next to her ear. He spoke in a low voice. "Watch Yegor, and keep your eyes peeled for suspicious people. Report by wristwatch radio about questionable activity."

Ginger blushed. "Yes, sir."

Rory considered her for a second. "We'll nab Yegor or additional suspects only on my command. But do take immediate action, if violence ensues."

Ginger nodded. Then she and the blond CIA agent, Sonja, inched closer to Yegor.

Rory rubbed his temple. He had a slight headache. *Something will happen soon.*

Rory saw a Raven Robotics employee give Yegor a business card. Then Rory saw the FBI Agent, Henry, moving toward Yegor.

Rory sent Henry a subtle signal to back off. He drew near

Henry and whispered, "The Raven Robotics man who handed Yegor the business card is undercover working with us."

Henry gestured he understood.

Rory sighed. *The team's edgy.*

* * *

3:16 P.M., TUESDAY, POPPINS PROVING GROUND

As Lord Thorpe neared the rear of the robotic tank, he felt sweat leak down his torso from his armpits. He touched a high-density computer memory card in his right-hand trousers pocket. With his fingers, he grasped the postage-stamp-sized memory device by its thick edges.

He felt his heart beat too fast, like a defective clock speeding ahead faster and faster. He inched closer to the computer card slot on the tank's aft end. The baron took a deep breath, but his pulse didn't slow. *I must appear to lean against the machine for a reason.*

His throat hurt worse, and he began an uncontrolled cough. He felt his face turn red. *A lucky cough. This is a great excuse to support myself against the tank's steel wall.*

He fell backward against the tank's armor plate. Though he tried, he couldn't stop coughing. *Goddamn, my whooping has to stop if I'm going to succeed.* The sun-heated exterior of the steel beast felt toasty to his touch. In five seconds, the higher temperature of the metal calmed his body. *Thank God, I stopped hacking.* He took a soothing breath, trying to reduce his heart rate.

Though his pulse continued to pound, he willed himself to slip the memory card from his pocket. He began to cough again. *Bloody hell, quit coughing.*

Shaking, he still managed to insert the card into the tank's computer update slot and press the button next to it. An amber light glowed behind his back, as he peeked behind him. An instant later, the tiny light turned a steady green. He took a cleansing breath. He knew the robot tank's artificial intelligence brain had been copied onto the high-capacity memory card. With another press of the button by the slot, the card popped back into his hand.

Did anyone see me?

* * *

LUKE HAD OBSERVED the baron fall backward against the tail of the US tank as he coughed. His face had become as red as the cheeks of a blushing bride. Luke then took notice of the amber glow from a tiny LED light near the aristocrat's back. Luke cocked his head. *Did the baron bump something when he fell against the tank?*

The tannish glow of the circular bulb, an eighth inch in diameter, turned solid green. Then Luke saw Lord Thorpe slip his right hand into his right hip pocket. His face faded from a bright crimson to a normal skin tone, and then it morphed into a pale, ghostly appearance.

The baron's Adam's apple went up and down. The aristocrat gulped as he glanced back and forth.

Luke felt Lord Thorpe's eyes settle on him. The nobleman nodded with a slight motion of his chin as if acknowledging Luke's presence.

The baron blinked fast, three times.

Luke returned the aristocrat's nod with a brief chin movement.

Lord Thorpe smiled, but he appeared nervous to Luke.

Glancing away from the nobleman, Luke rubbed his cheek whiskers. *I don't need the baron to think I'm watchin' him.* Walking to a position out of Lord Thorpe's line of sight, Luke noticed Yegor had begun to move toward the nobleman.

Luke felt his pulse rise. *What are those guys up to?*

Yegor said something to the baron, but Luke could not make out what the Belarusian spy had said.

Lord Thorpe reached into his right hip pocket.

* * *

3:25 P.M., TUESDAY, POPPINS PROVING GROUND

A happy mood seeped throughout Yegor's total being. His brain switched to his familiar Russian tongue. *America, here I come.*

Yegor held his hand out toward the baron. "Nice to see you, Lord Thorpe."

The Belarusian spy saw the aristocrat's pale face turn bright pink, like a chameleon's skin displaying another hue. Grasping the baron's hand, Yegor felt the high-capacity computer card in the nobleman's palm. As Yegor shook the man's limp hand, he took hold of the card.

Yegor grinned and felt elated. *It should contain a clone of the tank's neural net brain. If not, I'm screwed.* He felt perspiration roll down his temples.

When Yegor saw Luke peer his way, the spy felt a slight jolt of caution. But with the logical side of his brain, Yegor dismissed his initial gut feeling. *No reason Luke would think the baron gave me anything. I should escort Luke and Layla to the chopper and get back to the embassy.*

Yegor's brain switched back to English. "Lord Thorpe, where's men's room?"

The aristocrat appeared to decompress. "On the right side of the visitor center by the golf carts."

LUKE WATCHED as Yegor walked at a slow pace toward the men's room on the side of the visitor's center. Then Luke glanced at the helicopter he, Layla, and Yegor had taken to the Poppins event. *I wonder if we'll stay the whole day.*

Luke looked back toward the tank just as Mickey, the joystick operator, emerged from a hatchway on its roof and then jumped to the ground.

Then the massive robotic tank began to move. Mickey

gasped and ran to his table where his joystick sat. He lunged at the controller and fumbled with it.

The tank began to move faster. Mickey clicked his mouse over and over again, staring at the tank as it picked up speed. He appeared frazzled.

Rory jogged through the crowd to Luke's side, glared at Mickey, and in a strong voice asked, "What's wrong?"

Mickey's body shook as he slapped at his joystick. "The tank won't respond to commands." His voice sounded an octave higher. "I don't have control."

Luke heard the tank's gun turret motor whine. The metal beast's cannon turned and pointed at the ancient, display-filled, DC-3 airplane next to the visitor center. All of a sudden, the massive tank fired a 76 mm round at the old plane. It exploded in a ball of orange flames. Bits and pieces of jagged aluminum flew skyward. Metal debris fell on the concrete where the old propeller airliner had stood. Expanding black surges of smoke poured up from the wreckage.

A woman screamed, her voice as shrill as a wounded animal's cry. People ran toward the expansive parking lot. Frightened attendees tumbled into golf carts and sped away. In less than twenty seconds most of the 2,500 spectators were fleeing in all directions.

Luke watched the wild robotic tank as it swiveled and inched sideways as if it were assessing a battlefield. Luke felt sweat on his forehead. *I gotta stop this thing.* He saw the tank's top hatch was open.

When the massive, treaded vehicle came to a full stop, Luke sprinted to the rear end of the steel monster. A twinge of fear cascaded throughout his torso as he grasped a hand-hold and pulled himself atop the rogue machine. He tumbled down into the crew compartment.

At the same time as his eyes became used to the dim interior, he heard the tank fire its machine gun. *Damn.* A moment of panic struck him. *Where's Layla?*

He scanned a control panel with lots of lights, buttons,

and levers. He felt visual overload. *A hundred buttons must be lit up.*

The tank lurched into motion. Luke stumbled. He fell. Pushing himself up, he grabbed the side of the control panel. *Where's the off button?*

As he scanned the confusing array of flashing lights, he spotted a silver-dollar-sized button labeled "Manual." Quick as an alley cat batting at a rat, Luke punched the button. The sixty-five-ton, death-dealing machine came to a stop.

Luke shook his head and closed his eyes for a long second. He leaned back against the steel wall. His heart began to beat at a slower pace.

Mickey dropped down from the hatch and stood next to Luke. "How'd you stop it?"

Luke pointed. "I punched the manual button."

"Nice. Thanks, mister."

Luke nodded. "I gotta go. I'm workin' with law enforcement."

Mickey raised his brow. "Thank God."

Luke blinked. "Anybody hurt?"

Mickey frowned. "I'm not sure."

Luke began to climb through the hatch and peered down on Mickey. "I saw a man lean back against the tank's backside near the computer update slot. An amber light turned green."

Mickey rubbed his forehead. "Be sure to tell our people."

"Okay."

Mickey puffed out a breath and then grinned. "You saved the day."

FORTY-SEVEN

GRASPING AT HIS PAINFUL THROAT, the baron watched as Luke climbed down from the idle robotic tank. *The American copper could have seen me slip the memory card into the tank's slot.*

The aristocrat also noticed a shapely black woman cowering behind a pickup truck. *Didn't I see her with the American copper? Could she be his girlfriend or colleague?*

Although Lord Thorpe's neck throbbed, he stood taller. *I have nothing to fear. Yegor has the memory card. If he says I passed it to him, I'll claim he lied. But he has other proof I can't refute.*

The baron sighed. He couldn't think of an easy way to get himself out of his bind. *I must protect the Thorpe name, even if my days are numbered.* He narrowed his vivid blue eyes, steeling himself. He knew he had throat cancer, a result of heavy drinking. He'd be lucky to live another two months, according to his doctor.

I should go down fighting. The nobleman reckoned he could save a portion of his family legacy if he would be brave. He'd be admired for valor, ready to be killed instead of kneeling to authority. *The general public will know me. I won't be a forgotten, secret SIS employee.*

Lord Thorpe eyed the wide variety of helicopters sitting near the runway 300 yards distant. *I could hop in a golf cart and speed to the choppers. Everybody's running. What's one more desperate man trying to escape? I'll leave in the confusion. I could get away with this.*

Because he was a former military helicopter pilot, the baron knew most of the military whirlybirds would not be locked, and he did not need a key to start them. To avoid detection by radar, he'd guide the chopper close to the ground, following roads, riverbeds, and ditches, the same way he had learned to fly during Nap-of-the-Earth warfare exercises. He'd zigzag by trees and past power lines. *My reflexes are still quick enough.*

* * *

LUKE SAW the baron cough and begin to walk at a steady pace toward the parked electric carts. Then Luke spotted Layla. She hunkered down behind an abandoned pickup truck. *She's street-smart.* He smiled and began to run in her direction.

* * *

AS THE BARON marched toward the parked electric carts, he had to pass by Luke, who had almost reached the crouching black woman. The American saw him.

Lord Thorpe took a deep breath. *Does the Yank guess what I intend to do?*

As Luke approached the gorgeous black woman who hid behind the pickup truck, he turned. The baron felt Luke's dark eyes focus on him.

Luke spoke. "What did you hand Yegor?"

"Nothing."

"I saw you fiddlin' with the computer card slot, and then the tank went crazy."

Lord Thorpe blinked. He glanced sideways. Rory, the London policeman, stood seventy-five yards away.

Luke waved, beckoning Rory to come to him.

The aristocrat's eyes focused on the black woman. *It's time to go.*

A sharp pain poked at Lord Thorpe's throat like a hypodermic needle sticking it over and over again. The baron grabbed his switchblade from his trousers pocket. He pressed the weapon's button. A razor-sharp blade popped outward and flashed in the sunlight. With his free hand, Lord Thorpe grasped the black woman's upper arm. He pulled her upward.

* * *

LAYLA FELT the well-dressed man grip her bicep, squeezing it. Pain shot through her arm. Staring down for a microsecond, she watched as a shiny, steel blade moved under her chin. A high-pitched shriek pierced the air.

That was my scream. The shrill sound of it surprised her.

* * *

THE WOMAN'S screech impacted the baron's left eardrum like a slap. The aristocrat caught sight of a tear-sized drop of red blood as it dribbled down her neck.

Lord Thorpe glanced at Luke, just as the American took a step toward him and the woman. The baron heard himself speak. "Stay back or she dies."

The American's eyes were steady. "Hurt her anymore, and I'll break yur neck."

DCI Rory Calvin slid to a stop on the pavement. He yelled, "Drop the knife."

The aristocrat blinked. He glimpsed at the line of light

airplanes and helicopters on the nearby airfield. *I'll take an electric cart and head for the aircraft now.*

"I'm leaving." His voice was scratchy and weakened. Numbing pain spread across his throat.

Pulling Layla with him, the baron backed up toward a golf cart. Layla's heels slid across the pavement as he yanked her along.

The tall American followed as did DCI Calvin, until the baron stood ten feet from the nearest cart, still gripping Layla.

* * *

LUKE FIXATED on the blade the aristocrat held against Layla's throat. What felt like a shock zapped Luke. His heart pounding, doubt hit him. He froze. *Is this fear?*

Watching a tear run down Layla's cheek, Luke saw her shake like an aspen tree in the wind. Luke gritted his teeth and eased yet closer to the baron.

* * *

PAIN INCREASED THREEFOLD in Lord Thorpe's esophagus, like the mounting discomfort of a dentist's needle probing deep into gum tissue.

Like a movie clip, a vision flashed into the baron's mind. Lord Thorpe saw his physician's lips moving. Dr. Ralph Malcolm said, "You have Stage 4 throat cancer."

It won't be long, and I'll join Anne. But sure as hell, I'm not going to die here.

* * *

EVEN CLOSER TO the aristocrat than before and poised like a cobra ready to strike, Luke stared at the baron. Luke felt a sudden calm, as if he were observing an event taking place on TV. *Is this my way of dealing with danger?*

* * *

LORD THORPE GLARED at Luke while tightening his grip on the black female. The baron wrinkled his brow. *How am I going to get this woman into the cart and control her?*

He felt the black woman breathing fast. She wheezed. *Is she going to hyperventilate?*

A coughing fit hit the aristocrat. He blinked. Cool blackness enveloped his vision for a microsecond.

* * *

LUKE SAW Baron Thorpe's face turn vivid crimson. Whooping, the aristocrat waved his blade away from Layla's neck, coughing into his palm and the weapon's handle.

Luke leaped forward like a long jumper.

* * *

A BLURRY, fast motion caught the baron's eye. *What's that?*

* * *

AS LUKE FLEW FORWARD, he saw Layla muscle herself sideways.

Good girl.

As Luke landed on his two feet, he launched his right fist against the baron's chin.

* * *

THE ARISTOCRAT FELT his jaw go numb. His knees buckled. He tripped on the black woman's ankle. Lord Thorpe fell like a chain-sawed tree. Watching in slow motion as the pavement below him loomed closer, the baron plummeted downward. A sharp pain like a punch to his chest impacted him. His world became silent. All turned black. Peaceful coolness enveloped him.

* * *

LUKE FELT relief as Layla scampered away. He peered down at the fallen lord. The aristocrat's legs moved as if he ran, and a slow, high-pitched hiss came from his mouth, like air whistling from a punctured bicycle tire. Then he stopped moving, and his blood oozed across the concrete from under his torso.

Rolling the baron onto his back, Luke saw the man's knife stuck in the left side of his chest above his heart. Luke touched Lord Thorpe's neck and felt no pulse.

FORTY-EIGHT

AFTER THE EXPLOSIONS CEASED, Yegor opened the men's room door with caution. Deciding it was safe enough to exit, he walked out near two dozen parked electric carts.

Fear hit his stomach like a sharp arrow when Yegor caught sight of Luke standing over the baron's crumpled body. Lord Thorpe appeared unconscious, if not dead.

Yegor reckoned it was not a good idea to linger at Poppins Proving Ground.

I must go. He felt the high-capacity computer memory card in his hip pocket. *Should I toss it in the grass? No.*

KGB headquarters in Minsk required him to deliver the memory card to Viktor, his handler.

Can I get away? Yes.

He squinted and spied the parked helicopters. Yegor thought he spotted George, his chopper's pilot, in the distance at least 300 yards away. The man wore a unique, blue outfit. The uniformed man walked toward the whirlybird Yegor had rented. *I could fly away with him.*

Yegor felt dread. *I must move fast. No one knows I have the memory card. What the hell were the KGB so-called "computer experts" thinking when they decided to create a diversion with the tank? Even if things have gone bad, I still have time to flee.*

Panic-driven, Yegor slid onto the seat of a golf cart. He twisted its key and turned the vehicle on. When he stamped on its accelerator pedal, the cart leaped forward like a sprinter trying to win a gold medal. A vision of Anne invaded Yegor's mind. *Too bad she had to die.* He felt deep regret. *In an alternate time, in a distant place, I would've married her.*

* * *

LUKE SAW Yegor race off in an electric cart. The spy headed straight for the chopper he'd rented. *Yegor could've guessed I'm workin' with the police, but he wouldn't be sure of it. Layla and me can catch up to him, and say we want to fly outta harm's way.*

Luke noticed the nearby carts had roll bars. He locked eyes with Layla and pointed. "Get in the cart, and put on yur seatbelt."

Layla hurried into the cart while Luke slid into its driver's seat.

When Luke smashed the accelerator pedal to the floorboard, the cart flew forward like a pronghorn antelope pursued by a Yellowstone wolf pack.

"Where are we going?"

"After Yegor to tell him we wanna ride the chopper outta here."

"Why?"

"I think the baron slipped a computer memory card to him with secrets on it."

Layla grabbed the steel roof support as the cart bounced and flew ahead. "Won't the police catch him anyway?"

"I *am* the police. And I can stop him easier cuz he thinks I'm a farmer."

262 JOHN G. BLUCK

Luke scanned ahead. Yegor's cart sped forward and climbed a steep hill.

Layla squinted. "What's ahead?"

"The vehicle test tracks and the obstacle course."

* * *

4:13 P.M., TUESDAY, POPPINS PROVING GROUND

Rory was examining the baron's body. Ginger followed Rory to the collapsed aristocrat.

Kneeling beside Lord Thorpe's corpse, Rory held his fingers on the man's throat, rechecking him for a pulse. Rory turned his head to focus on Henry and Sonja, who had sprinted up to the collapsed baron. "He's dead as a rock."

Ginger stared at Luke's electric vehicle speeding after Yegor's cart. "Luke's after Yegor."

Rory stood. "Follow me." He got into an electric cart. Henry joined him. Rory pushed the cart to its limit as he raced after Luke and Yegor.

Her short red hair bouncing, Ginger shoved Sonja toward another cart. "I'm driving, sweetie." Ginger's eyes were fiery as she put the cart in drive.

* * *

AS YEGOR'S cart zipped toward the helicopters and the airstrip, a pang of fright stabbed at his brain when he crested the steep hill. A water-filled, muddy ditch was dead ahead. It stood between him and the parked choppers.

He jammed his foot against the brake pedal. Sliding on muddy grass like a sled on ice, the fast-moving cart careened into the ditch and rolled over. Yegor felt water drench his clothes as he fell into the dirty muck. *I'm glad the memory card is in a plastic bag.* He paused while his brain recalculated. *I better get rid of it.*

From behind, someone grabbed his shoulders with strong hands and lugged him out of the overflowing ditch.

Blinking to clear the murky water from his eyes, Yegor saw a blurry image of Luke staring down at him. "You hurt?"

"No." Yegor rubbed a hand through his wet hair, and water dribbled down his face.

"I'm glad I caught up to you. Layla and me want to git out of here on the chopper."

Yegor grinned. "Okay. But we need ride in your cart." *When Luke turns, I can dump the card in the water.*

* * *

LUKE WATCHED as Yegor spit grimy water from his mouth. Luke heard a woman scream near the parked helicopters, and he focused on the whirlybirds in the distance. The yelling woman didn't appear to be injured. Then out of the corner of his eye, Luke saw Yegor reach into his wet, slippery trousers pocket. The spy slipped out a plastic bag with a computer memory card in it.

As if on autopilot, Luke made a fist. "Don't do a damn thing with the card. I don't want to slug you."

Without warning, Yegor ripped at the bag, but his fingers slipped from its muddy surface. *He's gonna throw the card in the water. Will that ruin the card?*

As fast as Mohammad Ali, Luke smacked Yegor's chin, and the man fell backward. The spy collapsed onto the weeds growing on the shore of the waterway. Luke snatched the bag. For a second longer, Yegor remained unconscious. Then he opened his eyes and shook his head.

"Sorry I had to hit you, Yegor."

* * *

LUKE HEARD an electric cart's brakes screech and bring the vehicle to a sudden stop behind him. As he turned, he saw Rory and Henry get out of the cart. Three seconds later, a second cart slid to a stop on the wet turf. A stocky, redheaded woman was behind the steering wheel, and Sonja sat next to her. Sonja smiled at Luke. "You got him."

Luke shrugged.

Yegor, covered in slimy mud, sat slumped on the weed-infested bank of the ditch. A fly landed on his nose. Yegor swatted the insect away. The spy appeared stunned to Luke. He grabbed Yegor's arms and hefted him to his feet.

Rory neared Luke and Yegor and focused on the spy. "Yegor Bulot, you were seen entering Baroness Anne Thorpe's building the night of her death. I am placing you under arrest for her murder."

Yegor's brow furrowed, and he opened his mouth, about to speak. Ginger, the redheaded MI5 agent, grabbed his right arm and snapped a handcuff on his wrist. With vigor, she twisted the spy's arm behind him. He moaned.

Luke frowned. "Take it easy. He ain't resisting."

Ginger frowned, and her eyes flickered. She paused, and then said, "Okay." She snapped the second cuff on Yegor's left wrist and pulled on the manacle. It pinched the spy's skin.

Yet another vehicle, this one driven by Sergeant Boutwell, arrived.

Yegor shook his head as if he had just come out of a daze. Luke reckoned the Belarus KGB spy's senses were growing sharper.

Luke heard someone. He turned and saw Rory had moved closer. "Luke, are you okay?"

"Yep."

Yegor coughed and spit muddy water into the ditch. Rory redirected his gaze at Yegor. "You don't have to say anything, but neglecting to talk may harm your defense, if you fail to mention something you later rely on in court. Anything you say may be given in evidence."

Yegor hacked and sprayed filthy water from his mouth. "I am not guilty. The baron killed Anne. I have video proof."

Rory eyeballed Yegor for a second. "Video proof?"

The spy showed a slight smile. "I hid an SD card in my left shoe's heel."

Rory stared at Yegor. "Sit down." Rory caught Ginger's attention. "Hold him still."

Ginger grinned. She held Yegor's legs and twisted his right leg. He grunted.

Rory untied Yegor's soaked left shoe and slid it off the spy's foot. Pulling a cotton handkerchief from his rear pocket, Rory wiped the shoe dry. "Sergeant, do you still carry a jackknife?"

Sergeant Boutwell handed Rory his unfolded knife.

Luke watched as Rory pried the heel from Yegor's oxford. A small plastic bag in a cavity in the heel fell into the London policeman's hand.

Rory glanced at Yegor. "We'll examine this after we find a computer." Rory paused. "But first, if this has a video on it, how did you obtain it?"

"I gave Anne gift, cell phone charger station with hidden camera inside." Yegor gulped and glanced back and forth at the gathered MI5 team. "Anne asked me to her flat. Said she had a surprise. I saw her body." A single tear dribbled down the spy's whiskery cheek. "I took the charger and left. Then I watched the video on the SD card from the charger. I saw the baron kill her with wheel brace." Yegor exhaled.

Luke recalled a wheel brace is the same thing as an automobile lug wrench. Then he remembered the baron's car had had a flat tire. Afterward, Lord Thorpe's butler had mentioned he couldn't find the car's wheel brace and had needed to phone an auto service to fix the tire. *The baron must've got rid of the lug wrench after he killed Anne.*

Rory kept his eyes on Yegor, who sat on the wet, muddy turf. "If you're not a killer, we likely will charge you with espionage after we examine the larger memory card we believe the baron secretly slipped to you."

"I am not murderer." Yegor blinked three times. He made

a jerky head movement. "I know lot about Belarus KGB. Can we make deal?"

To Luke, the spy appeared defeated, not defiant. *Too bad he decided to spy. Otherwise, he could've been an okay guy.* Luke wondered what had led Yegor to become a secret agent. Did he make his choice with little forethought, or had he planned early on to join the Belarus KGB?

Rory turned to Sergeant Boutwell. "Let's put him in the van, out of view."

Luke stared at Yegor as the sergeant began to lift the spy to a standing position. *It's lucky most people have fled and didn't see what happened here.*

Luke watched as Boutwell helped Yegor steady himself while Rory focused on the spy. "We'll talk this through right away."

* * *

USING AN ELECTRIC CART, Sergeant Boutwell drove Yegor toward MI5's long passenger van parked near the visitor center. With great care, Boutwell maneuvered the cart around jagged bits and pieces of the destroyed DC-3 airplane that littered the ground. Finally, he stopped near the van.

Several minutes later, Luke and Layla watched as paramedics rolled their gurney and the baron's body toward an ambulance. Luke turned and saw Rory approach. He stopped near Luke. "The Raven Robotics man in charge wants to see you."

Luke saw a clean-cut, middle-aged man in a rumpled suit power walking toward him.

Rory said, "Luke, this is Josh Burnside, Vice President of Raven Robotics."

Josh held his hand out to Luke, and the two men shook hands. "Luke, it's a pleasure to meet you. DCI Calvin told me you saw Lord Thorpe put a memory card in the tank's update slot." Josh paused. "Thank you for saving our butts by stopping the tank before it killed someone." Josh glanced at the ambulance as paramedics loaded the baron's body into it. "DCI Calvin told me Lord Thorpe died when he fell on a jagged piece of debris."

Luke figured Rory had a reason for falsifying how the baron had died. Luke lowered his head. "Lucky the hatch hadn't been locked, and the tank was near me." He glanced across the field at the wreckage of the destroyed DC-3 airplane. "You sure nobody was killed in the explosion?"

"Pretty sure. Workers were renovating the DC-3 display, but they weren't in it today." Josh gestured toward the idle tank, around which a half dozen people stood. "Let's go inside the tank, so you can show me what you did to stop it."

As Luke and Josh neared the tank, Luke recognized Mickey, the joystick operator.

Josh halted near the tank's rear and turned to Luke. "Three MI5 computer experts are working remotely with our chief computer engineer, Etta Jasek. They've found a computer virus in the robot's brain which, in layman's terms, drove it insane."

Josh climbed atop the battle tank and held his hand down to Luke, to help him climb up on the metal beast. In seconds, the two men were inside the crew compartment. Luke noticed it seemed roomier than when he'd stopped the tank.

Josh caught Luke's attention. "So, how'd you stop it?"

Luke hovered his finger over the control panel. "I pushed the manual button."

Luke heard someone climbing down the metal ladder behind him. When he glanced backward, he saw Etta.

Josh stared at Luke's eyes. "Rory tells me you're with the FBI, you have a top secret clearance, and you know this tank has a computer brain able to run it."

"Yep."

"Etta, this is Luke Ryder. Tell him what we know."

Etta took a half step forward. "I analyzed the flash

memory card you seized from the spy. The entire robotic brain is copied onto it. The neural net copy is undamaged." She paused. "However, the brain in the tank's onboard computer was infected with a computer virus, causing it to go crazy."

Luke rubbed his eyebrow. "Can you fix the infected brain in the tank?"

"We could, but the simple solution is to install a backup neural net brain on the tank's computer after we ask the diseased, onboard brain more questions."

"If the infected brain is still in the tank, isn't it dangerous?"

"No, we've cut off its ability to control the tank." Etta paused. "We discovered it's delusional. It believed it was being attacked."

Luke's eyes widened. "The tank was having halluci-nations?"

"Yes. It's as if it took a psychedelic drug like LSD."

Luke raised his eyebrows. "Why'd the bad guys infect the brain if they could've simply copied it and not got caught?"

Etta sighed. "I guess they wanted to embarrass Raven Robotics and the United States. I think the virus did its job too well. I bet the hackers wanted to make the tank act weird, not start shooting."

Luke bit his lip. "If the tank relies on radar, video from its cameras, and pictures from its drone, why would it hallucinate?"

Etta crossed her arms. "What I'm telling you is top secret." She stared at Luke. "Like a human brain, the tank's brain enhances what it sees. It has a database of images of tanks, planes, soldiers, and weapons. If it does not get a complete picture from its cameras, sensors, and radar, it fills in what's missing from the database. Then it can better recognize enemies and their capabilities."

Luke nodded. "It added images of tanks, planes, and soldiers to create hallucinations?"

"Yes."

Luke drew his eyebrows together. *This artificial intelligence software ain't ready to go out on its own. It's too easy to drive it nuts.*

Knocking sounded on the tank's open hatch door. Luke peered upward. Rory leaned down from the hatchway. "Luke, come out. We're meeting in the van with Yegor."

* * *

WHEN LUKE ENTERED the long MI5 passenger van, he saw Yegor sitting on a bench seat next to Ginger. He was chained to a metal loop under the seat in front of him. Luke sat beside Rory, facing Yegor. Sergeant Boutwell sat a row away.

Rory stared at Yegor. "I've been in touch with MI5 Director General Ashton Boxman. He's coordinated with the CIA and FBI. Because we must act fast, the DG has made a quick decision to grant your wish to allow you to defect to our side. But we have conditions to which you must agree, or it won't happen. If you double-cross us, your days will be numbered."

Yegor showed a weak smile. "I agree." He paused. "Can I still go to America?"

"There's a decent chance of it, if all goes well."

Yegor's smile widened. "Thank you."

Rory turned to Ginger, and then to Sergeant Boutwell. "Take the sedan and transport him to Thames House."

"Yes, sir," the sergeant said. Ginger unlocked Yegor's shackles.

Rory caught Boutwell's attention. "Send the rest of the team in here."

* * *

4:43 P.M., TUESDAY, POPPINS PROVING GROUND

After sliding into the driver's seat of the eight-passenger police van, Rory buckled his seatbelt. He pushed the start button.

In the last row of bench seats at the back of the vehicle, Luke sat with Layla. He felt the van ease forward to begin its trip back to London and Thames House, MI5 headquarters. In front of him, the majority of the task force filled the rest of the seats.

Rory switched on a music track. Vivaldi's *The Four Seasons* permeated the van's cabin. Luke thought the rich tones of the symphony orchestra's violins were uplifting.

But as Luke held Layla's hand, he noticed it shook every once in a while. Her tremors were not due to the van's movement. He moved his lips close to Layla's ear. "You okay, hon?"

Sealing his body against Layla, Luke watched her dark eyes move back and forth, examining his. She blinked. "I'm jumpy. You saved my life a second time." She sat silent for a moment. "But I can't stop thinking about the baron's knife against my throat."

With a soft touch, Luke turned her head toward his. They kissed. Luke studied her face. He felt as if he were diving into her being, and they were one. "Ain't no way I'd let a bad guy git you."

Luke felt her sigh. She held him in a strong embrace as the van left Poppins Proving Ground and turned onto a highway.

Rory turned down the music. "Everyone, since we're on our way out of here, I'll give you a brief update because not everyone knows all the details of what's happened. After-ward, you can nap or listen to the concert." He cleared his throat. "Listen up…"

* * *

4:50 P.M., TUESDAY, MI5 SEDAN SPEEDING TOWARD LONDON

Sergeant Boutwell had ordered Ginger to remove Yegor's handcuffs. As the MI5 sedan flew at top speed toward London, Yegor relaxed.

Turning toward Boutwell, Yegor exhaled. "Thank you for driving fast. I need to report to my handler tonight to make the deal work."

Boutwell sat straight up with his chest out. "Be assured you'll arrive on time."

* * *

4:53 P.M., EN ROUTE TO LONDON

Rory coughed. "Later, we'll stop for takeaway sandwiches and drinks. You'll have time to use the loo." He paused. "After we arrive at Thames House, we'll go to a conference room for a team debriefing. This will be audio and video recorded."

Luke saw Drake raise his hand. "What about Yegor?"

"He'll undergo a thorough interrogation inside his cell. We plan to release him at once, if all goes well with his defection."

Sonja stroked her blond hair. "Has MI5 been in touch with Langley to coordinate?"

"Indeed we have. And DG Ashton Boxman continues to talk to your CIA director." Rory glanced in the rearview mirror. Luke figured Rory was watching for Sonja's reaction. Luke saw a relaxed smile form on her face.

Rory scanned the road ahead, and began to speak again. "DG Boxman, SIS, CIA, and the FBI have approved the actions we've taken." Rory again stared at the rearview mirror. Luke saw him gauge Henry's reaction to the news about the coordination of the four intelligence agencies.

Henry widened his eyes. Luke reckoned the seasoned FBI agent had not often seen the bureau work so fast.

Rory continued, "Right after we took custody of the computer memory card Luke had grabbed from Yegor, we copied it. Our MI5 computer experts and the Raven Robotics chief software engineer, Etta Jasek, then erased the card. Next, they saved an early, flawed, and unworkable version of the tank's neural net brain on the KGB's card."

Henry leaned forward in his seat. "What will you do with the doctored card?"

"Tonight, Yegor will deliver it to his handler. The faulty version of the tank's brain on the card will fool the Belarus KGB analysts. They will conclude the US tank cannot operate on its own. They'll think it needs to be run by a joystick operator."

Sonja sat up straight. "How are we going to use Yegor?"

"We hope his KGB handler will follow through on a promise he made to Yegor—to reassign him to the US." Rory glanced backward at Sonja. "The CIA and FBI directors say they love this possibility. They could feed the Belarus KGB false intelligence through Yegor."

Luke heard himself speak. "Y'all acted fast for a bunch of bureaucrats."

Rory laughed. "Our clandestine agencies had to expedite, or we'd have lost our chance to use Yegor. For once, we didn't tie ourselves up in bureaucratic knots." Rory paused. "We'll cover the rest at the debriefing." He pushed down on the van's accelerator, and the vehicle sped ahead.

FORTY-NINE

THE MORNING SUNSHINE SOOTHED HIM, and his bare feet relaxed on the warm concrete. Matéo Guerra, who headed the *Nuestro Club* drug cartel, sat near his Olympic-size swimming pool. A beach umbrella shaded him from the rising sun.

Surrounded by a fence and guarded by four men, the pool and his large compound were a safe refuge.

Matéo held a glass of orange juice as the delicious smell of bacon and eggs wafted up to him from his plate that sat on a wrought iron table. His mouth watered. A lovely young woman in a bikini approached, carrying a bottle of whiskey. He smiled.

As he lifted the petite glass of juice toward his mouth, his satellite phone rang. Frowning, he set his drink down. "Damn."

After picking up the phone, Matéo held his finger over an icon on the device's display, ready to answer the incoming call. He waved the well-endowed young woman away. She set the whiskey bottle and a shot glass on the table and left.

Matéo touched the icon labeled Javier Lagos. Javier was in California where José's broken wrist was being treated. "*Holá*. Javier? How's José?"

"Better, *jefe*." Javier paused. "I'm sorry we couldn't get near Lucas. He was working with MI5."

Matéo lowered his head and pressed his lips into a grimace. "Okay. It was a difficult situation. Return to Tijuana with José. We'll regroup. When Lucas comes back to the States, you shall try again."

"Sí, *jefe*."

Matéo smiled. "I have faith in you. You are doing your best considering the obstacles. You never give up. One day you will swat him like a nasty horsefly."

"*Sí*."

"I must hang up and attend to important business." Matéo waved for the young lady in the bikini to return. As she neared him, he disconnected the call, and she kissed his neck with her soft lips.

* * *

8:00 P.M., TUESDAY, MI5 HEADQUARTERS CONFERENCE ROOM

A waitress brought the catered dishes from the nearby kitchen and set them in front of the joint task force members, who sat around the long conference table.

Rory stood. "First, I salute and thank our American team members, Henry of the FBI; Sonja of the CIA; and Luke, a Kentucky deputy sheriff. Also Layla, who chose to assist her husband, Luke."

Luke felt a blush spread across his face.

"Sergeant Rick Boutwell and his street team did a tremendous job."

Boutwell peered aside for a moment.

Rory shifted on his feet. "Since our debrief is over, Rick, please ask Dr. Baumhauer to come in."

Rick left the room, and moments later he held the conference room door open.

Luke turned to see an old, skinny man with stringy, white hair enter. His skin looked as wrinkled as the peel of a drying apple. But like someone who rarely stepped into the sunlight, his face was pale.

The elderly man sat at the table. His eyes scanned the people sitting around it.

Rory walked to the timeworn man's side. "Dr. Gustav Baumhauer has joined us for dinner. Gustav is our chief MI5 psychiatrist and will chat about his analysis of the robotic brain as well as his examination of Yegor Bulot. By the way, Yegor signed on as an MI5 undercover agent thirty minutes ago."

Gustav took a sip of tea from a cup near his plate of food. He rose and bowed a fraction of an inch. "Thank you, Rory." He had a thick German accent. "Ziss computer tank brain went crazy because of a computer virus that mixed up its neural network. This shows how easy it is to overcome artificial intelligence." He studied the people's faces around the table. "Any questions?"

Luke raised his hand. "How come the tank attacked the DC-3 airplane?"

The old doctor focused on Luke. "The tank took pictures of the DC-3. The computer brain enhanced those images, combining them with pictures of an enemy fighter plane. The tank shot at what it thought was a threat."

Luke wondered if any country at war would risk using a battle tank able to operate without human intervention. *A tank like the Raven Robotics model could destroy a US city, if a computer bug drove it insane.*

Gustav continued to talk. "It vill be easy to defeat enemy robotic tanks by infecting their artificial brains." The old man crossed and then uncrossed his arms.

Rory furrowed his brow and glanced at the psychiatrist. "Did you learn anything interesting when you analyzed Yegor?"

Gustav grinned and showed his worn teeth. "Yes. We gave him our in-house truth serum. He said he loved Anne Thorpe and had vished to marry her. He started to weep when he told me he found her corpse."

Rory focused on the old psychiatrist. "Tell them what you told me about Yegor."

Gustav laced his fingers together. "Under zah truth serum, he said he would be loyal to MI5, but hopes he can quit the spy game someday."

"Thank you, Gustav." The old man eased back onto his chair and took a sip of tea.

Rory sat down. "Let's eat. Any of you may ask Gustav questions after dessert, if you wish."

The discordant noise of silverware clinking against china plates began. Luke watched Layla as she began to eat. He touched her soft shoulder. "I can't wait to git back to Kentucky."

Layla swallowed. "Me, too."

Luke leaned close to her and whispered. "I gotta be careful in the future. I'm gonna be a dad."

Rory took a seat next to Luke. "You have questions about the case?"

"Yes. What about the news media?"

Rory shrugged. "We've lied. To begin with, we told the director of Poppins the tank had an unlucky malfunction. We informed him and the Raven Robotics team that the one person to die as a result of the incident was Baron Thomas Thorpe. We said he dove away from the exploding DC-3 and fell on a razor-sharp shard of steel debris from the airplane's explosion."

Luke ran his fingers through his hair. *Rory must be feelin' bad about being a liar.*

Rory cleared his throat and peered at the floor for a second before continuing to speak. "The Poppins director held a press conference. He told reporters our false story. Thus, the Belarus KGB will believe Yegor when he gives his handler the bogus computer memory card tonight."

Luke blinked. "The baron will be remembered as a loyal British nobleman."

"Yes." Rory sighed. "We've learned Lord Thorpe had throat cancer and would've died within a short time. I wonder why he decided to steal top secret information even if Yegor blackmailed him?"

Luke exhaled. "I bet he did it to protect his family name. Thought he could get away with murder and espionage, and nobody would've been the wiser."

Rory narrowed his eyes. "If you hadn't spotted him at the back of the tank and seen the LED light glow amber, the baron could've succeeded in stealing the neural net brain undetected. He may well have gotten away with murder, too."

Luke shifted in his chair. "What about the investigation into Anne's murder?"

Rory sighed. "We'll let the case go cold."

"Will you call Arnold, the pro golfer, to tell him he's in the clear?"

Rory leaned forward. "Yes. We'll let Arnold, Estrella, and even the banker, Robert, know they are not suspects in Anne's murder. Of course, we'll arrest Robert for embezzlement."

Luke squinted. "We're lucky Yegor decided to defect."

Rory shrugged. "It happens a lot. Like football players, spies switch sides for better deals."

Luke yawned. "I'm as tired as a bear about to go into hibernation."

Rory leaned back in his chair. "MI5 has suites in Thames House. I've reserved one for you and Layla. Tomorrow, you can work with our travel office to arrange a flight back to the US."

"Thanks, Rory." Luke shook the DCI's hand.

FIFTY

YEGOR SAT and waited on a park bench one intersection from the Embassy of Belarus. Street lamps lit the roadway and sidewalk.

Chilly in the semidarkness, Yegor also felt jumpy. *When will Viktor be here?*

Had the sixty-eight-year-old spy learned Yegor now worked for MI5, SIS, the CIA, and the FBI, too?

Yegor tapped his foot on the pavement below the wooden bench. Peering at his watch, he saw the minutes tick by as if in slow motion. He bit his lips and then rubbed his hand down his trouser leg.

At 9:37 p.m., Viktor emerged from a dark shadow and walked into the bright light illuminating Yegor and the bench. The veteran spy handler sat on the bench and turned to examine Yegor. "You appear nervous."

Waiting for a reply, Viktor displayed an easy nod as if to urge Yegor to speak.

Yegor felt his leg muscles tighten. Forcing himself to exhale a half breath, he spoke. "Carrying this memory card is scary."

Viktor's thin lips formed a smile. "You have it?"

"Yes." Yegor slid a newspaper toward Viktor.

The elderly man slipped his thin fingers between paper folds, and with an expert hand, removed the memory card.

"Excellent work, Yegor." He slipped the card into his trench coat pocket. "We'll check this at once, and if all's well, tonight I'll ring you and say, 'You've earned a holiday.' Then you will be reassigned to the US."

Yegor felt his muscles relax. "I was lucky to leave Poppins alive after the tank went crazy firing at an old plane." Yegor raised his eyebrows. "What was on the card the baron slipped into the tank's computer slot?"

"We're investigating. We planned to create a slight diversion, not cause mass murder." Viktor's pale ears turned red in the bright lamplight.

"I hope somebody didn't try to sabotage the operation."

Viktor nodded. "If so, that person will pay with his life, if he did this knowing what the tank would do."

Yegor took in a breath of cool air. "I hope so."

The gray-haired spy coughed. "I saw the news." The old man's probing stare seemed to slice into Yegor's body. "You took a while to return to London."

"The helicopter pilot flew the rental away in a panic. I caught a ride with a random attendee who also fled."

Viktor continued to eyeball Yegor. "An online report said the baron died when he fell onto a jagged piece of metal."

Yegor nodded. "We were lucky he died after he slipped the card to me. Do you see how close to disaster we came?"

Viktor stood. "At times you need luck. Still, you did an outstanding job." The old spy walked away in the direction of the Belarus Embassy.

* * *

10:32 P.M., TUESDAY, YEGOR'S LONDON FLAT

Yegor sat on his worn easy chair holding his mobile phone. It rang. The device's display read "private number." His heart beating as if he were sprinting, he tapped the icon to answer the call. "Hello?"

"You've earned a holiday." The voice sounded deep. Viktor had called.

Yegor opened his mouth to reply, but he heard a click. The call had ended.

Yegor laughed. He felt like dancing, like singing. Though it was September, the air seemed spring-like, even inside his stale, one-bedroom flat.

I'll be on a plane to the US in a day or two. He grinned. He poured a shot of whiskey and nursed the amber liquid.

FIFTY-ONE

A MEXICAN EMPLOYEE of a Kentucky horse farm sat on a bench facing the exit from the Blue Grass Airport's secure passenger boarding/arrival gates. In his hand, he held two snapshots. One was a picture of Luke Ryder, and the second was a photo of Layla Ryder. He saw a dozen passengers walking toward him along the almost vacant airport hallway. He narrowed his eyes. Yes, he'd spotted Luke and Layla.

The Mexican turned his back on the departing passengers. He phoned Tijuana.

Drug lord Matéo Guerra answered. "*Holá.*"

"They arrived."

"Good. I'll tell Javier. Come home now, and help him plan the hit."

"Sí, señor."

* * *

9:50 P.M., THURSDAY, LEXINGTON, KENTUCKY

Now in the Blue Grass Airport's parking lot, Luke unlocked Layla's old sedan, a "beater." After his new wife fastened her seat belt, Luke stared deep into Layla's eyes. "I bin thinking. I've been good at not touching alcohol for about a year. But instead of booze, I got addicted to adrenaline rushes. I've been takin' lots of chances. I need to stop doin' that cuz I'm gonna be a father."

Layla sighed and then smiled. "But it comes with your job."

"I guess. But still, I'm gonna be more careful."

He backed out from his parking space. He stopped, glanced at Layla's youthful face, and smiled. "I can't wait 'til we're home in our own bed."

Layla touched his shoulder. "Me, too. I'm going to surprise you when we make love, honey." She held her breath for a moment and then trembled. "I've been thinking of something you're going to like a lot." She kissed his cheek as he put the vehicle in drive.

He felt himself flush in the darkness. "I ain't lyin' when I say I can't wait." He felt his heart begin to pound.

ACKNOWLEDGMENTS

I thank my wife, Sheryl, a retired English teacher, for her thoughts, critical edits, and encouragement. She has helped me with this and my other books as well. I'm also indebted to my editor at Rough Edges Press, Rachel Del Grosso, for her patience, expert suggestions, and friendliness.

IF YOU LIKE THIS, YOU MAY ALSO ENJOY: THE FINGER TRAP

A TONY FLANER MYSTERY BOOK ONE
BY JOHNNY WORTHEN

When half measures don't get you the whole truth...

Tony Flaner is a part-time comedian and full-time commitment-phobe who has never been able to stick with anything in his life. After his fourteen-year marriage ends in divorce, Tony's life takes a dramatic turn when a drunken party ends in murder.

With his life on the line, he must uncover the identity of the mysterious girl who was murdered and how they ended up together in the first place. This undertaking is not just about clearing his name—Tony needs to prove to himself and everyone else that he can finish something for *once in his life*.

But when Tony discovers that his fate is intertwined with that of the mysterious girl he hardly knew—and that their lives are connected like a Chinese finger trap—he unknowingly embarks on a journey full of twists and turns around every corner.

Can Tony Flaner finish this one task and clear his name before he gets sent to prison for a murder he didn't commit?

AVAILABLE NOW

ABOUT THE AUTHOR

John G. Bluck was an Army journalist at Ft. Lewis, Washington, during the Vietnam War. Following his military service, he worked as a cameraman covering crime, sports, and politics—including Watergate for WMAL-TV (now WJLA-TV) in Washington, D.C. Later, he was a radio broadcast engineer at WMAL-AM/FM.

After that, John worked at NASA Lewis (now Glenn) Research Center in Cleveland, Ohio, where he produced numerous television documentaries. He transferred to NASA Ames Research Center at Moffett Field, California, where he became the Chief of Imaging Technology. He then became a NASA Ames public affairs officer.

John retired from NASA in 2008. Now residing in Livermore, California, he is a novelist and short story author.